---- ★ ----

The last piece of first-class mail had no return address. A small off-white envelope of good quality, postmarked REVERE. I slit it open and pulled out a plain sheet of matching paper.

My throat tightened as I scanned the neatly typed lines, then reread every word.

KEEP OUT OF POLICE WORK. TAKE UP SEWING. END YOUR NEW POLICE CAREER, OR I WILL.

My fingers gripped the note. I looked around quickly, as if the author might be standing over me with a coatrack, ready to push me out the door and down my own staircase.

---- ★ ----

"A solid, grown-up series, well plotted and well peopled. With dialogue that keeps you smiling."
—Shelly Singer, author of *Royal Flush*

Previously published Worldwide Mystery titles by
CAMILLE MINICHINO

THE BERYLLIUM MURDER
THE LITHIUM MURDER
THE HELIUM MURDER
THE HYDROGEN MURDER

Forthcoming from Worldwide Mystery titles by
CAMILLE MINICHINO

THE CARBON MURDER

The Boric Acid Murder

Camille Minichino

WORLDWIDE®

TORONTO • NEW YORK • LONDON
AMSTERDAM • PARIS • SYDNEY • HAMBURG
STOCKHOLM • ATHENS • TOKYO • MILAN
MADRID • WARSAW • BUDAPEST • AUCKLAND

For my husband, friend, and benevolent reviewer,
Dick Rufer

THE BORIC ACID MURDER

A Worldwide Mystery/June 2004

First published by St. Martin's Press LLC.

ISBN 0-373-26495-X

Printed in U.S.A.

Acknowledgments

My special thanks go to Robert Rice, Director of the Revere Public Library, not only for countless pages of information and photographs, but for his inspiration and great patience while I turned his building into a fictional crime scene, and him into a female murder suspect.

Other valuable assistance and advice came, as usual, from Robert Durkin, my cousin and expert in all things mortuary, and from Detective Sergeant Chris Lux of the San Leandro, California, Police Department.

Thanks also to the many writers and friends who reviewed the manuscript in progress, in particular: Judy Barnett, Dr. Eileen Hotte, Jonnie Jacobs, Anna Lipjhart, Peggy Lucke, Lynn MacDonald, Ann Parker, Sue Stephenson, and Karen Streich.

I am most grateful to my wonderful editor, Marcia Markland, who has been with me in one way or another from my first book, and to my patient, remarkable agent, Elaine Koster.

ONE

"MOST GRUESOME THING I've ever seen," Frank said. He shook his head, loosening strands of fine gray hair. "The little girl's head was completely severed from her torso. Caught in elevator doors at the mall."

I dropped my fork into my marinara sauce and made a slight gagging sound, earning a worried look from Matt Gennaro, my first romantic partner since we put a man on the moon.

"Are you all right with this, Gloria?" Matt asked me, concern in his droopy brown eyes. Al Pacino eyes, I called them. I'd yet to come up with a similar complimentary label for my own baggy lids.

The four Galiganis—Frank, Rose, and their grown sons Robert and John—were watching me, too. Frank had been in the mortuary business for more than thirty years, and I guessed macabre dinner conversation had been the norm. Matt, a homicide detective, was no stranger to grisly scenes either. Even though I'd consulted with the police on a few murder cases, I was the weak one at the table, not quite comfortable with the mixture of embalming and endive.

But, as a retired physicist, I'm also overly curious. I picked up my fork and cleared my throat. "I'm fine with this," I said. "Absolutely fine."

"The parents insisted on an open casket," said Rose Galigani, the hostess and my best friend. "The mother was one of the six Basotti girls from Beachmont, the one who married a Fantone."

We thought of Rose as the human database for residents of

Revere, Massachusetts. With these statistics, however, I heard an undercurrent of prayer in her gentle voice. Rose nudged her husband. A proud smile lit her face and spilled over Robert—heir to the family business—and John—a journalist with the local paper.

"Tell them how happy you made little Casey's family, Frank," she said.

Frank pushed his tomato-streaked plate away to make room for gestures. "I took a piece of skin about this long from the girl's thigh"—he used his hands to mark off approximately ten inches of air—"and I wrapped it around a cardboard tube, to make a neck. Then I stitched…" Frank's fingers sewed imaginary thigh flesh to an invisible chest.

I finally summoned the nerve to look at his photos—not prints from an ordinary camera, but images stored on a floppy disk and displayed on a handheld monitor, a computer screen no bigger than the last slice of Italian bread in the basket in front of us. I shuddered as the scenes shifted into view, the high resolution giving the images a you-are-there quality. I stared at the latest in camera technology. Casey's head carefully lined up next to her small torso. Close-ups of the stitches holding her flesh together at her chin and her chest. The little girl's sweetly coiffed hair discreetly spread over layers of makeup that covered the patchwork.

Frank shook his head, as if reliving the experience. "It's hard enough to have your little girl come back from the mall in pieces. The least I could do was put her back together for them."

"Great work, Dad," Robert said.

Nods all around the table.

"Very nice," I managed to say. I knew Frank was a professional, eager to share his work as part surgeon, part artist, part beautician. Not unlike particle physicists, I thought.

But I was glad I'd chosen physics, not mortuary science, as a career. My lab had been clean, if not sterile. I'd used lasers instead of trocars. I'd calculated the density of inorganic crystals, not human hearts and livers. During my thirty years of research, the worst smell might have been from a burnt-out 6.3-volt filament winding on a power transformer.

"This morning's case…" Frank began.

"I think we've had enough shop talk," John said. His voice was temperate, but with an edge that said he meant it. As a journalist, he usually had bizarre stories of his own to tell. But this evening he'd been quiet and preoccupied.

Rose smoothed things over in her typical perfect-hostess style. "This is Gloria's welcome home party." Deliberately or not, she was dressed to match her Wedgwood serving bowls, in cream slacks, a short-sleeved blue jacket, and beads that set off her auburn highlights. Even as children, Rose and I were separated by several dress sizes, but I loved her anyway.

"I've only been gone ten days," I said, but I caught a look from Matt that confirmed our mutual feelings—it had seemed like months.

"Tell us about your West Coast adventure," Robert said.

Frank snapped his hi-tech photo display shut. "Police work is turning into a second career for you, isn't it, Gloria?"

"We're happy about that," Matt said, his casual, bulky presence a contrast to the trim Galigani men. Another comforting look passed between us. For a woman who had spent three decades with as many dates as your average nun, I'd adjusted quickly to a pattern of suggestive glances. I smiled at him over Rose's beautifully pressed linens and fresh flowers.

A year ago, I'd retired from my lab in California and returned to Revere, Massachusetts. Back to the town I was born in, a few miles north of Boston—home to America's first public beach, the travel books noted. I moved into the small apartment in the Galigani Mortuary building, three floors above Frank's embalming table. An address that had proved more exciting than I'd imagined.

If I had any doubts about settling again in my hometown after thirty years away, they'd been squashed by my new relationship. I'd met Sergeant Matt Gennaro when he'd hired me as a science consultant, and we grew closer with each case.

"Dr. Lamerino on the job," Rose said, with a twirl of her

monogrammed spoon. "Catching another killer, coming home from battle without a scar."

I frowned, exaggerating my pain. "I have scars. My feet are all torn up," I said with a mock whine. "I had to run across a nasty waste pit, through broken glass and gravel and who knows what corrosive material." I pointed to the copper metal cane my Berkeley friend Elaine Cody had given me as a send-off present after my quasi-vacation with her. She may have meant it as a joke, but I'd found it very useful. My wounded soles deserved to be spared the entire weight of my full-figured body.

I showed my own photos, this time simple, low-tech paper snapshots with lovely California landscapes, as we ate dessert—Rose's homemade cannoli, a rare treat that we all exclaimed over.

Except for John, who picked at crumbs.

Matt looked at his watch. "We have to leave soon," he said. "I need to get Gloria home, and then go to work. I told Berger I'd stop by his house to get briefed on a new case."

"Yolanda Fiore, I suppose," Frank said.

Matt nodded. "Her body was found in the library yesterday morning. I've been out, so I don't know what we have." He looked at me as if to say it was my fault—he'd been busy picking me up at Boston's Logan Airport. Without a lot of practice in my adult life, it had taken me a while to see the affection in his eyes when he teased.

"Very sad," Rose said. She shook her head and clucked her tongue. "We knew her." I waited for statistics—age, ancestry, number of siblings. Instead, Rose cast a sympathetic look at her younger son. "Yolanda and John used to date."

"Everyone and John used to date," Robert said with a grin.

"That was a long time ago," John said. He gave his older brother a playful punch, but his face was strained. He turned to me with an explanation. "We were pretty close once. I can't believe she's dead."

I felt sad for John, and glad to know the reason for his somber mood. "Were you, uh, close for very long?" I tried to remember a mention of Yolanda in John's letters to me while I lived in California. Nothing came to mind.

"About a year." John's voice was low, his fingers playing with the corner of his lacy placemat. "She was a writer for the Public Affairs Office at the lab and at one time I worked that beat for the paper."

I straightened up. Another murdered labbie. My emotions swung from sympathy for John at the death of his friend, to excitement—if there was a possibility Yolanda's murder was related to her work at the Charger Street lab, I'd be called on to help.

The doorbell rang, and as Frank went to answer it, I pondered the possibility of a new contract with the Revere Police Department.

"How long did she work at the lab?" I asked John, spinning my crystal water glass on its axis, striking a casual tone.

"Don't even think about it," Matt said before John could answer. He laughed and stretched his chunky legs under the table until he bumped against my ankle. "Take care of those feet first."

The small thrill I felt at his touch kept me quiet until Frank returned to the dining room with Sergeant Ian Parker, one of Matt's colleagues whom I'd met at the station. He was accompanied by a uniformed officer.

Their look said they hadn't come for cannoli.

"Gennaro." Parker's young, thin face registered surprise at seeing Matt. "Didn't know you'd be here. We'd have given you a heads-up."

Before I was aware he'd moved, Matt joined the two officers in a huddle by the door leading to the kitchen. "What's up?" I heard him ask.

The rest of us stayed in place, motionless.

I focused on Rose's expression as she stared at the cluster of representatives from the Revere Police Department. From her calm, curious look, she might have been wondering why they'd come to spoil her perfect decor.

Parker moved toward Rose and Frank, his badge barely visible at his waist, under his jacket. He addressed them in a soft voice. "I'm sorry to interrupt you like this."

Rose's eyebrows reconfigured into a frown. Frank put his arm around her as Parker turned his attention to John. The chamber music that had brightened our lunch stopped abruptly, the CD player seeming to respond on its own to the force of law.

"John Galigani, we'd like you to come down to the station. We have some questions…"

Before Parker was finished, John shoved his chair behind him and stood. He let out a low moan, a sigh of resignation, as if he'd been waiting all day for the summons. In his loose T-shirt and tennis shoes, he looked younger than his thirty-six years and too fragile for police custody.

Frank drew in his breath. Rose threw up her hands. For me, it was an experiment gone wrong.

"Questions about what?" Rose asked, her voice high-pitched and weak.

Parker responded softly, a sign he wasn't enjoying the moment any more than the rest of us. "…in connection with the murder of Yolanda Fiore."

I fell back onto my chair. A shiver ran through me when I caught Matt's eye. *Nothing I can do,* was his silent message.

TWO

TWENTY MINUTES after the police led John away in an unmarked sedan, Matt and I sat on a sofa in his partner's Fenno Street living room. I was relieved they hadn't handcuffed John, at least not in front of his parents. We'd brushed past Rose and Frank, in silent acknowledgment that it was better for us to work on the case than to stay around offering consolation. Matt had put up no fuss when I asked to accompany him.

"Jeez, I'm sorry, Matt. Gloria." George Berger looked at each of us as though condolences were in order. I felt enough like a grieving parent to welcome his concern. "It happened pretty quick. One minute, no suspect—the next, John Galigani. Parker asked me to help out. I agreed, but"—Berger turned to Matt and shrugged his shoulders—"of course, officially, you're off the case."

I knew police department rules. Matt had known the Galiganis since he was a rookie cop, and detectives were prohibited from investigating cases where their objectivity might be compromised. But the immediate effect of the policy hadn't struck me until Berger's reminder. Matt nodded, apparently reconciled to the situation.

Unlike me. I'd already resolved to find the real killer. I saw myself in the victim's home, workplace, places of recreation. Interviewing, using the Internet, reviewing her address book, police files…until Matt's voice gave me some perspective.

"I realize we can't work on this," Matt said. "I'm just curious what you have."

"Can't see the harm."

Although he was Jewish, Berger's short, heavy physique and dark hair gave him the look of most Neapolitans, Matt and me included, if you subtracted about twenty years. He was in suit pants and shirt, apparently considering this Saturday a workday.

Every visible surface of Berger's yellow clapboard home held signs of a modern tot—bulky plastic toys, tiny shoes, and strange-looking contraptions with wheels, all in primary colors that clashed with the soft mauve carpet and pale blue upholstery in the living room. It was a relief to hear that Baby Cynthia was out with her mother—I was never up for relating to an eight-month-old child, least of all this evening.

Berger pushed a few red and blue plastic creatures off the coffee table and spread out pages from an accordion file. I twitched involuntarily when I saw the label—GALIGANI—on a police department folder.

In a file marked FIORE was a photograph of the victim. Leaning against the lab's large maroon and gold sign at its Charger Street entrance, Yolanda Fiore appeared tiny, her hands folded below a wide, multicolored belt tied around her slim waist. Even in the long-distance shot I could see her neat pixie haircut, bright round eyes, and disarming smile. I guessed she raced through a day's work and had energy to spare.

I could see why John Galigani might be attracted to her. I tried to imagine why someone would want to kill her—not that I ever understood the motives for murder. Could Yolanda have been the victim of random violence—someone burglarizing the library? *Of what?* I had to admit, the idea of a hooded thief attempting to steal overdue fines was shaky at best.

I grimaced at the next photo—the same lovely body, lifeless, at the bottom of the interior library stairs. The crime-scene photographs presented every angle, although there was little difference among them. Yolanda's head seemed to be folded under her chest, bringing back the image of Frank's decapitated client.

I breathed deeply and turned my attention to Berger.

"Evidence says she was hit on the head—probably with a

coat rack we're looking at—then she was pushed, or she fell down the stairs as a result of the blow. We can't place Galigani at the scene at the time of the murder, but a few things point to him.''

Berger's words seemed to come from a black hole. I swallowed hard. What could point to John, this man I'd known since his birth, other than a mistake?

"First, several letters from Galigani in the victim's apartment. Apparently she'd dumped him for another guy." Berger pulled photocopies of the correspondence from a thin file.

"He sounds pretty angry," Matt said as we followed Berger's fingers down the lines of John's handwriting.

I read the harsh words, threats, and name-calling, and winced at labels like *conniver, cheater, liar,* that jumped from the pages. I groaned inwardly at John's closing line in one of the letters. *I'll have you back, one way or another, I swear.* Surely a prosecutor's dream evidence.

I remembered the times I'd seen John angry. He was definitely the most hotheaded of the family, lashing out at his sister, now living in Houston, for not coming home to Revere often enough, or at his older brother for canceling a fishing trip. And he'd been almost proud to tell us how he'd often storm out of meetings at the newspaper office. He was known around town for questioning the ethics of his editor, railing against the incompetence of his colleagues, harassing any group whose policies and practices he thought inhumane.

But angry enough to kill someone? I knew better. And I intended to prove it.

I bent over to look more closely at John's letters to Yolanda Fiore, checking the dates. *Aha!* "These letters are more than a year old. Why does it matter now?" I asked, a note of triumph in my voice. Had I already come up with enough to clear my best friends' son?

"Doesn't matter. Everything's important in a murder investigation," Berger said. He used a teaching tone, as if he were instructing a rookie. Not far from the truth.

Why would Yolanda have kept the letters so long? I asked

only myself, afraid the answer might cast even more of a shadow over John. Maybe it was part of a pattern of harassment and Yolanda was building a case against him. I shook the thought away.

I knew John had dated several women in the intervening year, and had planned to take his latest significant other, Carolyn Verrico, on a cruise to Bermuda. I held back the information until I could determine whether that would make him look better or worse in the eyes of the law.

I wished I knew more about Yolanda Fiore. Was she as sweet and innocent as she looked in the publicity photo—or had she provoked her killer? Was she a blackmailer? A jealous lover? A killer herself, perhaps, murdered by someone defending himself? I winced at how far I'd strayed from reason.

Matt leaned forward and scratched his chin, a sure sign he was paying close attention. "Is that it?"

Berger shook his head. "There's more."

I wanted to clap my hands over my ears so I'd hear no more incriminating details, but I needed to know everything if I was going to help John.

"His prints were on her purse, next to the body."

I gritted my teeth. I can deal with that, I told myself. Maybe it was a very old purse, one she'd used when she and John had dated. I'd heard fingerprints last for years.

But Berger wasn't finished.

"And we have a couple of witnesses who claim they saw John and Yolanda having dinner at Russo's on Thursday, likely only a few hours before she was murdered."

I groaned. "I suppose they were arguing."

Berger nodded. "Loud and clear."

I sat back, trying to push away a feeling of defeat. It didn't help that I was tired, after a long flight and a hectic ten days in California. I longed for my apartment, a refreshing shower, quiet time with Matt. Not yet.

I tried to keep my mind off John the murder suspect, and focus on Berger's summary of the details in the case. Derek Byrne, assistant director of the Revere Public Library and Yolanda's current boyfriend, told police he'd let her into the library building on Thursday after hours, so she could use the Internet. He left her around eleven o'clock, adjusting the security system so she could leave when she wanted to without setting off an alarm. When the director, Dorothy Leonard, came in early the next morning, she found Yolanda's body at the foot of the stairs to the basement and called the police immediately.

I mentally listed the facts of the crime scene as Berger read from the report. Yolanda's purse with the usual contents—wallet, hairbrush, tissues, cosmetics, keys. Traces of blood on the coat rack near the top of the stairs. No sign of a break-in. Nothing else disturbed.

My mind drifted to the chief suspect, journalist John Galigani, and to an article he'd written a few months ago on the city jails, housed in the basement of the police department building. Last winter, a prisoner had escaped by pushing the bars away from the decaying old masonry and John took the opportunity to plead for state funds for a new facility. How ironic that he was virtually a prisoner there himself. I pictured him escaping—snapping a rusty old lock in two, running through the building, racing across town, breathlessly climbing the stairs to my apartment for refuge. Would I harbor a fugitive? I wondered, as if I had to make the decision any moment.

"So we've got the letters, the prints, and the alleged argument," Matt said. I was glad one of us was in the proper mood for objectivity.

"Right," Berger said. "And he does have a record."

My head snapped up. "A record? John Galigani?"

Berger moved a sheet of paper to the top of the stack. "Afraid so. He's been arrested for trespassing and disorderly conduct. Twice, in the last ten years."

I sank back on the sofa. "Good Fridays."

Berger clucked his tongue. "That's right."

How could I have forgotten? The Good Friday protests against the weapons program at the Charger Street lab. Every year, anywhere from a few dozen to hundreds of protesters were arrested for blocking the entrances to the lab. Rose and Frank were so upset when John was among them, their feelings bouncing back and forth between anger at their son's criminal behavior and pride that he had such strong convictions. Rose blamed herself for not keeping better track of John's activities. Frank claimed John's sociology professors at Boston College put him up to it. Robert and Mary Catherine thought their brother was on something.

"Now I remember," Matt said.

"Once in the seventies twelve hundred people were arrested outside my Berkeley lab," I said, eager to give a context to John's actions, make him part of the culture, not a lone criminal, capable of anything.

"But it does show he's willing to break the law," Berger said.

I pressed my lips together to avoid speaking before I was ready. I reminded myself that Matt, and even his partner, probably wanted to clear John as much as I did.

"Is that how it's perceived?" I finally asked. "Civil disobedience leads to murder?" I hoped my voice sounded more controlled to them than it did to me.

"You have to think like a DA." Matt screwed up his Roman nose—only slightly bigger than mine, and with one extra bump—and shook his head. His signal for bad news. "They're going to pull up everything."

I sat back, willing myself to think clearly. I remembered John's comment on how he'd met Yolanda—she'd been a writer at the Charger Street lab when he'd worked that beat for the *Revere Journal*. I wondered how her employment there squared with John's anti-lab leanings.

"What exactly did she do at the lab?" I asked, carefully phrasing the question. I didn't want to remind them of another possible motive for John—differing political positions, in addition to a romance gone bad.

Berger sifted through the papers in front of us. "Here's a memo that says she was fired a week ago. That's why she was in the library—to use the Internet since her home computer evidently belonged to the lab and she'd had to return it. Before that her job was to put together material for the lab's outreach programs. Public Affairs Office, Visitor Center, Education Division, things like that. Here's a page with Parker's notes on her latest project."

Berger handed me the sheet. I squinted at Detective Ian Parker's tiny script. His list of questions under "Lab" sparked my interest.

I read out loud.

"*Controversy?*

"*Nuclear reactor—safety issues?*

"*Cooling water?*

"*Spent fuel pools?*

"*Boron (i.e., boric acid)?*"

I breathed deeply and smiled broadly at my partners. "There it is. Yolanda uncovered a problem with boron and she was fired."

Matt looked at Berger. "I think that's an 'aha,'" he said.

IT SEEMED TOO GOOD to be true, but I saw myself digging up the boron connection, setting John free.

"Am I the only guy here who doesn't know what boron is?" Matt asked after Berger and I spent a few minutes discussing how a work-related controversy could have led to Yolanda's murder.

Matt and I both knew Berger would appreciate an opportunity to use his one year of college chemistry. When I first appeared on the Revere Police Department scene to help investigate the murder of a Charger Street lab hydrogen researcher, Berger had resisted.

"How much detective work have you done?" he'd asked me.

Matt had answered for me. "About as much science as you've done, Berger," he'd said with a grin. Although I'd proven my worth a few times, I still took great pains to play down my expertise when Matt's partner was around.

Berger rubbed his hands together, clearly delighted at the

prospect of tutoring Matt, who at fifty-five was at least twenty years his senior. "Boron is the fifth element in the periodic table," he said. "And the most common boric acid is H_3BO_3."

I wondered if he'd researched boron in his old chemistry text before Matt and I arrived. When he announced, "Boron was discovered by Humphry Davy in 1808 but not identified as an element until 1824," I was sure he had done some cramming. Most scientists I'd worked with would never pass a test on historical trivia. It was the present that mattered.

"The main use of boron compounds is as a bleaching agent in detergents," Berger said, continuing to sound like a textbook. "The most popular one is called sodium perborate. It's obtained by mixing boron with two other—uh—some kind of -ides that I can't quite remember."

"Like 20 Mule Team Borax?" Matt asked. "My father always had that around the garage."

"Exactly," I said. "That's one of the common products that contains boron."

Matt looked at Detective Parker's list. "How's boron used in nuclear reactors?"

Berger cleared his throat. I had the feeling he'd come to the end of his expertise on boron. "Gloria probably knows more about that than I do." He smiled at me, as if to indicate there were no hard feelings.

"I'm a little rusty, myself," I said truthfully. It had been a while since I'd read *Nuclear News*.

"Do you need some paper?" Berger asked. He pulled a child-size bright red easel from the corner. The image of me sitting on the built-in seat, formed for the one- to three-year-old set, must have hit all of us at once and we laughed out loud—a nice relief for the tension in my muscles.

Knowing the boron tutorial had to do with John Galigani's arrest for murder made it less fun to talk science, but I organized my thoughts and went on.

"Boron is what we call a neutron poison."

"So it's no good for neutrons?" Matt asked.

I shook my head, aware the term was confusing. "Just the

opposite. It *absorbs* neutrons. That means it doesn't allow them to interact with each other, or with whatever other nuclei are in the way. It's important in a nuclear power plant because we don't want runaway reactions.''

"Right," Berger said.

"Huh?" Matt asked.

"We need to be able to control the reactions of the neutrons. Putting a neutron absorber like boron into the system does that for us. Usually components will be made of boron, and a solution of boric acid will be used in cooling and waste systems.''

"OK. That's enough for now," Matt said.

"But I'm just getting started.''

"Later." His grin took the edge off the abrupt curtailment of my lesson.

"We'll have to look at Yolanda's notes," Berger said. "Whatever she might have had with her in the library when she was killed is gone. There were no notes or disks near the body.''

"No briefcase?" Matt asked.

Berger shook his head. "Nothing like that. But I'm sure Parker's checked her apartment and I don't know what he found there. Sorry you're out of the loop here, Matt. Rules are rules, I guess.''

Matt nodded. "It'll be hard not to get involved. But I have plenty to do. There's Rigione, Peters, Gong, Sforza…'' He wiggled his fingers, indicating there were too many other cases to count.

I tried to determine if Matt felt as acquiescent as he sounded, but his face was turned from me.

The noisy whoosh of a minivan door floated through the screen door. I looked out the picture window and caught a glimpse of Roberta, Berger's wife, unfolding an elaborate stroller, with enough pockets and shelves to rival a lab locker. I was thrilled to hear Matt's next suggestion.

"We probably should be going. I'm sure Gloria's exhausted from her trip.''

After a brief visit in the driveway with Roberta and Cynthia,

Matt and I waved good-bye to the family. The nuclear family, I mused.

"Are you really going to recuse yourself from this case?" I asked as I buckled myself into Matt's Camry.

He nodded. "Department policy."

Good thing I'm not in the department, I thought.

THREE

AS HE PULLED ONTO Broadway, Matt turned and gave me a wide smile. "Nice work, letting Berger in on the chemistry lesson," he said, reminding me of his own attractive qualities.

"I'm glad you're not egotistical," I told him.

"You mean you're happy I'm not sensitive about my ignorance?"

I laughed. "Something like that. By the way, have you been to the library lately?" I used a nonchalant tone, as if I hadn't been plotting a trip to the crime scene for the past hour.

Matt reached over and rubbed my shoulder and upper arm, a proprietary gesture that I loved, although it had taken several amorous evenings for me to stop wishing I had leaner, firmer biceps for the occasion. His, after all, were in similar soft, cushiony shape.

"You're thinking there'll be a uniform there and he'll let us in," he said.

"Exactly."

"And since we're not on the job, you must want to check out the New Releases shelf?"

"Right again."

We took a slight detour down Pleasant Street, past the police department, and parked on Beach Street near the front of the Revere Public Library. Bereft as I was of any literary sense, I had always admired the building itself, which dated from 1902, according to the numerals on the new-looking sign—brick-red printing on white—that decorated the front lawn. In my day, Revere High had been next door to it, before being rebuilt in another location a few years ago. I guessed I hadn't visited this spot since Rose had dragged me to a fund-raiser around the holidays. I remembered hearing about plans for remodeling and expanding the library, and the importance of preserving the architectural lines and materials of the original Georgian structure. The Carnegie style, they'd called it, after philanthropist Andrew Carnegie.

Now the beautiful building was a crime scene, but the only indication of that was the uniformed officer sitting on a brick ledge that protruded from the left front of the edifice. No yellow tape, no sign on the door. I didn't even notice a cruiser in the vicinity. A coffee run in progress, I guessed.

"The director probably wants to keep it low-key," Matt said. "A highly publicized murder is not the best way to inspire donors."

"Is he planning to open on Monday?"

"She," Matt said. I slapped my forehead, figuratively. Matt's grin told me he was pleased he'd caught me in a sexist assumption. "Dorothy Leonard's had the job since the first of the year. She's spearheading the plan for renovation and expansion." I'd forgotten the name on the police report. Jet lag, not old age, I told myself. And lack of interest, I admitted. I'd never used public libraries on a routine basis since they couldn't compete with a lab or university for the specialized books and periodicals I liked to read.

In spite of thirty years of effort by my well-read friends, I'd never sustained an interest in fiction or any other nontechnical reading. The farthest I strayed from a book with numbers was to scientific biography.

Once inside the building—a small wave of Matt's hand was all it took to get us access—we were surprised to find we weren't alone. The impeccably dressed Director Dorothy Leonard greeted us as Matt and I climbed the half flight of stairs from the entryway to the main floor.

"Working late?" Matt's smile said they were well acquainted.

Professional associates, I assumed. *Hoped.*

"I lost a lot of time yesterday and some things won't wait," she said, in the resigned tone of one who didn't like working on a Saturday night. Several inches taller than Matt and me, Leonard wore smart slacks and a blazer, in taupe, and seemed the kind of woman who did the dishes in a similar outfit. I was conscious of being in my airplane clothes—green knit pants and top, now sticking to my body in disconcerting places. After ten days in the dry heat of California, I had to reacquaint myself with the humidity of Massachusetts in June. Even in Leonard's imposing presence, however, Matt seemed perfectly comfortable in his casual pants and faded brown polo shirt. I figured he must have learned the attitude in detective school.

"This is Dr. Gloria Lamerino," he told her. "A science consultant for the department."

Leonard nodded in my direction. A polite gesture, with no warmth or accompanying greeting. I hoped her apparent lack of interest in me stemmed from the distraction of dealing with murder on her premises and not disgust at my appearance. I was glad I'd at least left my cane in Matt's car.

She invited us into her office, an ample room a half flight up from the main floor, on the mezzanine level. My eyes ran over the rich mahogany furniture, an art deco lamp, and a large bay window onto the back lot. The ugly orange carpet seemed out of place, as if it might be a temporary fix while the city government replenished its stock of the pleasant, light blue fabric that lay over the main floor.

But it was the walls that captured my attention. They were covered with nearly a dozen art prints of the old Revere Beach Boulevard. Bluebeard's Palace. The Virginia Reel. Carousel horses. Popcorn and cotton-candy stands. The Cyclone rollercoaster, seen from a car on its topmost hill. DO NOT STAND UP warned a cracked wooden sign. Several views of the ocean side included boxy old cars lining the street, dumping out bathers in cumbersome black suits. The colors were muted, as if they'd aged along with the people in the scenes.

I wanted the prints, and it showed.

"I can get you a set," Matt said softly. He pointed to a chair and I guessed I'd missed an invitation to be seated.

I made a note to request another detour before Matt took me home—to the real Revere Beach Boulevard, a mile from my apartment. The Atlantic Ocean would always be *the* ocean for me, even after thirty years by the Pacific.

"I can't stop thinking about what happened here," Leonard said to Matt. "It's too…bizarre."

It, I assumed, was finding Yolanda Fiore's body in her establishment. I wondered at her choice of *bizarre* until Matt explained. "Mrs. Leonard's husband was killed by a fall down the same staircase." He turned to her. "About ten years ago, wasn't it?" he asked.

Leonard nodded, running a well-manicured hand through her short gray-blond hair. Unlike mine, the gray in Leonard's hair seemed strategically placed, designed by a professional. "An accident that time, of course. And, fortunately, I wasn't the one who discovered Irving's…" She hunched her shoulders, as if to ward off a sudden chill, and swung her chair halfway around to look out the window onto the back property. I thought she left us for a moment to visit an earlier decade, and her husband's death.

I made a note to ask Matt for more details, wondering why he hadn't mentioned the incident before. Two deaths in the same spot, ten years apart. In my mind, no coincidence was too small to investigate when John Galigani's life was at stake. I looked at Dorothy Leonard's tall, slender figure and constructed a variation on the black widow theme—she brushes back her stylish bangs and shoves first her husband, then Yolanda Fiore down the same narrow metal staircase. Why, I'd yet to figure out.

Matt stood up, bringing me and Leonard back to the present.

"Sorry," she said, in a monotone, as if she wasn't sure why or to whom she owed an apology. I wished I were better at reading faces. Did a flat stare mean guilty or not guilty?

"Why don't we let you get back to work. We'll take a walk around by ourselves," Matt said.

"Would you mind? I've already been through everything with Detective Parker and his team. I'll be here another half hour or so, if you have any questions."

"Uh, technically, I'm not on the case."

Leonard made a silent snapping gesture with her fingers. "Oh, of course not. The Galiganis."

I wondered how she'd learned about John's alleged involvement so quickly and mentally filed it under "suspicious behavior." Any suspect but John would do.

Matt touched his forehead, as if to salute the director, and followed me down to the main reading room.

When we were out of earshot, I cleared my throat in a deliberate *ahem*. Matt picked up on my unspoken question. "I didn't think of Irving Leonard's death until I saw Dorothy," he said. "As I remember, it was ruled an accident after a brief investigation. Nothing suspicious. No extra bruises or bumps on his body."

"Still…" I said, leaving the rest of the thought in the air.

We stopped in front of a small redbrick model, a three-dimensional rendering of the library-to-be—the present structure, with renovations, plus a new wing extending into the back property. I had a vague memory of seeing the model at the fund-raiser.

A city councilman had listed the shortcomings of the current facility, from its lack of handicap accessibility to the treacherous—in fact, twice lethal—stairway to the basement, not up to code by several measures. I'd found myself rooting for the grant proposal they'd submitted to the state, though I doubted I'd frequent the new building any more than I had the old.

Matt and I walked to the northwestern corner, to the top of the deadly stairs. As we started down, I held on to the wooden railing, as if to brace myself against a sudden forward thrust.

One of the cleaner crime scenes I'd visited, the area where Yolanda Fiore's body had been found was now bloodless and unremarkable. A door marked CUSTODIAN was immediately behind the staircase, the children's reading section spread out to the side. We looked in on the staff lounge and a storage area, completing the tour of the north wing's bottom floor.

Matt took notes, though I couldn't imagine what he found worthy of recording. Especially since he wasn't "on the job" as he'd put it. I hoped I'd be able to read the official police report, figuring Parker and his crew had combed the whole building for physical evidence. But how likely was it the library would be free of fibers and prints from John Galigani, a writer and a great reader who worked in the *Journal* office, only a few blocks away?

"There's nothing more we can do here," Matt said. What have we done? I wondered, growing more anxious every minute John was in custody. He flipped his notebook closed. Jet-lagged though I was, I hated to leave the building. I felt we were just beginning to explore its nooks and crannies.

The area above the circulation desk was open to the roof, past two unconnected mezzanines, one of which housed Leonard's office. I stretched to survey the strangely arranged lofts. What rare books might be stored under their rafters? More to the point—where might a murderer lurk? I resolved to return soon.

As we passed the model library again on the way out I stared at it, as if it might come to life. I wished it could provide a mini-reenactment of the murder John had been accused of. I'd hoped to return to my apartment with a long list—suspects, motives, evidence. All I had from an evening's work was an unidentified controversy over boron and a respectable widow of ten years.

I climbed into Matt's car, straining to see the vacant lot designated for the library expansion, hoping John would be freed before the first shovel went into the ground.

MATT HAD PICKED ME UP at Boston's Logan Airport at three-thirty in the afternoon, East Coast time, and driven me directly to the Galigani residence. I'd been away only ten days, but Rose had planned what was supposed to be a happy reunion.

"Come straight to our house, Gloria, and we'll have an early dinner,'' Rose had told me over the phone the night before. ''Robert and John will be here, too. Besides, I want to see you and make sure you're home to stay.''

Although her voice was full of laughter, Rose had good reason to worry—thirty years earlier, after my fiancé died in a car crash, I'd left my oceanside hometown and gone to Berkeley, California, where I stayed until a year ago. At fifty-five I decided to return and find out if I'd missed anything. It turned out, I had.

My luggage was still in the trunk of Matt's steel-blue Camry—my clothes stuffed into a duffel bag, unlaundered. I felt like a level four biohazard worker running from one crisis to another. But the circumstance of John's arrest had sent enough adrenaline through my system to sustain however many more waking hours I needed. Besides, I had three hours on everyone else in town.

We carried my luggage up the two flights of stairs. Neither of us liked to ride the elevator in the Galigani Mortuary. Spots of blood and other displaced organic material haunted my fantasy of the closed, padded space that Frank and Robert used to transport their clients, as they referred to them.

When Matt's beeper went off, I knew a long kiss was all I could hope for before Matt would leave.

''Don't make any plans for tomorrow,'' he said.

''Day or night?''

''Both,'' he said, and we kissed again.

IT TOOK LESS THAN an hour to reconnect with my life. My E-mail and phone messages were light since I'd accessed them from Elaine's house in Berkeley. One phone message had come in during the morning from Peter Mastrone, an old friend who expected more than renewed friendship from me. I deleted it, with a resolution to be clearer than ever about how I felt, or didn't feel, about him.

One quick look at the U.S. mail, a call to Rose, then I'd take a nap. It was only six o'clock California time, but I felt I'd already lived those extra three hours. I sifted through flyers,

magazines, and bills, filtering out the first-class letters. A few
letters from former professional colleagues, sure to be part
business, part personal. A bright pink envelope from my cousin
Mary Ann in Worcester, probably a late-arriving bon voyage
card. A thick letter from the youngest Galigani child, Mary
Catherine, a chemical engineer living in Houston. I wondered
if she'd been told yet about her brother's arrest.

The last piece of first-class mail had no return address. A
small off-white envelope of good quality, postmarked REVERE.
I slit it open and pulled out a plain sheet of matching paper.

My throat tightened as I scanned the neatly typed lines, then
reread every word.

KEEP OUT OF POLICE WORK. TAKE UP SEWING. END YOUR NEW
POLICE CAREER, OR I WILL.

My fingers gripped the note. I looked around quickly, as if
the author might be standing over me with a coat rack, ready
to push me out the door and down my own staircase.

FOUR

IT MEANS NOTHING, I told myself as I chained my door and set the intrusion alarm. I carried the letter, stuffed back into its envelope, to one of my pale blue glide rockers—the only furniture that survived my cross-country move—and put it on my lap. Was I hoping it might have a different message when I pulled it out again?

I'd looked forward to returning to my neat apartment—simple furnishings, framed prints of San Francisco and the Bay Area. I hoped for a little breeze to carry the smell of salt air to my window onto Tuttle Street and St. Anthony's Church. A threatening note was not part of my welcome home plan.

I read the letter again, and annoyance replaced my initial reflexive panic. *Sewing* indeed. I thought of astronomer Maria Mitchell and her complaints about needlework. When she was a young woman, she'd been forced to learn to sew although she wanted to study astronomy, her father's profession. As a treat to counteract the nasty note, I made an espresso and took a copy of her diary from my bookcase. I found my favorite passage, from an entry in 1853.

> *The needle is the chain of woman, and has fettered her more than the laws of the country. I would as soon put a girl alone into the closet to meditate as give her only the society of her needle.*

Too bad I don't have a return address on my threatening note, I thought. I'd send him—or her—this quote.

I'd received intimidating notes and phone calls working on other cases with the Revere Police Department, but not so early in the game. The only person I'd met so far in connection with Yolanda Fiore's murder was Dorothy Leonard, whom I'd left less than an hour ago. Certainly not enough time for a posted letter to reach me.

I studied the cancellation mark, but couldn't make out a date. While I was in California, Rose, whose office was one floor below my apartment in the mortuary building, had piled my mail into a basket on the floor of my small foyer. I decided against asking if she remembered which day this letter had arrived—no need to worry her over what would probably be useless information.

It had been less than forty-eight hours since Yolanda had been killed. Not much time, unless the killer had dispatched Yolanda down the library stairway with one hand and mailed the letter with the other. It was even more curious to think the note could have been written before the murder. Curious. And not a little frightening.

I abandoned the idea of a nap and took out a notebook. I headed the first page SEWING LETTER, to remind me of the perseverance of Maria Mitchell, who eventually discovered a comet and became the first female member of the American Academy of Arts and Sciences. The impact of the rude note was softened by the title I'd given it, and I was able to analyze it with a level head.

I made a list of potential meanings.

Possibility number one—the note had nothing to do with the current case. Perhaps the writer thought I'd receive it before my trip to California. He could have been warning me off the now-completed Berkeley murder investigation.

Number two—the revenge of an unhappy relative of someone I'd helped put behind bars. I scribbled the names of the key people in earlier cases. No one stood out as the likely author.

I briefly considered a misdelivery, but since there wasn't

another Dr. Gloria Lamerino in Revere, or in the state as far as I knew, I didn't bother to write it down.

On to possibility number three. I was being warned off investigating Yolanda Fiore's murder.

The implications were clear and chilling: the murder was committed by someone who knew me, or knew about me. I shuddered at the idea that I was specifically sought out by a cold-blooded killer. More probably, I decided, the person was aware of my contracts with the police department or my connection to the Galiganis, and figured I'd get involved.

At the bottom of the page I wrote my view of the case so far:

1. Possible motive: controversy over boron? Suspects: nuclear scientists at the Charger Street lab.

2. Possible motive: unrelated to boron? Suspects: everyone else.

3. Killer's strategy: frame John Galigani. Dissuade Lamerino from investigating.

Under ACTION, I wrote

1. Visit Charger Street lab.

2. Get library card.

My work on the Fiore case was under way.

THE TELEPHONE woke me from an unintentional nap in the rocker. My notebook had slid to the floor, my espresso cup was perilously close to the edge of the end table.

"You were asleep," Rose said, her own voice far from upbeat.

I groaned when I realized I'd forgotten to call her. "I didn't mean to be. I took a couple of pain pills."

"Are your feet still bothering you?"

"A little." I paused. I had so many questions for Rose, but I wasn't sure how to phrase them and I was worried about the answers. I settled for the simplest one first. "How's John?"

Rose sighed. I heard a pain beyond the reach of little white pills. "They're keeping him overnight, Gloria. I didn't think they could do that."

"I didn't either." Rose sounded so fragile, I hesitated to ask even the most basic questions, like whether they'd retained a lawyer for John.

"Frank called Judge Sciacchitano," she told me. I waited for Rose to give me the stats on Sciacchitano—parish, number of children, recent deceased loved one laid to rest with Frank's help. But this was not a normal conversation, and even the judge's gender remained undisclosed to me.

"So John might be home soon?" I asked in a hopeful tone.

"Yes. He told us there was no reason John shouldn't be allowed to come home, and he's going to look into it."

Neither of us wanted to articulate the worst—that John might be detained. Surely a judge who knew the Galiganis well enough to talk to them on a weekend would work hard to get John home. I carried the phone to my window and stared across Revere Street to the gray brick tower of St. Anthony's Church. The prayers of my youth came back to me, as if it hadn't been decades since I'd knelt at Tuesday night novena services. *Saint Anthony, our patron and our advocate, grant us what we ask of thee.*

I knew the Galiganis had no financial problems, but I made the offer anyway.

"Thanks, Gloria. I'm sure we'll be able to take care of it. We need you to..." Rose's voice broke.

"I'm already on it."

SATURDAY NIGHT was not a handy time to begin an investigation. Both the lab and the library would be closed until Monday morning. I wandered around my apartment, halfheartedly unpacking, uninterested in reading or television. I wondered where Matt was, and how I was going to acquire necessary information without his formal participation. I knew he wouldn't cross the line drawn by department canons.

I blamed my impasse on how pitifully few friends I'd made during my year back in my hometown, leaving me no resources, no contacts. When John was cleared, I decided, I'd be more responsive to Rose's attempts to draw me into Revere society. As if I hadn't made that resolution before.

If Rose and Frank could command the services of a judge on a weekend, I should be able to do some small thing off-hours. My friends are a small group, but of high quality, I told myself. I picked up the telephone and pushed Andrea Cabrini's number.

"Hi, Gloria. It's great to hear from you. I knew you were coming back from California today."

"I got in a little while ago. I hope I'm not calling too late."

"Oh, no, I'm a night person. I hope you had a good time."

I'd met Andrea, a technician at the lab, on my first case with Matt. A friend of hers—a hydrogen researcher—had been murdered. Since then she'd attached herself to me as a kind of disciple for my work on homicide cases. She'd introduced me to scientists and engineers I needed to interview, taken me to seminars, given me the scoop on the latest in laboratory politics. Andrea was what plus-size clothing ads called a big, beautiful woman. She had fewer friends than I did, and I'd convinced myself that she really enjoyed helping me.

I thought I'd spare Andrea the details of my harrowing ten days and wounded feet. "I have a souvenir for you," I told her instead.

Andrea's delighted gasp sent a wave of guilt through me—first because I planned to exploit our friendship one more time, and second because I hadn't even picked out her souvenir myself. At the end of my stay in Berkeley I'd taken advantage of my slight disability and talked Elaine into shopping for me, something I dreaded even with perfect soles.

"I read the awful news about Yolanda Fiore's murder," Andrea said. "She used to work here. I didn't know her though."

"But you knew I'd have some questions for you."

"Yeah. About boron, right? I've already copied some material from our library. And I got you a pass in case you wanted to get on-site tomorrow."

"Andrea, you're a gem."

"I love helping you. It's the most fun thing I do." She paused and I heard a small cough. "Not that I hope for more murders or anything."

I pictured Andrea in one of her oversized tunics, her pudgy hands flying to her mouth in dismay at the thought of giving me the wrong impression.

"I know, Andrea. And I would love to get into the lab tomorrow. Why don't I take you to lunch first? Say, Russo's, at noon?"

"Yeah, I'm free for lunch. That would be perfect. Thanks, Gloria."

After we hung up, I wondered why I hadn't told Andrea how John Galigani's near-arrest made this case different from the others we'd worked on. Could I be in denial about the serious trouble my friends' son was in? I knew I would never believe John capable of murder.

During the years I'd lived in California, the Galiganis had visited often. At least once a year the whole family would fly west, crowding my condo, filling its small rooms and me with pleasure. Rose and I had seen each other more often, one highlight a week-long trip to Rome in our fortieth birthday year.

The Galigani children had also spent time with me separately. I loved each one equally, except for a slight bias toward Mary Catherine, the youngest and only girl. And the only one to enter a hard-science field, chemical engineering. Mary Catherine had been married to a lawyer for a short time. Her letter to me this week told of a new love, a petroleum chemist.

"I know you love him already, Aunt Glo," MC had written.

Though only a year apart, Robert and John might as well have been separated by a generation. I remembered their college days—Robert, the conservative dresser, studying biology, headed for mortuary school; John, the sociology major with long hair, wishing he'd been born early enough to join the protests of the sixties.

Nostalgia was getting me nowhere.

I checked my watch. Ten after seven. Still on California time. I turned the hands three hours ahead—with older eyes, I found analog watch faces much easier to read than digital—as much to put an end to Saturday as to be in sync with the East Coast. On Sunday, John would be home, I was sure, and I'd be at the lab uncovering a boron motive.

For now I should go to bed early, and be ready for a full day. I looked at the summer linens on my bed, an inviting white cotton knit spread and a soft pillow.

I groaned and rubbed my eyes. Not yet.

I changed the bandages on my feet and grabbed my cane. I had no idea what I hoped to accomplish by a visit to a public building locked up for the night, but I knew it was more than I'd get done sitting in my apartment.

A half hour later, dressed in cotton pants and a new Cal Berkeley T-shirt with long sleeves, I parked my long black Cadillac—another perk from living in the Galigani Mortuary—in front of the Revere Public Library. The officer was gone. I assumed some time limit had been reached and there was no more to be gained from keeping the crime scene isolated.

I limped around the property. The old redbrick structure was so beautiful, I felt almost inspired to read something literary. Years ago, Elaine had talked me into a card for the Berkeley Public Library—also a good-looking brick building—and I remembered taking out classics under her direction. I'd tried Jane Austen, Emily Brontë, George Sands, George Eliot.

"They're early feminists," she'd told me. "You should love them."

I shook my head. "It's hard to read a book without equations."

Eventually Elaine gave up her attempts to convert me to well-roundedness of the intellectual kind.

Lights were on up and down Beach Street as I took a lame walk along the side of the building. I pictured the model I'd seen inside the library and found the area designated for the new extension, stretching about sixty feet in back.

To the right of the building was the vacant lot where my old high school once stood, and just beyond that was the only cemetery in the city—the Rumney Marsh Burying Ground. I walked as far as the entrance and peered in through the wrought-iron gate.

The headstone closest to me had a date of 1809, but I remembered from civics classes that there were even older graves, some from the 1600s. Isolated from the activity on the main street, I faced the musty overgrown gravestones, dim forms in the darkness. I felt light-headed thinking how likely it was that the fence had been moved many times during the city's four-hundred-year history. I could be standing on the remains of pilgrims, Minutemen, patriots. I imagined the bulldozers unearthing the bones of doughboys. Or ordinary churchgoers and grandfathers.

The mixture of gravel and broken glass under my feet reminded me of the reason for my copper-colored metal cane—my flight from a killer in a Berkeley waste pit. At the same time a shadow fell across my path, cutting through the moonlight, as if a soundless, invisible airplane had passed over my head. I spun a full three hundred sixty degrees and scanned the area for an attacker.

The lot was empty.

Before I lost my balance completely and summoned up a ghost from another century, I turned and hobbled toward Beach Street and my Cadillac.

ON THE WAY HOME, I stopped at a supermarket on Broadway, grateful for the longer store hours of modern times. I picked up essentials for my empty larder—two flavors of ice cream and the makings of an eggplant parmigian. I made a special stop for Matt's favorite kind of bagel—plain—a vote of confidence that he'd be having breakfast in my apartment some morning soon.

My foresight was rewarded by the presence of a black unmarked Revere Police Department Ford in front of the mortuary. When I drove up, Matt got out of his car and stood near the shrubbery that lined the driveway. I knew he enjoyed watching me squeeze the Cadillac between a hearse and a limousine in the Galiganis' specially designed garage. I'd gotten good at it, but still held my breath, waiting for a scraping sound, until I shifted to PARK.

"Have you been here long?" I asked him.

"About fifteen minutes. I took care of that call and came back for a cup of coffee. When you weren't here, I figured you were breaking into the lab, reading boron documents."

I laughed and shook my head. "Just doing some errands." I handed him one of the grocery bags and preceded him through the mortuary foyer, giving slight nods toward Mr. McCabe, in cherry wood in Parlor A, and Mrs. Tucci, in walnut in Parlor B.

Matt continued his guesswork as we climbed the stairs, past Rose's office on the second floor, up to my apartment on the third. "Well, then, you have a meeting with Andrea tomorrow and she's going to get you in on a weekend visitor pass. Or something like that."

I stopped midstep and looked down on him, still in his airport casuals.

"How did you know that?"

He shrugged his shoulders. "It's what I do." His grin made me want to skip coffee.

We entered my apartment, both slightly out of breath. Matt put his nose near the top of the brown bag he was carrying. "Umm. Breakfast bagels. Is that an invitation?"

I felt my face redden. My motives were entirely too transparent for comfort.

We postponed our food and drink.

FIVE

AT MIDNIGHT, eastern daylight saving time, Matt and I sat across from each other, the remains of a snack on the coffee table between us. My piles of science magazines were dotted with cannoli crumbs and powdered sugar—not even her son's legal predicament had prevented Rose from sending us off with a plate of treats earlier that day.

Matt had managed to bring copies of the police report, but the additional pages didn't add much to what I'd already learned at Berger's. I needed to know more about Yolanda Fiore, her family and friends. I needed to get into her apartment, but couldn't count on that with Matt off the case.

While Matt cleared the dishes, I glanced toward the desk drawer where I'd stored the warning note left in my mail basket. For a moment I wondered whether I should contribute it to the police folder, at least figuratively, by showing it to Matt. I decided against mentioning it—an unnecessary complication that might spoil the evening. It wasn't as if the note held a clue, I told myself. Besides, the threat might have nothing to do with the Fiore case.

But I had to admit, the biggest reason I withheld the note had to do with Matt's concern for my safety whenever I undertook police work without his supervision. The last thing I wanted was for him to try to curb my investigation into Yolanda Fiore's murder.

"Give me another installment on how Yolanda's looking into boron might be connected to this," Matt said. "Twenty-five words or less,'' he amended, probably when he saw the excited gleam in my eyes.

"Twenty-five words. I can do it." I cleared my throat and made elaborate counting motions. "Boron is put in the cooling water system to keep the reactor core from overheating, plus in the pools where the waste is stored." I smiled. "Twenty-four."

"Very good. You mean otherwise you could have a reaction take place in the pile of waste outside the reactor building?"

I waved my hand in a sort-of gesture. "Yes, but not likely, even though the fuel assemblies that come out of the core are highly radioactive. It's just a precaution."

"So what could be controversial?" Matt asked.

I thought a moment. "The only safety issue I can conceive of is not enough boron in either the cooling or the disposal system. But it's hard to imagine. Boron is not that expensive. And it's certainly not new technology that anyone would be fighting over."

I was surprised when Matt stood to leave, gathering his jacket and files. "Too much science?" I asked.

Matt smiled. "No, I just don't think these clothes can take another on-off cycle. Can I have my bagel to go?"

"Help yourself."

"I'm sorry," he said, apparently hearing the disappointment I'd tried to mask with a yawn. He bent down to kiss me. "Maybe I should leave a change of clothes here."

The statement came out like a true/false question on a math test.

I smiled. "Good idea."

Ordinarily such a move forward—in my mind I bought a new toothbrush to leave at his Fernwood Avenue house—would have been enough to give me the sweetest of dreams. But Matt wasn't finished.

"Maybe I should bring all my clothes here. Or you could bring all of yours to my house. Your furniture, too." He grinned and swept the room with his free arm.

My body went rigid. My internal organs seemed to stop

functioning. I stared at Matt, then my eyes drifted to the ceiling, to escape the reality of the moment.

"I…I…" Not only couldn't I finish my thought, I couldn't even start it.

Matt slapped his forehead. "Sorry. It must be the cannoli talking." He gave me a big smile and kissed me good-bye.

I sat in my chair for a long time after Matt left. How could such an important moment have come and gone so quickly? I wondered if I'd lost him by my unenthusiastic response to what might have been a proposal—to live together, or—I also considered that he might have been joking all along and I'd narrowly escaped making a fool of myself by shouting *yes!*

I couldn't decide which interpretation was less appealing.

I'D SET MY ALARM for eight on Sunday morning, determined to call Rose before the day got out of hand. I took an espresso back to bed and punched her number—the first button on my speed-dial panel—from a barely upright position.

Matt's remark was at the front of my brain. Ordinarily, a heart-to-heart about my love life was among the top five of Rose's favorite topics, coming right after her husband and children, and I desperately wanted to talk to her about it. But I knew it would have to wait. The only topic for a while would be the pending murder charge against her son.

"John will be home at ten o'clock this morning," she told me, sounding wide awake and more positive than the day before. "And I know you and Matt and the whole RPD force are behind us. John is innocent and that's as clear as a rainbow in winter." I smiled at Rose's usual ineptitude at metaphors and analogies, relieved that her characteristic positive attitude had returned. "Can you come over around noon?"

"Much as I'd like to, I have an appointment at the lab with Andrea Cabrini."

"Wonderful, wonderful. That's more important." I thought I heard Rose snap her fingers. "I'll bet Yolanda's murder is connected to her work at that lab."

I sensed Rose's relief, as if the case had just been solved. In line with her optimism, I pictured a boron physicist already in custody.

Then Rose took me in another direction. "I can't believe I didn't think of this before. Yolanda was active in the group that's always protesting the lab's weapons research. They're the ones that complain about bomb-making and radiation leaks and such." She lowered her voice. "You remember when John went through that phase."

Not hearing a question, I chose not to pursue the reason for John's arrests—his record!—especially after Matt's warning that it could be used against him. It didn't surprise me that Yolanda could be an activist and a lab employee at the same time. Perfectly legal, if not welcomed by lab management.

"I'll bet someone wanted to silence her. You know how the lab hates bad press and she was in the news a lot," Rose continued.

It was as good a theory as any, I had to admit, and it seemed a more likely motive than a boron cover-up. Of the many parts of nuclear power that people worried about, the boron in the temporary waste pool was not high on the list. Lower than meltdown, lower than the permanent disposal of waste, to name two.

"I'll check it out," I said, as if I were the lead detective in the case. "While I have you on the phone, maybe you could help me with some basic information." I took a few sips of espresso and sat up straighter, giving me a better view of the Tuttle Street trees in the morning sun.

"Sure. What did you have in mind?"

I pulled my notebook and pen onto my lap. "I don't know exactly. But I'd like to get a better feel for John's relationship to Yolanda and why it ended."

"Oh, well, I wouldn't know exactly. Frank and I only met her a couple of times, but she was not right for John. Too—intense."

As if John were laid-back. I took another road. "Berger—remember Matt's partner?—said her current boyfriend was

Derek Byrne. Do you know if she went right from John to Derek? Things like that will help me get to know Yolanda better.''

''Right. Well, Derek is the councilman's son. Did you know that? Councilman Brendan Byrne. Must be in his seventies, but he still has a lot of sway at City Hall, and he's a big shot in the VFW. Awful tragedy years ago when his parents—they would be Derek's grandparents—drank a bad batch of moonshine liquor. Father died, I believe. Mother blinded. Or vice versa.''

Rose, the unofficial historian of Revere, was back, with statistics tumbling out of her mouth.

''What a disaster,'' I said. ''Did they find out who made the liquor?''

''Oh, yes, they knew it was the Scottos. They had a still over on Malden Street, before the bend in front of the old St. Mary's Church. One of them was arrested, but then he skipped to Italy while he was out on bail. Hasn't been seen since, as far as I know. Of course he'd be in his nineties. And then the rest of the family moved out west somewhere. Chicago, I think.''

I laughed. Only a native Bostonian like Rose thinks anything west of New England is *out west*. Rose had traveled to Europe and visited me in California, but she had no connection to the states in the middle of the country, mostly rectangles, she'd observed during her flights to the West Coast.

''Very interesting.''

''Oh, and I remember hearing that the councilman, young Brendan Byrne, who was about eighteen at that time, took off for the army right after all this happened.''

''Terrific. That's the kind of information I need.'' Not really, I thought, but I didn't mind stretching the truth now that Rose was back in her census mode. Anything to encourage normalcy. ''Tell me more about Derek Byrne. Apparently he was the last one to see her alive, except for the killer.''

''Unless he *is* the killer,'' Rose said, with another snap of her fingers. I imagined her adding Derek to a list of suspects that didn't include John.

''Of course.''

"Well, he's Dorothy Leonard's assistant at the library. You know that, but maybe you don't know that Dorothy was promoted over him. Unpleasant situation for a while. But Derek's a nice young man. In fact, you probably met him yourself, at the fund-raiser last Christmas."

I wrote "Derek upset—lost promotion" in my notebook, then closed my eyes and tried to picture him at the fund-raising punch bowl. It was hopeless. I paid little attention to people I met at social gatherings, while Rose probably remembered what color tie he was wearing, and whether he wore a matching hanky in his outside breast pocket. I'd agreed to attend the event only because Frank had the flu and Rose wanted company. Not my idea of a fun evening.

"Do you remember anything from when John and Yolanda were together? How long did it last?"

"Let's see. I'd say they dated close to a year. Kind of a big commitment for John. Not that he's fickle or anything."

"No, no."

"Just hasn't met the right one."

"That's understandable."

"Although he's pretty serious about Carolyn. You know he's taking her to Bermuda?"

I knew Rose was pacing as she talked, a habit when she was nervous. For my part, I sat up in bed making agitated doodles on my notepad. Not hard to figure which of us burned more calories.

"You told me. The Dalassandros hired him to be the official reporter for a charter cruise."

"Right. Lots of Revere people going. It'll be quite a spread in the *Journal,* and maybe even the *Globe* will pick it up. Big responsibility for John." I heard a pause and a coffee-sipping sound. "I think he'll stick with Carolyn."

The Galiganis always spoke of their children with pride, but today Rose sounded more like a confused character witness in a murder trial. To escape the sadness I felt, I'd scribbled a list of questions while she talked, some more sensitive than others. I was running out of nontouchy ones.

"Why did Yolanda call it off with John?"

I'd mumbled the question, half to myself, unaware that it would thunder across the phone line and strike at Rose's heart.

"What?" Rose's voice was sharp, and up a notch or two. "Who told you she called it off? It was John's idea. As I've been telling you, he doesn't get into long-term relationships." She sounded exasperated that her best friend didn't get it.

Her response, defensive and contradicting what I already knew about who had ended the relationship, provoked more frantic doodling. I made huge, wide Xs as if I could obliterate the last thirty seconds of conversation. I should have learned my lesson in California with Elaine Cody, when I investigated a case involving her boyfriend's teenage son. I thought of lettering a sign for myself. NEVER INTERVIEW YOUR CLOSE FRIENDS.

I also realized I was unequipped from a legal standpoint. What was the protocol? Could I tell her about the letters I'd seen in the police file—John's angry words when Yolanda dumped him? Was I even supposed to know about the correspondence? Was I Rose's friend or an investigator on her son's behalf? I wished there were such a thing as an Amateur Sleuth Handbook, or better yet, that Matt were around.

"Gloria?" I heard desperation in Rose's voice.

In the few seconds I had to decide, I opted for conservatism. I hoped it wasn't because I didn't trust my best friend with the truth.

"You're right, Rose. I shouldn't have phrased it that way." I cleared my throat and smoothed out the section of bedspread I'd been pulling apart. A cloud passed overhead and cast the notes on my lap in shadowy gray. "How about the dinner John and Yolanda had on Thursday night? Did you know he was going to see her again?"

"John had dinner with Yolanda? Where are you getting this, Gloria? I'm not sure you believe John is innocent." Rose's voice had reached such a high pitch I was concerned about her blood pressure. I hoped Frank was home.

"Of course I believe John is innocent. But I have to know

everything if I'm going to be able to help him. We can't have surprises.''

I heard an intake of breath. ''What surprises? How can you have any doubt?''

''To ask for information is not to doubt.''

''This is my son, Gloria. Don't give me a lesson in logic.'' My heart sank. A lifelong friendship was at stake. What made me think I was capable of an objective investigation under these conditions? ''I'd better go now,'' she told me.

My friend's cracking voice and the click of the telephone sent a wave of anguish through me. First Matt, now Rose. I leaned back on my pillow and stared at the ceiling, the painted off-white swirls matching my emotional state.

I COULDN'T REMEMBER the last time Rose and I had a serious disagreement, unless you counted the controversy over whether to eat inside or out when we were in Venice twenty years ago.

I tried the Galigani number several times in the next hour, but hung up each time I heard the outgoing message on their answering machine. I wished they had E-mail at home. Probably just as well, I realized. It was even easier to be misunderstood electronically.

The phone rang while I was dressing. I picked up on the first ring, hoping it was Rose. Instead, the call was from Erin Wong, the twenty-something general science teacher I'd contacted at Revere High School. To meet one of my retirement goals—contributing to science education—I'd promised to mentor students who showed a special interest in science and technology. Although I didn't remember writing ''murder investigations'' on my to-do list for old age, I'd spent more time at that than at any of the hobbies I'd envisioned.

''Have you given any more thought to a project for my seniors?'' Erin asked me.

''How about building a model nuclear reactor?''

''Cool.''

IT WAS ONLY ten o'clock and I wasn't due to meet Andrea at Russo's until noon. I considered driving first to the Galigani home across town, but in the end, I decided the best thing was to wait until I had something tangible to show them. Because that would be more efficient, I told myself—and because I couldn't risk face-to-face rejection.

My computer provided the distraction I needed to fill the time until lunch. I clicked on a search engine and downloaded the first ten matches to "boric acid + reactor."

In spite of my careful choice of key words, I got three leads to boron as a nutrient in the human diet and its use in wine-making. I read ads for boron fertilizer and a dietary supplement—boron the "Calcium Helper," assisting calcium absorption in the body. I also noted in passing that the market value of boron was three hundred fifty dollars per ton for raw material, and the U.S. and Turkey accounted for 90 percent of world production. News of a multipatient clinical trial of an experimental treatment for brain tumors, called boron neutron capture therapy, caught my attention until I remembered my mission.

Here was one problem with the Internet I knew too well—it was so easy to become sidetracked by useless information.

The good thing about it—there's no one to offend on the other end of the line.

SIX

I PARKED IN THE BACK lot of Russo's Cafe, an upscale coffee shop around the corner from the police station on Broadway. I'd signed my first Revere Police Department contract at one of the tables in the back of this restaurant. Matt had been waiting for me, his long nose deep into crime-scene photos from the murder of a hydrogen researcher. I'd met him only briefly before that day, when I appeared as an expert witness for him.

Almost a year to the day, when I didn't know what he ate for breakfast. It seemed long ago.

On Sunday morning the weather had turned even warmer. I stepped from my air-conditioned Cadillac into the low nineties, with humidity to match. I wore an olive-green linen dress, sleeveless, but layered with a short-sleeved blouse in a sheer fabric. My upper arms hadn't seen the light of day since I was a teenager, no matter what the temperature.

Andrea was waiting in the small entryway, dressed in a purple and black print outfit I'd seen before—wide pants and a matching short-sleeved tunic. She stood and gave me a sweaty hug.

"I always love your pins," she said, studying the one-inch bronze computer on my lapel. I showed her how it opened, just like a real laptop, its tiny keyboard hanging from the collar of my shirt.

Russo's fine reputation was for food, not decor. I'd gotten used to the fake columns and broken sculptures, a shabby recreation of ancient Rome. But today the headless torsos reminded me of Frank's decapitated client and the bodies buried in the cemetery behind the library. I knew I wouldn't enjoy my roasted peppers with thoughts of a hand-fashioned neck stitched to a dead chest, so I focused instead on a faux marble cherub with a faucet for a mouth.

When we were seated I gave Andrea the souvenir I'd brought from California. A plastic sports bottle with the logo of Berkeley University Laboratory, my place of employment for thirty years. It was the kind of water container active people might attach to their bikes, or Andrea and I would keep on our desks, filled with pens and pencils.

"Wow. Thanks, Gloria." Andrea turned the mug around and laughed at the acronym BUL in blue and gold. "Everyone will want this." This in exchange for entry into the Charger Street lab and the inside scoop on boron problems. It didn't seem fair, and I thought of making it up to Andrea later. Silently I thanked Elaine Cody, my personal shopper. Andrea stuffed the souvenir into her tote bag, pulling a large notebook and folders out in the same motion.

I wasn't surprised to see Andrea had done her homework.

"Yolanda Fiore's supervisor was Anthony Taruffi. Tony. He heads the Public Affairs Office at the lab—one of those party-line guys. Nothing gets past him that might make the lab or any of our funding agencies look bad."

"He couldn't have been happy with her activism. I hear she was a troublemaker of sorts?"

Andrea nodded. "She started a newsletter for employees' grievances and environmental complaints from the community. It's called *Raid-iation News*." Andrea spelled the play on words. "Like 'raid the lab,' I guess. I've seen a few issues. She did a special one on boric acid solutions and how they can overflow from a waste tank onto the floor of the building and cause corrosion."

Boron again. Used properly it prevents meltdown, but if not handled correctly, it becomes a safety problem itself. "I'd like to see a copy if you have one."

Andrea made a note, and I knew from experience that she'd

follow through. "She got some volunteers to work with her. Supposedly it was all done on their own time."

"So technically it wasn't a reason to fire her."

Andrea tilted her head from side to side, in an "iffy" motion. "You know how these things work."

I did. It was always a contest between official procedures on the one hand and a supervisor's desire to get rid of an employee on the other. Although legislation was in place to protect rights on both sides, there were ways around it.

Andrea handed me a lab-issue orange folder. "I pulled the last few articles Yolanda wrote for the lab's official newspaper. They all have to do with boron and the state of the waste generated by nuclear power plants. Remember, the lab has a contract with the Nuclear Regulatory Commission to oversee the waste storage containers."

I flipped through the pages, noting titles like "The Quest to Bury Nuclear Waste," "Keeping Assemblies Subcritical," and "Safety Injection Systems."

"Thanks. I'll read these later," I said as a lovely young Asian woman—CYNDI, her name tag said—brought our pasta and beans. Russo's had become a melting pot.

"I've looked through the articles. They're pretty harmless. Taruffi would never let anything but happy talk get out to the public. Once in a while Yolanda slips in scenarios about breaks in the steam line and that kind of thing. And she talks about the quantity of boron that's required for safety in the waste pools."

"Maybe there's more inflammatory material in her newsletter."

Andrea nodded. "Maybe. And if Yolanda had found a controversial angle to nuclear safety, it could be another motive to fire her."

"Right."

Or kill her, I added to myself.

ANDREA ESCORTED ME through the building that housed the Public Affairs Office, the Visitor Center, and the Science Education Center—all the functions that had to do with the world outside the lab. I wondered what percent of the total budget was designated for "outreach" as my Berkeley lab had called it. Not much, in my experience—just enough to keep the activists at bay.

Yolanda had been fired a week before her murder, but according to Andrea, the police had visited her former work site anyway and carried off a carton of material.

"Would you like to see her old desk, too? Maybe you'll get a vibe or something."

I gave her a teasing look of disapproval, evoking a giggle from her small round mouth.

"I know—this is logic, not magic. But the police might have left something behind."

I didn't hold out much hope for a cubicle that had been gone over by the police and, presumably, by Yolanda's murderer, if he or she was a lab employee. It was as good a place as any to start, however, and I followed Andrea through the labyrinth of partitions that divided one large room into dozens of small work areas. The building was empty, but well lighted even on a Sunday. Its interior design was a relic of the seventies, when beams and pipes were painted bright colors and left exposed.

No one had claimed Yolanda's work space, still stacked with office supplies, but containing no personal items I could see. Andrea walked around the area, ran her hand under the desk and chair, pulled out drawers, and inspected the computer ports.

"I've seen this on TV," she said. "They find clues taped under the furniture."

I smiled. "I think it only works on TV."

As we toured the divided room, I felt I should be leaving a trail of crumbs. It was hard to tell one end of the windowless maze from the other. Name plates stuck to the fake walls with Velcro were a help—the third time I saw LORNA SANFORD on a brown felt partition, I knew we'd covered the area.

As supervisor, Tony Taruffi had a real office, closed in by glass on two sides.

"We call it the fishbowl," Andrea said.

We peered in, palms on the glass as if we were waiting for the gelato shop to open. In spite of the bright lights, the lack of noise from people, printers, or telephones gave me a creepy feeling that seemed to be following me around since I'd heard of Yolanda's murder.

What had I possibly hoped to find here? I wondered. A gun or a knife? The weapon was a coat rack. A blood-streaked carpet? The crime was committed in a building two miles away. The murderer lurking in the hallway?

"Can I help you?"

The voice echoed loudly in the cavernous building. Andrea and I jumped as high as our respective masses would allow.

"Hi, Tony," Andrea said. I was impressed at the tone she'd managed—as if she'd shown up on time for a Sunday afternoon meeting and he was late. Tony Taruffi was a large man, taller than a coat rack, I guessed, with a wide neck. Andrea kept up her cheery front, though I detected a nervous pitch to her voice. "This is Dr. Gloria Lamerino. She's a retired physicist from Berkeley, California."

Taruffi grinned broadly and extended his hand. "Yes, I've heard about you. A police consultant now, aren't you?" I looked up and down his long face, from his smile to his eyes. Both seemed cold.

"At times, yes." I presented my most pleasant countenance.

Taruffi had moved his body so he was between us and his office door. His brown hair, graying at the temples, was carefully groomed and his clothes were casual, but crisp enough in case a TV van pulled up unexpectedly. I placed him at about fifty, but I was getting poorer at such estimates as my own age crept toward a new decade.

"Is there something I can do for you?"

"Oh, no," Andrea said. "We're just on our way to the Visitor Center."

I nodded, happy to have Andrea directing the fiction. Taruffi looked dubious, but played along.

"Well, let me show you some of our latest publications," Taruffi said, leading us away from his office to a metal rack near the elevator. He pulled brochures and flyers from rows of vertical slots and held up a colorful pamphlet on the lab's laser fusion program. "Andrea helped us with this one. Very bright, this little lady."

I grimaced at the first-grade characterization of a competent adult woman in a highly technical field, but I'd heard it before. On the other hand, I'd never heard a professional man referred to as a bright little gentleman.

"Tony got us permission to do it in color," Andrea said. She pointed to dramatic photos of enormous round lenses and imploding targets.

"The government guidelines specify black and white only. But I found a way around it," Taruffi said, stopping short of beating his chest. He walked us through double doors, to the Visitor Center, an annex east of the Public Affairs Office, boasting the whole time. When the president of the United States visited the laboratory in '91, Taruffi himself showed his entourage around the property. Taruffi's latest plan for expanding the lab's education program had received accolades from the Department of Energy. Taruffi's portfolio of public information materials was nominated for a special award by the Society of Technical Communicators. Lucky for the lab, Taruffi had rejected many offers to head outreach programs for private institutions.

When I finally tired of his monologue, I tried a new direction.

"I suppose you heard about Yolanda Fiore's murder?"

As if on cue, Taruffi nodded. He threw back his broad shoulders and drew his face into a serious expression. "Very sad."

"I understand she used to work for you?"

Taruffi put his arm around my shoulder, and laughed. I felt a shiver up my back. "Dr. Lamerino, why didn't you tell me you were here as a police representative?"

"I'm not. Not today anyway." I made an attempt to match his frivolous manner, and came out with a small laugh of my own. "But I'll be back."

I heard Andrea's nervous cough and hoped I wasn't putting

her career—or her life—in jeopardy. It's Taruffi who should be tense, I thought—at least, I would be if a woman I'd fired was found murdered a week later.

When he left us, I turned around and caught a glimpse of him standing, legs apart, arms folded, leaning against the doors, as if waiting to intercept us if we walked back into his side of the building.

I let out a big sigh.

"Whew," I said, wiping my brow in an elaborate gesture, only half faking relief.

"Wow," Andrea said, shaking her wrist, her eyes wide. "You sounded like you suspect Tony."

"In my book everyone's a suspect, Andrea. Except you, me, and John Galigani."

SEVEN

AT FOUR O'CLOCK on Sunday afternoon, approximately seven hours and thirteen minutes after Rose had hung up on me, I stood on the lawn-green welcome mat of the Galigani home. I'd struggled over what to bring as a peace offering. Rose hardly ever ate candy, and as a nondrinker, I was hopeless at choosing wine. Flowers were out, since she had her own garden full of colorful blooms—we'd expect nothing less from the daughter of the late Mike Zarelli, at one time the owner of Revere's biggest nursery.

To put another damper on my spirits and my opportunity to bear gifts, our favorite bakery was closed on Sunday.

I settled for a supermarket selection of bread, cheese, and fruit. I bought a basket and a bright yellow kitchen towel and did my best to arrange an attractive package. It looked as artistic as the graphics in my Ph.D. thesis, which I'd also designed.

I rang the bell, half of me hoping there was no one home, the other half wishing the moment were over. I surveyed the prize rosebushes, the beginnings of a lattice Frank was building, the new light fixture Robert and his fourteen-year-old son Billy had installed at the edge of the driveway.

After what seemed like hours, Frank opened the door. His smile cheered me. Rose was right behind him, her eyes puffy and without makeup. She held out her arms and I knew there'd be no need to discuss our first falling out in more than forty years.

"Gloria, we've been trying to reach you. John is home."

I let out a long breath. "I'm so glad."
I meant it in many ways.

JOHN SAT ON the sofa in navy-blue sweats I recognized as Frank's. His longish hair was wet, and I imagined he'd gone straight to the shower when he'd arrived at his parents' home after a night in jail. He'd agreed to stay as long as it took to answer their questions.

On the chairs across from John were the Galiganis' lawyer, Nick Ciccolo, and a freckled young man introduced to me as criminal attorney Mike Canty. Both lawyers wore casual slacks and shirts and somber expressions. I'd experienced lighter moods at Frank's wakes.

When John stood and gave me a silent hug, I felt I was bearing all his weight. From reflex, I patted his back as I'd done when he was a child.

Rose had resumed her role as hostess, serving iced tea and beer. She'd turned my haphazard fruit basket into an attractive tray of hors d'oeuvres, adding tiny hot meatballs with barbecue sauce. I figured she'd channeled her nervous energy into food preparation. But, unlike me, she didn't eat everything she cooked.

"Matt called," Rose said. "He'll be here any minute. Robert and Karla went home to get Billy. They'll be back. And Mary Catherine offered to fly in from Houston, but we told her she didn't need to do that right now." Rose waved her hand. "She can come when we're all happier, when…"

She drifted off. We were all accounted for. Rose was keeping track of everyone close to her, as she usually did.

"Any news?" I asked.

Heads shook all around the room. "Matt said he'd tell us whatever he could when he got here," Frank said.

Rose beat a path from the living room to the kitchen, refilling drinks and picking up crumbs. When the doorbell rang, she jumped.

Matt stood on the threshold carrying a large watermelon and I wondered if he'd also aggravated Rose today. "It's hot out there. Couldn't pass this up.'' He pretended to toss the heavy ellipsoid to John. I was happy for his cheerfulness, hoping it meant good, or at least neutral, news.

Rose brought Matt, a teetotaler like me, a bottle of mineral water. All eyes were on him as he addressed the lawyers. ''I'm here as a friend.''

They nodded and gave identical waves of their hands, indicating they understood. I imagined the gesture had a Latin name, something with *mano* in it, something they learned in law school.

''They found a box of stuff in your closet, John,'' Matt said, his voice soft and caring, but with an unmistakable note of worry. I noted how he appeared to distance himself from *them*.

''What kind of stuff?'' Rose asked. I saw frustration take over her face, and hoped she wouldn't turn it on Matt.

''How did they get a search warrant?'' Frank asked. He'd moved toward Rose and put his arm around her.

The lawyers stood by, not participating in the conversation. I figured they knew what they were doing and that their silence had some legal significance. I imagined them later, in a courtroom, denying they had knowledge of the search warrant or of this conversation.

''The judge gave it to them, on the basis of some letters found in Yolanda's apartment, and also on the fact that Yolanda's briefcase, which she had at dinner with John, was missing.''

''But what about Derek Byrne?'' I asked him. ''Didn't he let Yolanda into the library? Did she have it then?'' I knew there were too many questions facing Matt at once, but I wasn't moved to make it easy for him. The messenger.

Matt nodded. ''Derek says she had the briefcase when he let her in.''

''So how could John have taken it?''

''They think he went back later, and—''

''Why would he want her briefcase?'' I asked, aware that ordinarily Matt wouldn't answer questions that threw him off track. But he was here as a friend, I reminded myself.

"Well, there might have been more threatening letters. Maybe Yolanda brought them to dinner in an attempt to extract something from John. Maybe she made her own threats, to go to the police with them." He held up his hands, as if to stem the tide of upset he expected to come his way. "I'm giving you potentials, here, because you asked."

Matt turned to John, regaining control of the unsolicited question and answer period. "The good news: no briefcase in your apartment. However, they did find the crate on the floor of your closet. The one with photos of you and Yolanda. Plus, programs that look like they might be from dates. Tickets from concerts, plays. Letters and cards."

"So he saves souvenirs. That doesn't mean he killed her." Rose crossed the room and stood behind John, putting her hands on his shoulders.

Matt took a sip of his water and let out a long breath. I realized I'd been holding mine in. This time he kept his eyes on John.

"There was a stack of clippings from newspapers. Back several years. All with Yolanda Fiore's byline."

"So he keeps clippings. He's a journalist." Although Rose moved her hands to her hips in a defiant posture, her voice was pleading. I hoped she wouldn't lose control.

"John?" Matt addressed him quietly, and I supposed he wished he had the suspect to himself. I was pleased and surprised that the lawyers still hadn't interfered, except through body language. Nick Ciccolo rubbed his fists together as he paced in front of the fireplace. Mike Canty bit his knuckles, a gesture that made me wonder if he was half Italian. In another situation, Rose would have filled me in on his ethnicity on the spot.

John raised bloodshot eyes to Matt. "I cared about Yolanda. I never wanted to break up. I know it was silly to keep that stuff, but I didn't think I was doing anything wrong."

"How did he know someone was going to kill her? Maybe I should go upstairs right now and see what I've kept, just in case someday..." Rose turned away, clearly making a great effort to stay calm and rational. Every time she addressed Matt I worried that she'd lash out at him, or dismiss him, as she'd done to me. I figured Matt was used to more abusive treatment than Rose would ever mete out, but I felt sorry for him nonetheless.

"I think Matt needs time alone with John, and maybe Nicky and Mike," Frank said. "I'm going back to my office for a while. How about you, dear?"

Rose responded to Frank's pleasant tone with a weak nod, while he rubbed a spot high on her back, as if he were giving a secret marriage code. I'd always admired their great trust and affection for each other and hoped it would carry them through what must be very painful for them.

In spite of the mood, I smiled to myself. It occurred to me that I was building a similar relationship with Matt. Unless I'd thrown it away last night. I realized I'd been avoiding Matt's eyes since he'd arrived, and we hadn't exchanged a greeting.

I hadn't had romance in my life since my engagement at twenty-one. That had ended with the death of my fiancé three months before the wedding. I'd handled the tragedy beautifully—I ran off to California and didn't come back for more than thirty years. So much for mature responses.

"I'm going to take a walk," Rose said. She looked at me, a plea written across her face. I was torn between wanting to stay for the interview and the desire to comfort my friend and renew our closeness. I plotted how to have the best of both worlds—go with Rose for now and grill Matt later for details. If we were still on speaking terms.

"Count me in," I said to Rose, earning a smile from her that lit up the room.

AT EIGHT O'CLOCK, Matt showed up at my apartment with the beginnings of a feast—fresh basil from Rose's garden. The aroma did wonders for the air in my flat since it had been closed up for ten summer days.

I noticed he didn't have a change of clothes with him. I was still unclear about my feelings. One minute I wished he'd whisk me away to St. Anthony's and make me his bride, the next minute I wanted to run to California again. It seemed romance was no easier at fifty-something than at twenty-something.

While we prepared a large bowl of penne and tomatoes, I searched Matt's face for signs of displeasure—or relief. Was he upset that I'd ignored his proposal to live together? Or was he happy I hadn't taken him up on what he'd intended as a joke? I read nothing in his expression, and imagined he was calling upon years of practice in interview rooms to maintain a neutral demeanor.

I retreated from the personal issue and welcomed his briefing on the session with John and his lawyers.

"The bad news is John doesn't have an alibi for the time after about eight-thirty Thursday evening, when he says he dropped Yolanda off at the library," Matt told me.

He says. I understood Matt's caveat. He used it out of habit, but I didn't like the implication.

"He went straight to his apartment, did some reading, etc., etc. He says Yolanda told him Derek Byrne would let her in, which checks with Byrne's statement. Byrne says he let her in around eight-thirty, stayed and worked a couple of hours himself, and left her a little before eleven."

He flipped through his standard-issue notebook, as if this were an ordinary case. What did I expect? I wondered. A bigger pad since the chief suspect was our friend? A smaller one since he wasn't guilty? A special color?

"What's Derek's alibi for after he left Yolanda in the building alone, allegedly?" I had a few caveats of my own.

Matt smiled. "Allegedly, Byrne went home to his place on Reservoir Avenue. His alibi's not a lot better than John's, but he doesn't have a motive. Apparently Byrne and the victim were getting along fine. No problems noticed by anyone who was interviewed."

"Maybe he saw John drop her off and got jealous, and…" I trailed off, embarrassed at the flimsy excuse for a motive.

Matt had the courtesy not to follow up. "Did you get anything from your trip to the lab?" he asked.

"Just a bad feeling from a public affairs officer. No surprise there. I still have Yolanda's boron articles to read."

"Was that boring articles?"

"I was hoping you wouldn't say that." I wondered if I should tell him about element number one hundred and seven, called bohrium, after nuclear physicist Niels Bohr.

"That was too easy a shot, I guess."

I nodded. For the first time since we'd started dating, I felt strained around Matt. In spite of the distraction of Yolanda Fiore's murder and John Galigani's predicament, it was clear that we were stepping around another important topic. *Us.*

Matt's pager went off just as we'd run out of excuses to discuss our future together. A wave of relief flowed through me.

"Another case," he told me after responding to the call.

I suspected he was equally relieved.

IN MATT'S ABSENCE, I took Yolanda's reports to bed with me, a scenario much more typical of my adult life than the last few months with a steady boyfriend.

One report was a treasury of data on the radioactive waste that's been gathering for the last fifty years, mostly in large pools right next to the nuclear reactors that generated it. Like lethal swimming holes all around the country.

In another of her articles, Yolanda had created an accident scenario: suppose a steam line in a power plant breaks, causing a rapid temperature change in the cooling system. Immediately the control-room staff would need to inject a solution that would safely shut down the plant—a solution containing boron. What if the plant didn't have enough boron on hand? Yolanda asked. A meltdown on the horizon, she answered.

All of Yolanda's articles had a definite antinuke slant—in one she managed to bring up the hazardous presence of weapons-grade material on lab property—but hard as I tried, I couldn't see anything worth killing her for. No individual would likely feel threatened by her pseudo-exposés. Ordinarily I'd be happy to find no scientific motive in a murder investigation, but this time I was ready to sacrifice one of my own species, a professional scientist, for the sake of exonerating John Galigani.

My eyelids drooped as my gaze and my fingers drifted off the pages.

Boron. Maybe Matt was right. Boron is boring.

An eruption of sound woke me. I couldn't place it at first. An overlay of at least three excruciating tones—a clanging bell clapper, a loud, annoying buzz, a boisterous honking.

An alarm.

Something—someone?—had set off the Galigani Mortuary intrusion alarm.

I hurried to get myself out of bed, my reading matter spilling onto the floor, my ears ringing from the din. I went to the window—why not under the bed? I wondered later. The metal box, just under the roof overhang, seemed to be shaking from its own noise.

My heart pounded in my throat, nervous tingles raced through my body. I tiptoed to the threshold of my bedroom door, as if my footsteps could be heard over the clamor. I looked across my foyer to the front door, the only entrance to my apartment other than third-floor windows.

I saw the chain, still fastened across the frame, and let out a deep breath. No one was in my apartment. Unless he'd replaced the chain behind him.

The cacophony from the alarm box went on at the same level, hurting my ears.

No doubt a false alarm.

Maybe I'd forgotten to lock one of the downstairs doors and the wind blew it open. I tried to determine which mortuary door could have swung free on this warm, still night. Or maybe an animal pushed against it. Never mind that I hadn't seen a stray animal big enough to do that since I'd left California.

I walked to the alarm pad, on the wall in my entryway. Even though my security chain was in place, it frightened me to be so close to where someone might crash in.

The building was divided into sectors, each one with its own light on the pad. I had to determine which door corresponded to the light that was blinking red. Why hadn't I memorized the correlation between the zones and the lights? I seemed to have left my good habits behind, in the pocket of my old lab coat.

The building layout ran through my mind like the video output of a camcorder. The whole first floor of Galigani Mortuary was wired to the alarm—the main front door, the back door, the parlor windows, the garage door, the door to the basement. Too many to guess which one had been violated, which little magnet in the system had sent a message to the sound box, commanding: SCREECH!

I found the security company pamphlet in my desk drawer, grateful I had at least some organizational skills left. The furiously blinking red light was from zone four, the prep room. A partially embalmed body crying for help? My thoughts ran as wild as my pulse.

Although I'd been expecting a response from the monitoring service, when it finally came—a telephone ring that wouldn't startle me in other circumstances—I gasped and nearly lost my balance.

The question was what to tell the dispatcher. *Send someone immediately,* and risk aggravating my neighbors even further with police sirens? Or should I say, *Never mind,* and take a chance on a real intrusion?

I picked up the phone, ready with the password. Rose had let me choose it—GALILEO, whose birthday was February fifteenth, like mine. I reminded myself to remain calm.

"Pilgrim Alarm Company," the dispatcher said. "Your password please?"

I took a breath, and composed myself. I thought I had myself under control.

Until, for no reason, I screamed.

"Help!"

EIGHT

THE ALARM OUTSIDE my window stopped clanging almost immediately, its clamor replaced by a patrol car siren. I supposed Pilgrim Alarm deactivated the signal once the police arrived. I wasn't ready to admit the intrusion had been real, let alone related to my embryonic investigation into the Fiore murder. But I allowed that if I continued in this career, I should learn more about the inner workings of my safeguards system.

I watched the proceedings from my bedroom window. When two more police cars arrived and six uniformed officers fanned out around my building, I ventured into the living room and undid the chain on my door. I opened it slowly, half expecting a burst of gunfire to my chest, either from the intruder or from cops who might think *I* was the intruder.

My tension was relieved significantly by a familiar face. One of the officers climbing the stairs toward me was Michelle Chan, a petite Asian woman I'd met through Matt. She and her partner trained extra-long flashlights on their path even though they'd thrown the switch for the foyer lights.

"Gloria, what's up?" Michelle's tone was friendly but her posture and her partner's expression told me they were on duty.

"I hoped you'd have the answer to that."

"Nothing so far. We'd like to check inside your apartment."

"My door was chained."

"Even so," said Michelle's partner, a tall black man—J. Daniels, according to his ID. He waved his flashlight toward the ceiling. I pictured a burglar in black spandex hugging the mortuary roof, ready to enter my flat through the attic. I nodded and stepped aside.

Michelle and Daniels swept through my rooms, tapping the furniture and walls periodically with their batons, as if they were testing for a trapdoor. Nothing sprang to life.

Fifteen minutes later I was serving coffee and biscotti to six guests, all in uniform. Party noise consisted of beeper signals, heavy footsteps, and radio static. I figured my small apartment was host to about twelve guns, six cans of pepper spray, and enough handcuffs for an X-rated flick. Some celebration. I wondered if Matt knew of the pseudo-gala and the alarm that provoked it. Outside his sphere of information, I hoped. With any luck he'd never know. He didn't need another reason to worry about me.

The gist of my guests' report to me—they'd found nothing suspicious on the grounds or in the building. The door between the main foyer and the stairs to the prep room was ajar, most likely not fully closed in the first place.

Conclusion: false alarm. Fallout: six of Revere's finest on an unexpected coffee break.

I was curious about the size of the response force sent out to my building.

"Not exactly standard," Michelle told me when I broached the subject. She'd begun what seemed a tricky process—stuffing her long dark hair back under her cap.

"Someone else would have gotten five cars instead of three?" I asked.

She laughed. "Hardly. I got the call and—given the circumstances, thought I'd ask for backup."

"The circumstances being…?"

"It's a business site."

I raised my eyebrows and grunted my disbelief. "Is that all?"

"And you're on our short list," she admitted.

"Well, I'm grateful for the service."

True to my Italian upbringing, I made sure everyone had enough to eat and encouraged the officers to wrap a few cookies for later. As they prepared to leave, my tension returned. Had they missed anything? I was too embarrassed to ask if they'd checked inside the dryer in the laundry room, inconveniently located next to the prep room where Frank and Robert embalmed their clients. Although Rose ridiculed my choice, I was a frequent customer of the Laundromat on North Shore Road.

Michelle patted my shoulder on her way out. "I can hardly wait for retirement, Gloria. Your life is more exciting than mine."

COMFORTABLE AND SAFE in my air-conditioned Cadillac the next morning, I talked myself out of worrying about the alarm incident. I'd spent my last waking moments planning my outfit for the trip to the library, starting with a costume jewelry pin Elaine had given me—a colorful ceramic stack of books she'd earned by tutoring in an ESL program in Berkeley.

As I drove, I reviewed the details of my eventful evening. Zone four, the one that was breached, was an inside door—a second wall of safeguard. Since there was no sign of break-in through any outside door or window, I reasoned, it was certainly a false alarm. I focused on how lucky I was to have so many police officers at my disposal.

One especially, I thought. Then reality kicked in and I realized it might be time for the first we-have-to-talk session for Matt and me. A session about our future. If we had one.

I approached the library for the third time in two days, surely a record for a noncardholder, and parked on Beach Street. My mission was to introduce myself to Yolanda's last-known boyfriend, Assistant Director Derek Byrne.

I could hear the arguing as I walked to the circulation desk. A meeting seemed to be breaking up on the mezzanine above me, at the doorway of Director Dorothy Leonard's office. I altered my strategic plan, deciding to remain anonymous for a few minutes.

A table in the adult reading section was close enough for me to eavesdrop. Only one other table was occupied, by teenagers who seemed more interested in each other than the library hold-ings. A nearby pamphlet on the history of Revere provided cover as I pretended to read it. Over the edges of the colorful tri-fold, I watched two men and a woman come down the stairs to the first floor.

The first comment I heard, right after Dorothy Leonard slammed her door, was from the woman. Tall, navy-blue power suit, bulging Italian leather briefcase. A lawyer, I decided. "This is not a battle you want to fight, Derek. The expansion proposal is dead," she said to the younger man. Derek Byrne, Yolanda's boyfriend—tall and lean, with light brown hair. "You should listen to your father."

"He never does," the older man said. Councilman Brendan Byrne, according to Rose's tutorial.

"Not since I was two." Derek's laugh came out more like a snort.

"You're out of your league here," the lawyerlike woman said. "I don't care what documents you claim to have."

Derek ignored her. "I'll talk to you later, Dad."

The repartee turned to whispering as the three entered the public area, but even without audible words, I sensed a heavy undercurrent of hostility in the banter. I lowered my eyes and skimmed a paragraph on the 1871 celebration when the town of North Chelsea became officially known as Revere.

Councilman Brendan Byrne stood a few inches over his son, and nearly a head over the woman, the slight round-shouldered bent to his posture the only sign of his age. Around seventy-five, Rose had guessed. It seemed the father-son disagreement I'd witnessed had to do with something more serious than a missed curfew. Something like the library expansion program, a major city project.

Derek returned to the circulation desk alone, after the other two left, and I made my move.

"Good morning," I said, extending my hand. Derek glanced at me, then scanned the area, as if to locate a clerk to take care of me. "I'm Gloria Lamerino, Mr. Byrne. I'd like to talk to you if you have a few minutes."

He gave me a distracted smile. "Oh, yes. I've heard about you."

Hasn't everybody? I said to myself.

"I'm so sorry about the loss of your friend."

Derek ran his hand through thick hair, set back from a high forehead. His eyes wandered toward the stairway where Yolanda had been shoved to her death. "Thanks. It's been tense around here."

Derek's smooth, fair skin and sad blue eyes made him look much younger than I knew him to be—like John Galigani, closing in on forty years old. "Would you like me to come back another time?"

"It's OK. Sorry to appear rude. And please call me Derek." He tilted his head in the direction of the front steps, as if his father and the woman I'd endowed with a law degree were still standing there, pointing fingers at him. "Sorry about that, too," he said. "We're in the middle of a small war."

I nodded, surprised at my sympathetic feelings toward him. I was prepared not to like Derek Byrne, hoping to find in him a viable alternative to John Galigani, currently the principal murder suspect. My experience with the Revere Police Department to the contrary, part of my mind held on to the idea that murderers should look the part and evoke negative vibes.

I pointed to the model of the planned renovation and expansion. "Is the war over this?"

"Uh huh. The woman is Frances Worthen, an attorney for the Archdiocese." I gave myself a point for a correct guess. That she had an ecclesiastical boss never crossed my mind, however. "The Church claims it owns the land surrounding the library. They say it's sacred historical ground and we shouldn't dig it up."

"But that's where the high school used to be. Immaculate Conception Church was across the street." I hurried to verify the little bit of Revere history I knew. "And the Rumney Marsh cemetery is much farther down the street."

"That's right. After the high school burned, the city built a park that lasted sixteen or seventeen years. Then the parish and the city did a land swap. The city got the old church site and the rectory, and the Church got some of the land surrounding this building. I'm sure you noticed that new church on the corner of Winthrop and Beach.''

''If they got the land that recently, how is it sacred and historically significant already?''

By now, two middle-aged women had taken over the business at the circulation desk and Derek and I had moved to the table from which I'd done my spying. He seemed eager to explain himself to someone who'd listen. I wondered if he'd be as forthcoming if he realized I was scrutinizing his smooth face for signs of malice, ready to turn him in at the least provocation.

''It's not one particular congregation that's opposed to the construction. There were a lot of churches along Beach Street in the old days. The Catholic Archdiocese is spearheading the resistance for all of them. They're saying at one time the land could have held a number of cemeteries of many different denominations.''

''They want to stop the construction because it *might be* the sacred ground of some *possible* early churches?''

Derek nodded and raised his eyebrows, creating a pleasant pattern of wavy lines across his high forehead. He seemed to say he was equally confused by the logic. He stood and motioned me to the model of the library-to-be, moving a pen along the miniature landscape as he talked. ''We're only going out sixty feet from the back of our building. The chances of hitting graves are very slim. About as likely as digging anywhere in the city.'' With every sentence, Derek became more animated. ''Not only that, but this building was erected in 1902, so we know there haven't been bodies buried out there at least since then.''

''And your father is on their side?''

''He is.'' Derek sounded sad, as if he'd give anything not to have to go against his father. ''He's Catholic. But I never realized he was *that* Catholic, if you know what I mean.''

Naive as I was about political dealings, I'd have thought

something like expanding the public library would be welcomed by all. Who can be against literacy? Of course, if it came down to allocation of limited funds—more library space versus a new laboratory wing—I might think differently.

"Is there competition for the funds?" I asked, still seeking a logical explanation for the controversy.

"Technically, no. But all the old city buildings are in bad shape. The people at the police station are making the biggest fuss—the chief and the administrators. Their building's in a state of decay, too. But our money's coming through a state grant specifically designated for libraries. The cops can't have the grant even if we don't accept it."

Interesting, and worth asking Matt about. I realized I'd gone astray of my motive for being in the library in the first place.

"I hate to bother you with this, Derek, but did Yolanda feel strongly about this issue, one way or the other?"

He shook his head. "She knew about it, but she had other things on her mind. She was caught up in causes at the lab." His voice choked slightly and he turned away. I tended to believe him, but just in case, I made a mental note to put the Church/State dispute on my list of motives for Yolanda's murder. Giving me all of two besides John's.

Derek Byrne seemed to be what my father would have called "a nice young man." I had to remind myself he was one of my murder suspects. It was to his advantage not to tell me if he and Yolanda had argued about the expansion proposal. I planned to check it out.

"I know you've only recently returned to Revere. Would you like a little tour of the building?" Derek asked, recovering his equilibrium.

I appreciated his allowing me a full year back to find the library again. I accepted and followed him up and down the stairs to the two unconnected mezzanines off the main floor. I'd already been, with Matt, to the one that held his office and Dorothy Leonard's. Her door was still closed.

The second mezzanine was more like an abandoned loft, filled with sealed cartons and rusty trunks and a collection of dusty artifacts that didn't seem to belong in a library. Its walls were uncovered brick, like the outside of the building. The slanted beams that formed the ceiling forced Derek to walk with his head hunched between his shoulders. I worried about dirt and snags in his expensive-looking suit, light brown, almost the color of his hair. I had no such problem with either my height or my washable cotton jacket.

"From the Historical Society," Derek explained as we passed two spinning wheels and stacks of old photographs in elaborate frames.

A long glass-covered case contained antique knives and guns and what looked like the precursor to the modern crowbar. Handwritten labels with a temporary look identified a colonial musket, a Civil War cannonball, a wooden gavel made from the keel of the *U.S.S. Constitution*. I grimaced as I calculated the number of years since my fourth-grade field trip to *Old Ironsides*. A bigger number than Derek's age, I was sure.

"I'm impressed," I said, checking out a thank you letter sent to a Revere resident by Jackie Kennedy a few weeks after the assassination of her husband.

"We're storing all this while they complete a new history wing in the City Hall."

Derek seemed proud to show me a special bookcase with original editions of stories by Horatio Alger, a Revere native. "Alger wrote more than a hundred books with 'rags-to-riches, onward and upward' themes right after the Civil War. Very inspiring message—if you do your best and always try to do the right thing, you'll succeed."

I let Derek go on about Alger, the poet, journalist, and eventually a minister on Cape Cod. I couldn't bring myself to admit I'd never read him and if I were on a quiz show, I would have guessed he was a spy during World War II.

A strange-looking contraption next to a musty dressmaker's dummy caught my eye.

"That's part of a still," Derek said, apparently noticing the direction of my gaze.

"From Prohibition days. When they made wood alcohol in backyards."

He nodded. "That's right. Moonshine. It gets its name from being made and transported at night, by moonlight. It was also called bathtub gin, because it was often stored in bathtubs so the user could just pull the plug if a raid was imminent."

Derek's tone was neutral, as if he were lecturing fifth-graders on a tour of the library. I remembered Rose's account and wondered how much he knew about how wood alcohol/moonshine/bathtub gin had ruined his grandparents' lives.

"Fascinating," I said.

My trip to the library was proving more interesting than boron.

Could that be?

NINE

WHEN I LEFT Derek Byrne, it was still too early for a one o'clock appointment I'd made with Matt. Since it was hot and muggy outside, I sat in my comfortable car and made some notes about my interaction with Derek.

A dispute over sacred burial grounds, the history of Revere, Horatio Alger lore, the etymology of "moonshine" liquor. I felt I'd learned a great deal, even if none of it seemed relevant to my investigation of Yolanda Fiore's murder. Maybe that's what libraries were all about—a collection of data and facts, with the responsibility for synthesis on the shoulders of the cardholder.

The more I thought about it, the more I realized it had been Derek's agenda, not mine, that we'd followed. Could he really have been simply exercising good PR skills, unaware that I was engaging him in an unofficial police interview? Had he skillfully steered me past anything that would help my inquiry? Or was Derek what he seemed—a nice guy distracted by the loss of his girlfriend and his involvement in a conflict with his father and the Catholic Church?

He hadn't offered to include the basement area on our tour, where the computer center was, and where Yolanda's body had been found, and I hadn't had the heart to ask. I figured it would be too difficult for him. Either because he missed his girlfriend, or because he killed her.

Although I didn't think it was pertinent to the murder case, I jotted down the salient points about the "war" over the library expansion project.

Pro: Dorothy Leonard and Byrne the younger.
Con: the Church (Attorney Frances Worthen) and Byrne the elder.
Unknown position: Yolanda Fiore, John Galigani.

I tapped my pen on the pad. Skimpy information, but I didn't rule anything out.

When you have nothing, everything matters.

AT ONE O'CLOCK, a smiling and efficient Michelle Chan walked me to Matt's office in the Revere Police Station. I estimated her weight at about the same as mine when I was eleven years old. I was more than usually aware of the cramped quarters, walls badly in need of paint, torn-up furniture, out-of-date office equipment, water stains on the ceiling. I was sorry for every time I'd declined to buy tickets for policemen's balls. I wondered if the police station staff was envious of the state grant to upgrade the library facility.

"Matt's always excited to see you," Michelle told me. I gave her a nervous smile. Was that before or after I refused his invitation to…to what? I wondered. "Finally get some sleep last night?" she asked.

"Yes. I hope you did, too."

"Not yet, but I'm leaving soon." She looked at her watch and smiled. "Hot date." She took off her hat and loosened her thick black hair, shiny as new filament wire.

"I have things to read while I wait," I told Michelle when we found Matt's office empty. "Don't be late for your date."

Michelle winked and left.

The last time I'd visited the office Matt shared with George Berger there had been only one picture on Matt's side of the room—a photo of his parents at their fiftieth wedding anniversary celebration, surrounded by him and his sister Jean and her family.

I was glad Matt wasn't present to see my double take when I glanced at his credenza today. He'd added a new photo. *Me,* in a blond wood frame, windblown and smiling for the camera, wearing a red fleece jacket Rose had pressed on me. I recognized the background as Jean's home at the Cape. I was thrilled to see the photo, though the event it recalled hadn't been as pleasant as I'd hoped.

When I began my dating life with Matt a year ago, in my mid fifties, I'd expected to be able to skip a lot of the usual problems—zits on prom night, grounding for a missed curfew, begging for an advance in allowance to buy a new dress.

Matt's sister, Jean Gennaro Mottolo, a real-estate agent ten years younger than Matt, proved an unexpected stumbling block, substituting for a strict mom and dad. The one time I'd been at her home in Falmouth was the previous Christmas. She was cordial, but not overly welcoming. I'd run through a list of possible ways I'd offended her—my mother, Josephine Lamerino, had trained me to blame myself first if anyone didn't take to me immediately.

Perhaps I'd chosen inappropriate gifts for her children. I'd given a valuable old biography of Marie Curie to her fifteen-year-old daughter, and one of Einstein to her thirteen-year-old son. I'd wrapped colorful posters of the periodic table for both of them.

Or maybe she was cherishing the memory of Matt's wife, Teresa, who'd died of heart disease ten years ago. Jean's husband had been killed in a boating accident a year later. I recognized she'd not had an easy life, raising two small children by herself. On the other hand, she was doing it in a beautiful beachfront home on Cape Cod.

I'd written Jean a note after the holidays, thanking her for the wonderful dinner and pink silk scarf. I hadn't heard from her since. Maybe she knew I never wore scarves, except for warmth. No need for more layers on my already ample chest. And I never wore pink anything.

A gentle hand ran across my shoulders. "That wasn't your favorite afternoon, I know," Matt said. "But it's the only decent picture I have of you." Matt kissed my cheek in between sentences—I was back in his good graces. Had I ever left them?

He squeezed past me to sit on his desk, crossed his arms, and smiled, seeming pleased with himself for having caught me in a daydream, staring at the photo.

I was more dismayed that he'd picked up the tension between his sister and me. "Has Jean complained to you?"

He shook his head. "I notice these things. It's…"

"I know. It's what you do."

"We can talk about it if you want."

"Maybe later. Let's get to work."

WE TOOK A QUICK lunch detour to Kelly's Roast Beef on Revere Beach Boulevard, sharing a sandwich and a look at the ocean from inside Matt's car. The beach and benches were crowded with bathers, diners, joggers, dog-walkers, Frisbee players. I wondered how so many people of all ages could be free in the middle of a Monday afternoon.

The drive to Yolanda's apartment on Bellevue Street, in the shadow of St. Theresa's Church, took only a few minutes, hardly long enough to cool our coffees.

"You haven't told me how it is that you can do this—go into a victim's dwelling, when you're not on the case?"

"It's all cleared from the top. Yolanda lived alone, so there's no one to disturb, and Parker's guys have been here already, so it's not as though I'm acting as part of the team. In fact, I'm sure they've taken anything interesting, but I still want a look around for myself." Matt unlocked the door to a flat on the ground floor of a white wooden two-family house. "See if anything strikes you."

I nodded, picturing a notebook titled "Incriminating Boron Evidence."

I wondered if I'd ever get used to riffling through the belongings of a murder victim. Seeing things Yolanda might have wanted to keep from a stranger's eyes. Rummaging around messy bookshelves, which she might have straightened if she expected company. All worth it, if there was a clue here to lead us to her murderer.

Yolanda's computer area was predictably busy, with the

usual overflowing disk holders and yellow sticky notes—and a large rectangular border of dust indicating where the lab computer had sat. What distinguished the environment were a child's drawings, "to Auntie Yo." Berger had mentioned Yolanda had a sister in Detroit, and no family in Revere. My eyes fell on a jumble of photographs, many of her with Derek Byrne. I picked up a framed snapshot of the two of them in bulky, bright orange vests, foamy white water surging around them. Rafting.

Why would anyone do that? And they were smiling. Whenever possible I kept away from amusements that called for protective gear or activities requiring safety precautions, except, of course, for a lab coat and safety glasses. In all the years I'd sold cotton candy under the Cyclone roller-coaster on Revere Beach, I'd never stepped into a car. The only ride I'd ever ventured to try were the bumper cars, but as soon as I thought someone was serious about slamming into me, I'd head for the sidelines and buy myself a frozen custard.

I looked at the photographs, piecing together a person. Yolanda's tiny waist and large bright eyes, fine threads of hair surrounding her round face. Yolanda at the center of a protest group outside the Charger Street lab, in a news story framed and mounted on the wall over her desk. Yolanda with a little girl under a Christmas tree. Big smile, happy countenance, unlike many sullen activists I'd been familiar with in Berkeley during the sixties.

I addressed silent questions in the direction of her photographs—*Why did you dump John Galigani? He's a writer, just like you. He likes rafting.* I stared at Yolanda's sweet face. *And who murdered you? A stranger? A friend? You know it wasn't John.* I resented that she wasn't present to answer, as if she'd invited me to a party in her living room and failed to show up. Then I realized my own selfishness, how little attention I'd paid to the violent death of a young woman. I was more caught up in proving the innocence of my friend, treating Yolanda's murder as an inconvenience to me and the Galigani family.

Old as I was, I was still learning a lot about myself, not all of it pleasant. I took a moment to consider that before continuing to browse the victim's disheveled rooms.

What might have been a dining-room table was strewn with wire baskets, binders, newspaper clippings, and flyers. I walked among floor-to-ceiling books and papers, some in bookcases, others stacked on the scatter rugs and kitchen linoleum. I looked through the piles, not sure whether to be disappointed or relieved that Yolanda hadn't kept mementos of John—no shoe boxes or crates full of ticket stubs like the material police confiscated from his apartment. Unless Parker and Berger had already taken them away.

I watched Matt scribble in his notebook. He'd picked up a disk, a book or two, and a mug from the counter, but apparently nothing struck him as worth taking. I remembered reading how police on the West Coast had solved the case of the Hillside Strangler—actually two cousins, who'd committed twelve murders—from a sprig of heather, a carpet fiber, and some scratches on a rock.

How did crime-scene technicians know what's important? What's a clue and what's just lint? I thought I should be doing something useful and looked down into Yolanda's wastebasket, almost as a private joke.

I felt my throat constrict, my knees weaken. I blinked and bent over the short black metal basket.

An envelope, off-white, of fine quality. I reached in and picked it out of the trash, shaking pencil shavings and cracker crumbs from its folds. I was sure the envelope was identical to one I had in my desk, still enclosing the note that threatened me if I didn't take up sewing.

I rummaged further, but there was no matching notepaper in the basket. I smoothed out the envelope and strained to read the postmark.

I jumped when I heard a voice behind me.

"Sorry. I didn't mean to startle you. I thought you might want to look through this." Matt handed me an accordion folder, marked BORON.

"Thanks. This is just what I was looking for." I cleared my

throat in an attempt to cover my nervousness. Matt's glance
went to the envelope I hadn't had time to hide. "Just trash,"
I said, dropping it back into the wastebasket.

I tried to sound more interested in the boron file than in a
piece of rubbish, which I planned to retrieve later.

We drove away from Yolanda's home in silence. I assumed
Matt's brain was processing what he'd seen in the apartment,
folding it into the rest of his case notes. For my part, I thought
I could feel the envelope heating up the side of my briefcase.
I didn't know for sure whether Matt had noticed that I'd taken
it, but I felt he probably did. I appreciated his trust in me and
hoped it was well placed. A year ago he would have reminded
me of the limitations of my involvement in police investigations, and probably would have told me to "be careful." It was
a sign of my growing self-confidence that I took his new attitude to mean he cared more about me, not less.

I rubbed the soft leather of my briefcase, as if to absorb a
coded message from the envelope. Had Yolanda been threatened also? Were we on a bulk mailing list? In a way, I felt
better thinking perhaps everyone in Revere got the same letter.
I couldn't remember if my note included my name anywhere
but on the envelope. I could hardly wait to go home and make
the comparison.

Matt dropped me off at my car in front of the police station
on Pleasant Street. I'd planned to go from there to the lab to
meet Andrea.

"See you tonight?"

I nodded and smiled. "Dinner at seven."

Matt cast a deliberate glance at my briefcase, slung over my
right shoulder. I felt it before I heard it.

"Be careful," he said.

TEN

I FOUND IT HARD to resist the temptation to go home immediately and check on the envelope in my desk, to match it with the one I'd taken from Yolanda's wastebasket. But it was nearly three o'clock, and I was already running late. Andrea had told me she was working an early shift, seven to three-thirty.

As planned, I called her when I got to the Visitor Center on the edge of lab property.

"Gloria, I was hoping you'd get here soon. I'll be right out."

Andrea met me at a wide turnstile meant to accommodate several people, or one person and a bicycle, or Andrea and me. She pushed her badge through a slot and entered a PIN code with great haste, nearly out of breath.

"There's someone I want to show you."

Someone to show me? Odd choice of words, I thought, but it became clear when Andrea wrapped her hand around my wrist and led me toward the fishbowl that was Tony Taruffi's office. She positioned us behind an orange felt partition. I hoped the cubicle's resident, a Jeff Bonivert according to the sign, wouldn't appear and call 911.

"See that man with Tony?" I nodded, and focused on a short, wide man in a tweed jacket, engaged in animated conversation with Yolanda's former boss. "That's Garth Allen." Andrea sounded as if I should know the name. The man had a jaunty air about him in spite of graying hair and half glasses perched on his nose. A talk-show host? A movie star? If so, I was lost. I'd abandoned my interest in popular culture right after the Kennedy administration.

"He's the safety manager for the nuclear power regulators. He oversees the contract they have with the lab—we give technical advice to the safety inspectors." My look must have betrayed my continued bafflement but Andrea remained patient. "Allen's the one who'd be on the line if Yolanda uncovered a problem with boron. I thought you'd want to see him," Andrea whispered, using her hands to emphasize a word here and there. "He could be a suspect."

I gave her a smile, hoping she'd interpret it as appreciation. "Interesting. Thanks." I had no idea what to do with the visual data Andrea had provided with such flourish. Evidently she'd taken to heart my comment that "everyone was a suspect." But I couldn't put Allen on a short list simply because he was in charge of safety at reactors. Or because he was in conference with the man who'd fired Yolanda. I might as well go with an indictment for a poor fashion choice—he wore polyester jean-like pants and a leather-elbowed jacket.

I regretted not having read the boron file Matt had given to me. Yolanda's thick portfolio might hold more possibilities than the articles I'd fallen asleep with last night. While I was sizing up my options, Allen and Taruffi left the office and walked toward us. Andrea and I slipped around the partition as if a grand coincidence had brought us all together.

"Dr. Lamerino. You're here so often, we'll have to get you a badge." Taruffi leaned into me, closer than I thought necessary for normal conversation. His silky tone and sweet-smelling cologne provoked me to move away from him, and from pretense. It seemed a "nothing to lose" moment.

"A badge would come in handy," I told him. "Since I'll be wanting to interview Yolanda's colleagues."

The look of consternation that took over Taruffi's face, though momentary, was worth the price I'd pay for stepping out of line, either by feeling guilty later or when the real cops found me out.

Allen cleared his throat and extended his hand. "Garth Allen. You're with the police?"

I smiled. "As a technical consultant. I understand you're familiar with such contracts."

Allen nodded and laughed. He seemed more relaxed—less guilty?—than Taruffi. "Listen, Dr....Marino?"

"Lamerino."

"Right. I used to know a Buddy Marino."

We Italians all know each other, I almost said, but I let Allen continue instead.

"I'd love to talk to you. But I'm only here till COB tomorrow."

"Garth works out of Washington," Taruffi said, apparently proud to be doing business with a true bureaucrat, one who knew the acronym for *close of business,* the end of the workday.

Andrea stepped back and leaned against our ambush partition. Her small dark eyes darted back and forth among us as we spoke. I figured her smile was self-congratulatory at having inadvertently set up the bizarre meeting.

"How about tomorrow morning?" I asked Allen, whipping out my electronic calendar at the same time. Busy police consultant that I am.

"It'd have to be early. Seven-thirty? I'll buy you a cup of coffee in Tony's office."

Very funny these government men. "I'll see you then."

Andrea and I walked off, heads held high, as if we'd just discovered evidence for hypergravity.

"Wow," was all she said until we got to her cubicle on the other side of the building, the wing with green partitions instead of orange.

I gave her a smile of genuine gratitude. "I'm really glad to have an interview with Allen. I wouldn't even have known about him if it weren't for you."

"You know I love to help." She retrieved a pile of papers from her desk and handed it to me. "I picked these up. They're copies of the newsletters Yolanda's group puts out. Some of them are old, but you never know." She raised her eyebrows in a conspiratorial gesture.

"Good work, Andrea." I looked at my watch. "And you're not even getting paid for this. Your shift is up."

She waved her hand. "It's OK. I'm free tonight. Maybe we could have dinner?"

I hoped I'd kept my reaction internal—a hard swallow and a silent "uh-oh." Lunch was one thing, part of the workday; dinner seemed more of a commitment to friendship. Andrea had come to the party Rose hosted to celebrate my one year back in Revere, but that had been our only purely social contact.

Matt was coming at seven. I didn't know what he'd think about a third person. I didn't know what *I* thought, except I suddenly felt very selfish.

"Come by my apartment at seven-thirty," I finally said.

Andrea's smile, buried in her cheeks, told me I'd made the right decision.

I ENTERED MY APARTMENT and went straight to my desk. I was almost surprised to find my letter where I'd placed it, as if the correspondence had a life of its own and had perhaps left for a while to visit Yolanda Fiore's trash.

To my unaided eye the envelope from my anonymous pen pal and the one from Yolanda's wastebasket came from the same batch. All the obvious features seemed the same—the fashionably rough texture, the size, the off-white tone, the slightly jagged edge on the flap. I sniffed each one, then looked around to be sure no one had witnessed the silly behavior.

I was reminded of expensive sets of letter paper popular as graduation presents years ago, with the name and address of the sender on the top sheet, and plain sheets meant for additional pages. Somewhere, I was sure, there was a companion sheet to my letter, with a name and an address.

If I gave the letter to Matt, there'd be considerable advantages—the police could canvass stationery stores, check for fingerprints, enlist the help of the post office. It pained me to acknowledge the superior resources commanded by real law enforcement personnel.

I felt let down. All I'd done was demonstrate to myself that Yolanda and I had received mail from the same person, or from two members of the same family, or two customers of the same card shop. Not much, once I thought about it.

I wondered what Yolanda had done with the contents of her envelope, and if it was also a threatening note. I envisioned a request to meet her at the top of the library stairs on Thursday night, by the coat rack. Or maybe it was just a party invitation.

The blinking light on my answering machine gave me an excuse to postpone further deliberation on our mysterious correspondent.

"Peter here," the first message started. Apparently Peter Mastrone was in one of his pretend-aristocracy moods. Probably watching British or subtitled films again. I'd been expecting the call.

Peter, who'd been teaching Italian at Revere High for decades, had been living a fantasy life since my return to Revere. In his mind, he and I were a couple, with him in charge. I'd dated him briefly in high school and he seemed to think I'd gone to California simply to give us a thirty-year breather before coming back to be with him again.

"Erin Wong told me you'll be helping her with science projects this month and that you might stay on and work with her during the regular school year also. She's thrilled." A pause, while he adjusted his voice to a lower frequency. "I hope that doesn't mean you're dropping my class." He laughed, as if the thought would never cross my mind.

Before I called him back I had to decide whether I wanted to continue my visits to his class. For a year I'd given monthly talks to Peter's students, on Italian and Italian-American scientists—Galileo Galilei, Enrico Fermi, Alessandro Volta, Guglielmo Marconi, Maria Agnesi. I hadn't run out of worthy subjects, but I was about out of patience with Peter's constant nagging. He didn't like my association with the Revere Police Department, either for business or social purposes.

I had a sudden brilliant idea, and picked up the phone to return Peter's call.

He answered, and lost no time getting on my nerves. "I know you got in on Saturday, Gloria. I was hoping you'd have called me by now."

"Yes, I had a good time in California, Peter. Thanks for asking."

Peter always seemed to bring out the petty, junior-high side of me. Not a good way to start our second year in the same state. I pictured his tall, thin Sicilian frame, cool and dry in a crisp seersucker suit, even on this day with 85 percent relative humidity. I was more comfortable with Matt, who wrinkled easily.

"Sorry. You know I worry about you, Gloria. I figured you were already back to work."

"Work?"

"The Fiore case. Don't tell me you haven't heard about it."

"Uh…"

I heard a long exasperated sigh. "I knew it."

"Did you know Yolanda Fiore?" I asked him. Maybe I could get some information out of this otherwise unpleasant interaction.

"Just by reputation. One of those fuzzy-thinking liberals who's always raving about one cause or another."

"Such as?"

"I don't even pay attention. Something about radiation leaking out of the lab. Then there was a fuss about nuclear plants and how they store the waste. People like that just like to get their pictures in the paper."

"Some people are like that." Peter didn't seem to know about John's involvement in weapons protests.

"I was hoping we could get together and talk about classes for the fall. I don't suppose you're free for dinner?"

"Not tonight." It's already crowded here for dinner, I thought. "And about the class…"

"You're dumping it, aren't you?"

"I have a great idea for it. Do you remember Andrea Cabrini? You met her at my party a couple of weeks ago. At the Galiganis'."

"The, uh, full-figured woman. How could I forget?"

"Peter." I made no effort to hide my annoyance.

"Sorry. What about her? You're not thinking of replacing you with her?"

"Why not? She's Italian. She speaks a dialect at least as well as I do." This was purely conjecture on my part, but I was sure Andrea was a quick study. "She's an excellent technician and knows a lot of the history of science and technology." I was winging the last part, too, and I hadn't yet asked Andrea if she'd be willing to do the classes. But this seemed like a good way to solve two problems—Peter's need for speakers and Andrea's excessive amount of free time.

"Has she ever done this before?"

"I'm sure she has." Another dubious statement.

"I like to give the students good role models for how to present themselves," he said.

"And also for professional competence?"

"Of course."

"And you want to teach them that personal qualities like kindness, intelligence, and generosity are not necessarily connected to candidacy for Miss or Mr. America?"

"OK, Gloria. I get it. I'll give her a try."

I smiled at my victory. Now all I had to do was convince Andrea. I felt I had some power over her—partly as her senior by at least twenty years—and hoped I wasn't abusing it.

I needed a treat first, however, so I made an espresso and punched the button for Rose's number. She'd also left a message, "just wanting to talk."

"I'm doing better," she said when I reached her. "I hope I have some friends left when this is over. Did I ever apologize to you?"

"Let's consider we've exchanged a mutual apology. How's John?"

"Holding up. You may have noticed the *Journal* left his

name out of the coverage. We're all happy about that. Any news on your part?''

The simple answer was ''no,'' but I hated to disappoint my friend. I gave her details of my encounters with Derek Byrne, Church attorney Frances Worthen, lab supervisor Tony Taruffi, and nuclear inspector Garth Allen. I told her about Yolanda's newsletter, the controversy over the library expansion, and even the root of the term ''moonshine liquor,'' as if it all mattered.

I omitted mention of my threatening note and the unruly alarm, surprised the security company hadn't also called the Galigani residence.

''Is there anything I can do to help?'' she asked me. ''It's nice to spend time pampering John, but I'm going a little crazy.''

It took me only a minute to work Rose's special talents into the needs of my investigation.

''I'd like to meet Derek Byrne's father, the councilman. Any ideas?''

''You want to have lunch with him tomorrow?''

''Tomorrow?''

I knew she was good, but this was impressive, even for Rose.

''You can go to the Civic Club luncheon. They'll be giving out the scholarships for the end of the school year. Byrne will surely be there.''

''How do I get an invitation?''

''I just gave you one. Frank and I are supposed to go, but obviously we're skipping it. Robert isn't in the mood either and Karla has a big case to argue next week. The Molinas are suing the school district over their son's suspension. They say it's caused undue hardship on the family. Can you imagine?''

''No, I can't.''

''So, you can represent the mortuary at the luncheon.''

''Perfect.''

''It wouldn't be the first time,'' Rose said with a laugh, echoing my own thought. More than once, my investigations had been helped by my informal status as adjunct mortuary staff.

''When and where?''

''The Oceanside, at noon.''

''Elegant,'' I said.

''It's still just rubber chicken.''

I laughed. ''I won't be going for the food.''

''Why do you want to talk to Brendan? He can't be a suspect.''

''Just a loose end.'' In a case full of them, I thought, having no idea what I'd say to Councilman Byrne. Is your son capable of murder? Can you vouch for his alibi? Do you have one yourself?

''Gloria, don't wear one of your crazy pins, OK?''

''I thought I'd show off my peach sweatshirt with the Peter Pan collar and butterflies on the front.''

Rose uttered a half laugh, as if she wasn't quite sure I was joking. ''OK, I'll mind my business.''

''That is your business, Rose. Would you like to dress me?''

''Gladly. I'll be over in the morning.''

Now that we were on good terms again, I gripped the phone and prepared myself for the inevitable.

''I'll need to talk to John at some point.''

I heard a humming sound. Rose's deep sigh of resignation. ''I know. It's OK.''

ELEVEN

ROSE AND I MADE a date for ten on Tuesday morning, after my meeting with Garth Allen. I hoped she wouldn't drag me to the mall for a new outfit. Especially during the daytime hours, the malls near us were a haven for young mothers. I had little patience with otherwise intelligent (I supposed) women in serious discussions about diaper bags and crib mobiles, and knowing their babies' ages to within two decimal points. I'd cringe when I'd hear, "Scott will be twenty-eight and a half weeks old on the seventh," or that nine-week-old Lindsey Anne loves the bookstore.

Maybe because I couldn't imagine Josephine Lamerino ever cared that much about baby Gloria.

In any case, my preferred shopping sprees were limited to discount electronics stores and pastry shops, and with the new opportunities to buy shoes and jackets on the Internet, I didn't see why I'd ever have to go to a three-dimensional clothing store again.

I needed to make one more phone call before I could sit down with Yolanda's newsletters and the boron file Matt found in her apartment—I thought I should tell Andrea my idea about Peter's class before she arrived for dinner, instead of putting her on the spot in front of Matt.

Her initial reaction was a loud gasp, as if I'd suggested immersing her soldering iron in water.

"I've never done anything like that."

I ignored the panic in her voice. "I know you've given technical presentations, and I think you'd be very good with high school students. You'll have the whole summer to prepare, and, of course, I'll work with you as much as you want.''

After a few moments of silence, Andrea's voice came back, shaky but upbeat. "It might be fun. I've been thinking I need a hobby or something. Does it have to be an Italian scientist? I just finished a book about Jenny Bramley.''

"The first woman in the United States to receive a doctorate in physics." I was surprised and pleased. Andrea had already passed my first test of a good role model for students—a reader of scientific biography.

"Yeah, she was only nineteen years old when she got her Ph.D.," Andrea said, her voice animated. "And she has patents for color TV tubes and the tubes they used in computer terminals in the early days.''

The early days—when I was in graduate school, and Andrea was barely walking.

"We can talk it over with Peter. He'll be teaching a new class in American history this year. Bramley would certainly fit there.''

"Great. I can make some vu-graphs or slides.'' Andrea paused. "Shall I still come over at seven-thirty?''

I realized she might be expecting me to cancel our dinner. "I'm counting on it. Matt will be here, too.''

"Detective Gennaro? Are you sure...?''

"We're looking forward to having you.''

Or I'm sure he will be when I tell him.

"WHAT? ANDREA WHO? I wanted to be alone with you,'' Matt said over the phone. My insecurity-driven call to tell him about my invitation to Andrea got an appropriate response. Teasing. And it took less than a minute for me to recognize it.

"Bring bread for three," I said, teeming with self-confidence.

I TOOK THE BORON FILE to my glide rocker and opened the first manila folder. DATA FALSIFICATION VERIFIED.

The headline on the most current issue of Yolanda Fiore's newsletter, *Raid-iation*, concerned an incident in Japan—a quality assurance problem with the containers used to ship nuclear waste. According to her and her staff, international inspectors uncovered falsification of neutron data. The flasks reportedly contained somewhat less boron than required to control the number of neutrons available for the fission reaction.

Since the loaded flasks were below allowable radiation limits, safety wasn't an issue. However, the incident had clearly widened the credibility gap between activist groups and nuclear facility managers. Focusing on motives for murder, I realized I'd have to stretch logic halfway around the globe to go from a boron predicament in Japan to an issue Tony Taruffi or Garth Allen would care about.

I skimmed reports on unequal pay scales for women and minorities, and the disbursement of funds between weapons and nonweapons research. A comparison of benefits programs put the Charger Street lab at the bottom of a list of similar employers around the country. Another column questioned safety measures in the tool and fabrication shops around the lab site.

It was easy to see why John was drawn to Yolanda, for more than her physical attractiveness and love of outdoor sports. They seemed also to share an idealism and a desire to speak out. Even when he stopped covering lab news for the *Revere Journal,* John's stories had a distinctively political bent, criticizing big business, fighting for consumer rights, speaking up for appropriate funds for education.

The March issue of *Raid-iation* featured a call for action—the annual Good Friday protest—that made me wonder how Yolanda had avoided arrest. I also wondered about her relationship to Derek Byrne, by all appearances more conservative than John Galigani. Derek had shorter hair, for one thing. He wore a conventional suit and tie, and was in favor of uprooting a possible ancient burial ground.

I tried to picture Derek lifting a coat rack and sending Yolanda to her death over political differences. Or over a disagreement about the library expansion plan. A stretch to places farther away than Japan, I decided.

Yolanda's views must have irked many conservatives—I wondered who might be irritated enough to kill her.

CONSCIOUS OF BETRAYING my mother's training, I'd planned a dinner of leftovers for my guests. On top of that, I broke another of her food rules by accepting offers from Matt to bring bread, and from Andrea to provide dessert. As far as I could remember no outside food or drink was allowed at Josephine Lamerino's table.

"We're not that poor," she'd say if anyone suggested they contribute to a meal in our house.

At seven sharp Matt appeared, having done his part by bringing three loaves—two baguettes and a fresh-smelling round with cheese and oregano.

"Anything in these files?" Matt took off his jacket and sat down in front of my coffee table, which was covered with papers from Yolanda's boron file.

"Nothing I can see. It's a set of articles Yolanda must have downloaded from the Internet. I found no order or logic to the collection except they all have the words 'boron' and 'boric acid' highlighted." I shifted the reports so Matt could see the topics—packaging requirements for waste transportation, temporary on-site storage, special reactor chemicals. "Most have to do with radioactive waste, but some are related to boric acid in the cooling system of the reactor itself."

Matt scratched his head. "This looks pretty complicated. Do you think Yolanda understood this stuff?" He pointed to a schematic of the pressure control system of Three Mile Island in Pennsylvania, the unit involved in this country's worst nuclear accident. A companion drawing showed the release path of gaseous fission products, carrying radioactivity from TMI's damaged core into the coolant water and ultimately into the atmosphere through the ventilation system.

I couldn't resist a little editorializing of my own. "Yolanda probably understood only one thing—radiation was released. Some people act on a little bit of knowledge. Nuclear waste management is a good example—fuel rods have been stored in pools next to reactors for almost fifty years. It was always meant to be a temporary solution until permanent sites could be licensed, but no state will take the responsibility. Technically, we're ready to deep bury the waste, but politically, it's the NIMBY Syndrome—not in my backyard.''

"Tell me more," Matt said.

Before I realized he was being facetious, I added to my sermon. "We've got feasibility studies, topological assessments, environmental impact statements—"

"Whoa," Matt said, holding up his hand. "A little defensive, aren't we?"

"I try to be objective."

Matt's smile and teasing jabs made me wish Andrea weren't due any minute.

THE DOORBELL RANG at precisely seven-thirty. I was sure Andrea waited on the stairway landing until her wrist alarm went off.

I adjusted my clothes and peeped through my security hole—mostly to impress Matt with how safety conscious I was—then opened the door to Andrea and an armload of pink boxes.

"I couldn't decide, so I brought a few things." Andrea emptied the contents of her boxes on my kitchen counter—cannoli, tortone, sfogliatella, and anise cookies, each with its distinctive sweet smell.

Before I could suggest we skip the day-old eggplant and go right to the bread and dessert, my phone rang—Rose Galigani, according to my caller ID box. Rose was one of the few people I knew who didn't block her number. Surprising, given her reluctance to use E-mail or computer technology in general. She handed off the spreadsheets and document preparation to Martha, her assistant at Galigani's, and had just begun to use an ATM card. I guessed she converted when I compared her Luddite tendencies to Peter Mastrone's.

I took the cordless receiver into the bedroom and left my guests to finish reheating dinner. I'd lost count, but I calculated this was at least the third or fourth violation of Josephine's dinner guest code.

"I know you have company, but I had to tell you," Rose said.

"They're doing fine. What is it?"

"I had the strangest call. From Councilman Byrne."

"What did he want?"

"At first he was just chatting, you know. Asked about John, and said he was sorry Frank and I wouldn't be at the luncheon tomorrow." Rose paused, as if she were still questioning the punch line that prompted her call to me.

"So?"

"Well I guess he knows you and I are friends. He asked if I could set up a meeting with you."

I SAT IN MY ROOM for a few minutes after I hung up with Rose. No, the councilman hadn't said why he wanted to meet me. And no, he didn't ask to meet anyone else. He wasn't running for office, so it couldn't be a vote-getting maneuver.

I couldn't avoid a creepy feeling. Did he know where I lived? I wondered. Had he sent me mail recently or set off the alarm in my building?

I've been doing too much police work lately, I decided. Maybe the councilman was merely being a good civic representative, introducing himself to the influential people in the city. An amusing thought—Gloria Lamerino as a force to be reckoned with in Revere politics.

Finally, the aroma of melting mozzarella reached the bedroom door, winning out over Andrea's strong perfume, and I went to join my guests.

Andrea and Matt were bent over my coffee table looking through the boron articles.

"I worked on a project like this for the lab last year," Andrea said, tapping a report called "Cask Designs for Spent Fuel." "We tested models of spent fuel containers. I remember creating neat scenarios, like what if a construction crane fell on a cask? Could it withstand the impact? Would acceptable limits—''

Matt held up his hand in a ''wait'' signal. ''What's spent fuel?''

''The antinuke people talk about the 'Spent *Fool* pool.''' Andrea laughed, then turned serious. ''You start out with this long, narrow container called a fuel assembly. It contains the uranium that's going to fission—split apart. Then, you know, the fission energy heats the water, the water becomes steam, and then it's like any other power plant.''

Matt nodded. I couldn't tell if he'd followed the explanation, which I considered very good. A hopeful sign that Andrea would do well in Peter's class.

Andrea continued, using her hands freely. ''Each assembly is used in a reactor for three or four years, then the fuel is used up.''

''Mostly,'' I said, wanting a piece of the tutoring action. Not that I was jealous because Andrea had taken over Matt's science education. ''There's some fissionable fuel left, just not enough to sustain the chain reaction.''

Andrea nodded. ''The uranium is depleted. It's...'' She spread her hands, palms up, and paused, as if ready for a drumroll. ''It's *spent*. But when the assembly is taken out of the core, it's still highly radioactive. So it has to be handled carefully and stored in a way that will bring down the radioactivity level, so to speak.''

''And not allow more reactions to take place in the waste pile,'' I added.

''And that's where boron comes in,'' Matt said. I was delighted he'd remembered our earlier session at Berger's house. ''It's a neutron poison, meaning it stops the neutrons from instigating more fission.''

''Wow,'' Andrea said.

Matt pointed to me. ''I have a good teacher.''

We shared a look that allowed me to feel generous toward Andrea and her moment in the limelight.

Later, it said.

TWELVE

I HEARD CHURCH BELLS earlier than usual on Tuesday morning. In my Sunday School days I'd have known to expect them—June 13, the Feast of St. Anthony of Padua, and a cause for celebration in the parish. I wondered whether the parishioners still gave out bread at the door, in honor of the healing powers of the food St. Anthony distributed to the poor. I had a vague desire to attend mass today. In the end, I chose not to, but I did hum the tune of a hymn I'd learned from Sister Pauline in 1946.

I wasn't worried about a dress code for my early morning meeting with Garth Allen, who'd be in his government-employee "uniform" of neutral suit and well-worn tie. And I was free to wear a pin since Rose wasn't monitoring my lab appearance. My choice was a stylized copper enamel replica of a nuclear plant. I'd picked it up at the Visitor Center of the Trojan nuclear facility in Oregon while I was living on the West Coast. The part I liked best was the tiny solar-system model atom sitting on top of the cooling tower.

Allen greeted me at the door of Taruffi's office, surrounded by the smell of hot-plate coffee—weak, burned, and bitter.

"Tony doesn't come in this early, but I know where he keeps the coffee." Allen smiled as if this were the key to a pleasure-filled experience.

"None for me, thanks."

"Too much already, huh?"

I nodded, keeping the real reason to myself—I didn't like coffee in large glass pots, especially when you could see through the brew. I grew up with rich, dark espresso. Before I was allowed to drink it myself, I'd watched my father, Marco Lamerino, begin and end each day with a small cup, sometimes spiked with a shot of whiskey. I thought often how staples in my house had become specialty items in the gourmet markets of today. Espresso, olive oil, ricotta, mascarpone. And macaroni—now called pasta in trendy restaurants. It was as if the whole country had gone low-income Italian.

Taruffi's posters also took away my appetite. Mountains, rapids, sunsets, seascapes, each with its own motivational phrases. ESTABLISH GOALS. MAKE AN EFFORT. BUILD A TEAM. In one, a human being foolishly challenged the law of gravity. He or she—I couldn't tell which from the silhouette—hung from a cliff that jutted out at an obtuse angle, with the top of the rock projecting out farther than the bottom. A single rope between life and death by impalement on granite. A different idea of inspiration. More inspiring to me would be a chart of the fundamental particles of the universe, or an attractive display of Maxwell's equations for the electromagnetic field, or the laws of thermodynamics.

"Clever pin." Allen leaned close enough to my collar for me to get a whiff of his aftershave, which didn't smell much better than the coffee. "I can get you a tie tack from the Harris plant in North Carolina if you're interested. It has the containment building, with the cooling tower in back."

I gave him credit for knowing how to win my heart. "I'd love it. Thanks."

"So, how did you happen to get into physics?"

My favorite question. Over the years I'd built up a reservoir of smart-aleck answers. *I fell off the kitchen stool and when I got up I was a physics major.* Or, *I started life as a boy, and before I knew it…*

Not wanting to begin on the wrong foot, I used a polite, generic response about how I enjoyed math and wanted to learn more about the universe.

"And Tony tells me now you work with the police. Fascinating. I assume that's why you're here."

I nodded. I was surprisingly free of guilt about not having a contract at the moment. "Just a few questions if you don't mind."

"Happy to oblige. Of course, I was in Washington, D.C., testifying at a Senate hearing both Thursday and Friday of last week. Up nearly all night Thursday going over white papers with my committee." A solid alibi if there ever was one—no wonder Allen was the most cheerful interviewee I'd encountered in all of my cases. I smiled and scribbled in my notebook, as if crossing him off my list. "And, of course," Allen continued, "I didn't see her on a daily basis. I'm just a work-for-others. Tony walked her through the projects, so I really only saw the deliverables."

Work for others, walking through talking points, deliverables. I was out of practice speaking lab talk. I remembered my first government contract in the seventies—I'd met fewer new terms in my quantum mechanics textbook.

Allen looked at his watch and put his feet on Tony's desk, which was remarkably clear of papers of any kind. A large picture frame dominated the area to the right of the blotter. The frame was at just the right angle for me to observe "happy family" snapshots—a child in a party hat, another looking with adoration at a soccer ball, even a portrait with Mom, Dad, kids, and dog.

I'm sure Allen thought he was helping me out by turning the frame to face me. "Nice family, huh? Tony's wife's a doll. Has her own business as a wedding coordinator—everything from engagement announcements to cutting the cake. Takes care of the kids, great cook…"

"How nice." I looked down at my notepad as if I had an organized set of queries for the interview. In truth, I'd had time to scribble only a few key words. "Yolanda seemed preoccupied with boron," I said, attempting a neutral tone. "In several articles she mentioned insufficient amounts of boron in reactor cooling water and spent fuel pools. Any reason you can think of?"

Allen looked past me, pursed his lips, and took a sip of

coffee. I tried to ignore the slurping sound. "Nothing comes to mind."

"I read about the problems the Japanese had. The political fallout could hold up their test program."

Allen snapped his fingers. "Oh, right. I do remember something about that. But as I recall there was no actual radiation leak. The casks met all the safety standards. You know how it is with politics. The truth doesn't matter. It's the *appearance of truth* they go by." I nodded, partly out of civility, and partly out of agreement. "Do the police think Yolanda's death had something to do with what happened in Japan?"

I wasn't sure whether Allen was leading me on or was really as dumb as he seemed, but I played it straight. "Not necessarily. But perhaps she suspected a similar problem with our systems?"

He shook his head, adding a frown for emphasis. "Not a chance. As I'm sure you know, Gloria, boron is only a backup for us." By *us,* I knew Allen meant the U.S. of A. I could almost hear the strains of the national anthem. He held up his left hand and ticked off points with his right. "First, there's the integrity of the cladding and the inner cask shell. Second, there's shielding—six to ten inches of heavy metal. Third, we keep the cask subcritical by controlling the amount in each load. Then, finally, we use a poison like boron." Allen spread his palms at the end of the list. His look and gestures asked, *What more does the public expect?*

I raised my eyes to Tony's posters and took my inspiration from the wheat field. DARE TO DREAM, it said.

"Can you think of anyone who'd have a reason to kill Yolanda?" I asked Allen.

He threw up his hands. "I'd like to help you, but all I can say is she was the kind of person who made enemies easily." He said this without rancor or judgment, as if he were reporting on a waste transportation schedule.

I lifted my eyebrows. "For example?"

He shrugged his shoulders. "She was on the warpath about everything. But her views didn't provoke *murder,* and no one

I know personally is capable of murder. In my opinion.'' Allen stood up, buttoning his jacket. ''Anything else I can help you with? Before I head home to D.C., I have to check in with some folks over in engineering.''

Folks. I thought I'd left that term behind in California. It always evoked images of men and women in red and yellow costumes dancing to accordion music.

I resorted to police procedure as I knew it and handed him my card. ''If you think of anything, give me a call.''

Allen ushered me out of Tony's office and walked me to the hallway, briefing me the whole time. I imagined bulleted items on transparencies, framed in cardboard holders, placed one by one on an overhead projector.

''For decades spent fuel has been safely carried by truck and rail in this country and abroad. Do you know every year the French move about one thousand metric tons of spent fuel to a reprocessing plant in The Hague? With nary an accident.'' *Who said* nary *anymore?* ''And our own American ships have extensive safety features.'' I felt a long list coming on, and I was right. I pictured the bullets as he spoke.

- Special Propellers and Electrical Supply Systems.
- State-of-the-art Cooling Systems.
- Satellite Navigation.
- Automatic Reports of Position, Heading, and Speed.
- Control Center Manned Twenty-four Hours a Day.

''Sounds like a perfect setup,'' I said.
''You bet.''

ON THE WAY HOME, I stopped at Russo's take-out annex and ordered a grande cappuccino. I talked to myself at great length, wishing I'd had the presence of mind to voice my opinions to Garth Allen.

I'd always been a proponent of nuclear power, but even the

biggest fan had to admit there were potential risks. No wonder people like Yolanda Fiore get angry, I thought.

However, in spite of my sweeping remark to Andrea, about suspecting everyone, I'd never seriously considered Garth Allen a candidate. Unlike with Taruffi, I thought of him as a harmless bureaucrat, and my meeting with him didn't change that perception. I detected no personal animosity toward Yolanda or any of the "radicals" that made his life more difficult than it would be.

And, I tended to believe Garth's assessment of waste pools, thus eliminating the boron angle as a motive for Yolanda's murder. Usually I'd be elated. I never wanted to keep scientists on my evil person roster very long. But even a Nobel Prize physicist might be preferable to John Galigani as a defendant.

I decided to reserve judgment on Taruffi. He had fired Yolanda, after all. Besides, he wasn't a technical person, just an administrator. I wondered what his stationery looked like.

I RUSHED INTO my apartment to answer the ringing phone—Elaine Cody. I hadn't talked to her since my quick call on Saturday to assure her I'd arrived home safely.

"Dare I ask what's new?"

"I just got back from a meeting to check on that boron problem I told you about. No leads."

"What a coincidence. There was a big accident in Boron over the weekend. I don't suppose it made the papers in Boston."

"Is boron a place?"

"Yes, don't you remember? It's a town off Highway 58, between Bakersfield and Barstow." I thought Elaine was about to give me all the cities in California beginning with B. "Anyway, these huge concrete pipes fell from a big rig and crushed a car."

"That's awful." I walked around opening windows as I talked, taking advantage of the cool morning air. No end in sight to the ninety-degree days. A school bus pulled up in front of a house across the street, alerting me to the hour. "It's not even six o'clock there, Elaine. What's wrong?"

"I broke up with Jose." Elaine's voice was suddenly low, her cheeriness gone. I'd met Elaine's boyfriend Jose Martinez the week before. "Too much baggage. That stuff with his son, and all."

"I'm sorry, Elaine."

"We're definitely still friends, so that part's fine."

"Do you want to talk about it?"

"Not really, I need a distraction."

I thought of Elaine's ability to attract men and maintain a social life any teenager would envy. "I'm sure one will be along in no time."

She laughed, and I knew she hadn't lost her sense of humor over one more breakup.

MY CONVERSATION WITH Elaine was cut short when Rose arrived. She'd made herself at home, sipping espresso and reading the *Globe* while I finished the call, but I wasn't eager to talk about my *Matt problem,* as I called it, in her presence. Already thin, Rose seemed to have lost weight in the two days since John's detainment. I hoped it was the loose-fitting sundress she wore. Her eyes, normally sharp and clear, were drawn and puffy.

I regretted I had nothing to make her life brighter except my willingness to let her plan my Civic Club luncheon outfit.

"It's only a little after nine. I'm glad you're here," I told her, "but I hope it's not going to take three hours to dress me."

"I'm not optimistic about the choices in your closet."

I grimaced, knowing she was right. I'd told Rose one of my favorite Marie Curie stories often enough not to repeat it to her. When Marie's sister offered to send her a dress for her wedding to Pierre, the scientist replied, "Send a dark one, so I can wear it to my lab the next day." I had no such excuse for the predominance of black apparel in my wardrobe.

Rose stood back from the rod that held my best clothes—

those that needed to be on hangers, and one or two outfits that required dry cleaning. I pointed out the too-small-at-the-moment group on the right, and the too-big-but-I'd-better-hang-on-to-them set on the left.

Rose groaned. My stomach tightened. It's only your clothing she disapproves of, I told myself. I pulled out my first choice, a black knit with short sleeves and a matching vest with a jacquard pattern.

Another groan. "Just what I thought. You don't have a thing to wear."

"There must be something here."

Rose shook her head. A smile broke out, transforming her face, and suddenly I knew why she'd come so early.

"What time do the stores in the mall open?" I asked her.

Her grin widened. "Nine-thirty."

The things I do to make my friends happy.

WORKING EFFICIENTLY, Rose and I finished shopping in time for coffee in my apartment. Under her direction, I'd bought a deep burgundy suit with matching shell top and a pair of flimsy sandals. I balked at wine-colored panty hose.

"All one color is in," Rose told me.

"Black is a color." Not in the electromagnetic sense, I added to myself, but certainly in the pigment sense.

Rose rolled her eyes and acquiesced to flesh-colored hose. "I can't wait to hear what Councilman Byrne is after," she said, her fingers marching through my jewelry boxes.

"What makes you think he wants something?"

"Byrne isn't the kind to waste time. He has an agenda, believe me." She pulled out a necklace of garnet and pearls, a present from Matt after a milestone in our relationship. "This is perfect."

I smiled at Rose's ability to multitask. I promised to call her immediately after lunch, happy for anything that distracted her from the sorry state of the Fiore murder investigation.

THIRTEEN

ONE LOOK AT the guests assembled for the Civic Club luncheon made me glad I'd taken advantage of a personal shopper. Men and women in different age ranges had dressed to match the elegant setting of the new Oceanside Hotel near the Revere/Winthrop border.

I looked around for someone I knew, but couldn't find a familiar face—not surprising since most of the friends I'd made tended to be pastry shop workers. Mingling was not my favorite pastime. *Networking,* I remembered to call it, not small talk.

A dark-haired young woman in a short black dress approached me at the bar, where I waited for a glass of ginger ale. I made a note to tell Rose about the many black outfits in the room, though I had to admit the ones hanging in my closet were dowdier than anything here at the Oceanside.

"Tina Ruggieri, Assistant Director of Communications for the Chamber of Commerce," the young woman said, extending her hand. Her smooth, freckled skin made me wonder if she'd been dropped off by her mother, but her professional demeanor kept me in check.

"Gloria Lamerino." I smiled and resolved to construct a title for myself before the next handshake. Police department consultant? I didn't have a contract at the moment. Retired Berkeley physicist? Irrelevant. Galigani Mortuary rep? Might be a put-off.

"Are you new in town?" Tina asked.

A deep voice answered for me. "Not exactly. She's a native

daughter finally returned home.'' I turned to see Councilman Brendan Byrne. He'd picked up my ginger ale from the counter and handed it to me, smiling broadly. ''Dr. Lamerino is a retired physicist working with the police, so be careful what you say,'' he said to Tina. He had two of my three titles right. And since he'd talked to Rose Galigani about me, I assumed he also knew my mortuary connection. I wondered if he was aware I'd been a surreptitious participant in his encounter with his son in the library.

Conversation was difficult in the densely populated room, its high ceilings echoing the chatter and the clinking of glasses. Only a minute or two after Byrne formalized introductions, Tina's eyes took on a glazed look, whether from the prospect of talking to a physicist or because she had outstanding warrants I wasn't sure. Perhaps she drifted off simply to find her peers.

The result was that Councilman Byrne and I were left alone to size each other up. The task was harder for me, given the councilman's height. I stepped back for a good view of his penetrating blue eyes and shock of white hair. I thought of his son and convinced myself there was a resemblance, though Derek's look was more somber, his eyes a darker blue. Both men dressed in fine style, except that Byrne had a dark spot at the bottom of his beige jacket. A bump from a martini-carrying networker, I decided.

''I've been wanting to talk to you, Gloria.'' He paused and put his hand on my shoulder. ''May I call you Gloria?''

''Please do, uh…''

''Brendan. I know you're looking into Yolanda Fiore's murder. And I realize you're very close to the chief suspect and would naturally like to exonerate him.''

Rose was right—the councilman didn't waste any time. He'd steered me away from the busy bar area, into the dining room where large round tables for ten were set up. At eleven forty-five, only a few people had made it this far, most still in the lounge. When we stopped walking, I looked down to find a place card with my name in fancy letters. *Dr. Lamerino*. The card to the left of it read *Councilman Byrne*.

Men in high places, I thought. I wonder what else he could get away with.

"You're doing fine so far, Brendan. You seem to know a lot more about me than I know about you." The perfect script for flirting—if it weren't for the difference in our ages and the seriousness of the topic.

Byrne pulled my chair out, a gesture that seemed to come naturally to him, but not to me. I stumbled onto the seat and struggled to slide into place, hampered by too much friction between the seat cover and the fabric of my new skirt.

Byrne turned his seat to face me, one elbow on the table. He raised his hand as if to shield our conversation, though there was no one near enough to overhear us. His voice was low. "I may be able to help you."

No truly useful information ever comes easy, I'd learned, in research or in police work. But I allowed myself a surge of excitement—this could be the one time in a million.

"I don't know how deeply you've looked into Yolanda's personal life."

"I know she was dating your son."

Byrne frowned and swayed a bit in his seat, as if he'd been knocked off balance. Surely he was aware the relationship was common knowledge. My guess—he wasn't prepared to give up control of the conversation.

Feeling the need for a little more power myself, I moved again before he recovered completely. "Wasn't Derek the last person to see her alive?"

He smiled. Back on track. "Except for the murderer."

"Of course."

"Before Derek, there was her boss," he said, out of the side of his mouth. "Her ex-boss, that is."

"Anthony Taruffi? Yolanda dated him?"

"'Dated' would be a euphemism. He has a wife and children." I remembered the nuclear family photographs in Taruffi's office. "Don't get me wrong. I like Taruffi. We've worked together on some projects—community relations between the lab and the city, you know. It's to our mutual advantage to keep things amicable.''

''So this…affair…would have been after Yolanda was with John Galigani?''

''Correct. I don't necessarily want to reveal my sources, but let's say very few people were aware of it. I don't think Claire, Taruffi's wife, ever found out. She's a businesswoman and I know her through the Chamber of Commerce.''

''Have you told this to the police?''

Byrne shook his head. ''It's not a good idea for a man in my position.'' The councilman leaned into me. ''Of course when I heard about your worthy pursuits, I sensed a perfect opportunity to get the information out without…'' Byrne trailed off and looked past me at the newcomers to our table. To my disappointment, guests were filling the room, and I didn't have time to ask what equation linked his ''position'' to talking to the RPD. I also wondered about this alleged affair that no one else seemed to know about—a perfect ruse for the councilman to steer me away from his son.

The last person to arrive at our table was Dorothy Leonard, who took the chair to my right. In my doddering attempts to seat myself gracefully, I hadn't noticed her place card. Dorothy's black outfit, a dress and short bolero with a subtle trim, rivaled any in the room for elegance. I delighted in the good fortune of being plunked down among the principals in a murder investigation. And for once, it wasn't at a Galigani Mortuary wake.

We sat quietly during the business announcements from the Civic Club luncheon committee, each preparing his or her own topics of conversation, I guessed. I struggled, not only with my slippery drumstick-thigh combo, but with words that would provoke a useful conversation without alienating my luncheon partners before I garnered information.

I started with a lie. ''I remember meeting you both at the fund-raiser last year. I was so impressed by the expansion plans for the library.'' Two lies.

Since I already knew Byrne's feelings about the proposal from my eavesdropping the day before, I focused on Dorothy Leonard. She brushed back her hair in the same elegant gesture I'd seen when I first met her.

"It's the best thing to happen in this city for many years. State grants are not easy to come by, and we should be very, very grateful." Leonard's slight overbite did nothing to detract from her forceful presence.

Councilman Byrne groaned. He clenched his jaw and stretched his upper torso. He might have been in agony. I was sure we were disrupting what he hoped would be a peaceful lunch, once he'd given me the scoop on the Taruffi-Fiore affair, but a peaceful lunch was the last thing I'd hoped for while John Galigani was about to be charged with murder. My job, as I saw it, was to encourage conflict. My strategy was to segue from the library expansion to the library slaying.

"I hear that some people are against the expansion?" I said, spreading cold, hard butter on a cold, stiff roll.

Byrne bit off a large chunk of his own dinner roll. Leonard put down her knife and fork.

"Amazingly, yes," she said. "There's a squabble over rights to the ground and some possible historical significance. But even the Revere Historical Society is in favor of the expansion, so I'm not concerned about the little protest."

This time, Byrne's response was a snort. "That's the first time I've ever heard the magisterium of the Holy Roman Catholic Church referred to as 'little' anything."

I dabbed my lips with the nonabsorbent white napkin. "Excuse my ignorance, but I don't know much about city politics yet. How will this issue be resolved?" I wondered about my position between two very tall, powerful people. I decided if they came to blows, the fists would fly over my head anyway. None of the other seven people at the table, all twenty-something I guessed, seemed the least bit interested in our drama.

"By documentation," Leonard announced. "As we speak, Amy Tung, the Historical Society's research director, is vetting papers that will show not only our proper ownership of the land, but the implausibility of its being sacred ground."

"As if someone named Tung would know anything about the history of Revere," Byrne said, not masking his sneer. Not only stubborn, but racist. "And who says the Historical Society is objective on this? Isn't your cousin married to their president?"

"That's just like you, Brendan," Leonard said. "When all else fails, make an ad hominem argument."

Magisterium. Ad hominem. Besides my wardrobe, my Latin also needed renewal. Who said Revere wasn't a classy city?

The luncheon seemed to be coming to a close and I hadn't made any progress in my unofficial investigation. I gave up my plan for a smooth transition.

"Any word yet on the Yolanda Fiore case?" I asked, swinging my head from Byrne to Leonard and back.

"Shouldn't we be asking you that?" Byrne asked. His tone seemed to carry a jeer, but maybe I was influenced by his recent Asian slur.

I stalled with a cough that required a sip of water. "We're looking into all angles." Nice generalization. "Did either of you know Yolanda personally?" Another swing of my head.

The "not very well" from Dorothy Leonard came out simultaneously with the "barely" from Congressman Byrne.

Evidently the murdered woman hadn't made much of an impression on either her boyfriend's father or his boss. Or the father and the boss were holding out on me.

FOURTEEN

I ARRIVED HOME to a telephone message from Peter Mastrone, irritating, as usual. This time he expressed concern about Andrea—she'd have to be fingerprinted if there were no prints already on file for her, since she'd be dealing with minors. I thought I detected an *aha* in his voice, as if Andrea Cabrini probably had a criminal record that would preclude her appearing in his classroom. I was surprised Peter didn't realize all lab employees were fully vetted by the Department of Energy before being hired.

Eager as I was to tell him the news—Andrea Cabrini was cleaner than his own immaculate oxford shirts—I called Rose first.

"Did you arrange the seating at the Civic Club?" I asked her. "I sat between Brendan Byrne and Dorothy Leonard."

She laughed. "I'm not that influential, Gloria."

"I disagree. But in spite of your efforts and my excellent position at the table, I didn't get as much information as I'd hoped. I picked up a souvenir program for you, however. There's a fine silhouette of Paul Revere and his horse on the front."

"Thanks," she said with another laugh. I was grateful for each one.

Unsatisfied by the congealed molecules masquerading as mashed potatoes at the luncheon, I'd started to pick on the leftover bread on my counter, Matt's dinner contribution last night from the bakery near his home. The home he'd invited me to live in. Or possibly he had. An image of my clothes and furniture at his Fernwood Avenue address was so distracting, I wished I could confide this new development, and my mixed feelings, to Rose. Ordinarily I would, and she'd be ecstatic at the idea of helping me in a romantic situation.

Instead, I told her about the alleged Fiore-Taruffi affair—as expected, she jumped on that as the likely motive for Yolanda's murder—and what little else I had to report from the luncheon. Eventually I had to broach the main reason for my call.

"Is John with you?" My fingers gripped the cord. I hoped there'd be no relapse into a strained conversation.

"Yes, he's staying here. I know you need to talk to him, Gloria. Anytime."

No sign of displeasure. I relaxed my fingers.

"Maybe I'll come over now." Before you have another negative reaction to me, I thought, but didn't say.

"HE'S ALL YOURS," Rose told me, leaving us on her air-conditioned porch, surrounded by white wicker furniture and floral cushions in pinks and reds. A pallid John Galigani in gray sweats sat across from me, a tray of iced tea and lemon squares between us.

I was relieved Rose didn't consider this occasion a version of a parent-teacher conference where the mother hovered over her recalcitrant fifth-grader. It was an added bonus that neither of the attorneys, Nick Ciccolo and Mike Canty, was present. It was awkward enough questioning a man I'd known all his life, about a murder. I felt close to John, and regretted every year of his life that I'd lived far away, as if his near-arrest were a reminder of my own poor choices.

We spent a few uncoordinated moments pouring tea, arranging napkins and straws, stalling. It took a great deal of energy for me to pull back and achieve a measure of objectivity, but I was finally able to get us started.

"I know this is hard, John, but I need to ask you some questions."

He nodded and waved his hand in a gesture of resignation, his head lowered. Although he'd greeted me with a hug, his expression was serious, and he still hadn't said a word. I noticed his hair was shorter than usual and wondered if his lawyers were responsible for the more conservative look.

I went on. "You know this is completely off the record, since your lawyers aren't present, and, anyway—" I paused for a laugh. "I'm not exactly an officer of the court, am I?"

Another nod and hand wave, but no smile.

"Is there anything you remember about the last time you saw Yolanda? Any strange behavior?"

John shook his head, ran his hands across his face, working his way up from his small round chin to his forehead. "We had dinner, is all. I never saw her after about eight-thirty."

It was a start. "You're sure of the time?"

He nodded. "I kept checking my watch because I had a deadline to meet at nine. Arnie was holding a spot for me on the sports page. He wanted to include the play-off results for the big bowling trophy. I was filling in for the guy who usually covers sports."

"Was it usual for you and Yolanda to have dinner together? Did you see her regularly even though you'd broken up?"

"No, just once in a while, mostly if business brought us together. I still did a feature on the lab now and then and she was my contact."

"So why dinner?"

John stood up abruptly. His knee banged against the table, sending our drinks into vibratory motion. "Why not?" His voice was too loud for the small quarters, and I glanced anxiously back into the house. I didn't need Rose worrying about my abusing her son.

I sighed, exasperated. "John, this is your friend, your Auntie Gloria, remember?" I spoke as if I didn't share his ambiguity over my current role in his life.

He sat back down, tears forming in his eyes. I walked around the table and leaned over to embrace him, my own eyes smarting. His hands were cold in spite of what I considered a minimum level of cooling on the porch. The outside temperature was over ninety degrees, presenting a big challenge to the small AC unit.

"I'm sorry," he said, while I rubbed his back. "This is crazy. Let's just start again. I'll tell you anything you think will help get me cleared of this."

I took my first full breath in a while, and gave him a big smile that was supposed to say, *Remember, I'm on your side.* "I don't know much about Yolanda at all," I said. "Did she have family, for example? Hobbies? Close friends?" I decided against telling John I'd seen the "Auntie Yo" drawings in Yolanda's apartment. I wondered if he'd ever been to her current residence—and if so, how recently.

"She had a sister in Michigan. Yolanda came here from Detroit about five years ago. Her family was from Revere originally, and she wanted to return to her roots, I guess. She had a little niece, about eight years old, I think, that she wrote to all the time. Cara was her name. And her grandmother is still alive. Her parents are both dead."

Would the sister come to the funeral? I wondered. I assumed Yolanda's body would not be waked in the Galigani Mortuary since John was involved in the case. A disadvantage for me—except for the absence of two-way mirrors, the Galigani parlors had been perfect as my own personal interview room when I worked on a case. For all I knew, Yolanda's body might be on its way to Michigan. I'd have to ask Frank, who was aware of the arrangements of all the dearly departed of Revere, whether his clients or not.

"Friends? Hobbies?"

"Not much of either, really. In spite of her public affairs role at the lab, she wasn't much for social life. She was a journalist at heart and loved to investigate. I guess you could call that her hobby—looking into things."

"Like safety problems and employee grievances?"

"Yeah, but that's not all." John smiled and I could tell he'd come up with a happy memory of his deceased friend. "One time she solved a mystery before the cops did—a series of thefts from the local schools. She compared the cafeteria food delivery schedules with the robberies and came up with a correlation. Cops picked up the delivery guy on his next try."

A woman after my own heart, I thought. I gave John a minute to enjoy his recollection, then went for a big question.

"Do you mind telling me why you broke up with her?"

John laughed, slightly, an uncomfortable snicker. "Incompatible philosophies, if you can believe that. We were always arguing over how we could make a difference in the world, which one of us was selling out, which one was maintaining the ideals that led us to journalism in the first place, instead of some profession that was locked into the establishment."

This was where I would usually step up to the lectern and deliver my speech about "how to make a difference." I'd always resented the idea that certain occupations were in themselves more noble than others. Didn't we all make a difference depending on how we did our jobs, the way we lived our lives? Did Walter Cronkite contribute more to the enrichment of humanity than Marconi, who gave us the ability to communicate with each other across continents? If it weren't for the technology, there wouldn't be a Walter Cronkite. And we'd never be able to see and correct human abuses on the scale that we do now.

I didn't share these feelings with John—even I could tell my musings were no more insightful than a better-things-through-chemistry commercial. Besides, I was sure there was a more recent example than Cronkite to make my argument, but I couldn't name one.

I cleared my throat of my opinions, swallowed my urge to preach. "Is that why you argued with Yolanda at the end of Thursday evening—incompatible philosophies?"

"Yeah, as a matter of fact. It was the same old story. She accused me of compromising my integrity by working for a mainstream newspaper, instead of some throwaway independent. And there *she* was working for the fr…for the government, for God's sake." I watched his face turn red, his temples throb. I told myself this outburst meant nothing in terms of whether John Galigani was capable of murder. He calmed down quickly, and sounded contrite. "I guess I said some pretty nasty things to her—like she was basically working for people who created weapons of mass destruction, and so was Derek for that matter, a yes-man at a government institution."

It wasn't the first time I'd heard John's passionate anti-lab sentiment. Now it seemed he was also anti-library, though I was sure that wasn't how he meant it. Probably out of deference for my relationship with his parents, John had never confronted me directly on my own role as a thirty-year veteran of a similar lab on the West Coast. It didn't hurt that we were separated by an entire continent for most of his life.

Time to switch topics.

"Were you aware that Yolanda and Anthony Taruffi... dated?"

John looked at me as if I'd told him a supermarket tabloid had won a Pulitzer Prize.

"Yolanda and Tony? I don't think so," he said. "Not in a million years."

I made no comment. I'd decide later whether to believe Councilman Brendan Byrne or John Galigani. In the meantime, John had come up with another recollection.

He grinned—a rare sight these days among the Galiganis. "We actually parted on a joke that night. There were these two huge lions in the lobby of the library, in crates."

I nodded, remembering the crates, parked against the wall, the evening Matt and I dropped in on the late-working Director Leonard. "We named them Patience and Fortitude."

I gave him a confused look. The punch line had gone over my head.

"Like the lions in front of the New York Public Library?" He looked at me as though I should know, and I finally did remember the lions sitting on pedestals on Fifth Avenue.

"Those lions have names?"

John nodded. "Yeah, Patience and Fortitude. Yolanda and I had been to New York together a couple of times, and we'd joke that neither of us had either virtue."

His voice cracked. I hoped he was wrong about the virtues.

"One more thing," I said. "About dinner on Thursday." It was the question that had caused spilled tea earlier, but I had to treat John like any other interviewee. I refused to give the word "suspect" any shrift. "Why dinner on that particular evening?"

John lowered his eyes, stared at his shoes, or at the new green indoor/outdoor carpeting Rose recently had installed. I didn't like the implication that he was about to be less than truthful. I cast my own eyes down, landing them on Rose's magazine basket, full of periodicals devoted to a range of topics from beautiful homes and gardens to current events and the latest business news. I'd heard her many times, holding her own with Frank and his colleagues in a discussion of international trends in trade, labor, and management disputes—topics that caused my eyes to wander, my mind to seek distraction by estimating the angles that made up the geometric wallpaper pattern.

John spoke softly. "Yolanda called me a few weeks ago, all excited about a project she was working on. She needed my help with some research. She knew I had access to old *Journal* files."

"Do you know what she was looking for?"

"No, just that she needed to see old newspapers, from the 1940s."

"That's all she told you?"

He nodded, his chin still hovering close to his chest.

"Couldn't she just go on-line for that?"

"For some of it, yes, but there's still nothing like doing things locally. And there are those of us who still like the feel of microfilm, you know."

John's smile was weak, tentative. When I'd left Councilman Byrne and Dorothy Leonard, I was convinced they were keeping something from me. I didn't expect that same feeling when I was finished with John Galigani.

But there it was, the certainty that John was hiding something.

FIFTEEN

"TOO LATE FOR ME to come over?" Matt asked, talking cell phone to cell phone.

Never, I thought. I was negotiating a STOP sign on my way home from a long afternoon and evening at the Galiganis'. I'd just about readjusted my driving patterns to accommodate the habits of Boston drivers. In California, drivers took turns, for the most part, politely—only one car at a time from each direction passed through a STOP sign; in Revere, as many as three or four vehicles would trail along after the first car in line came to a stop. Or merely slowed down.

California drivers saved their aggression for the open road and I didn't miss the freeway rage, nor the high stakes of accidents that occurred at seventy-five to eighty miles an hour.

"Not too late," I told Matt.

"Anything new?"

"I talked to John. I have a little more information, but not much. How about you?"

"Some nuggets from Parker and Berger. Not much either. Dying to see you, Gloria."

"Me, too." But I still couldn't be the first one to say it.

MY LATE-NIGHT APARTMENT smell was more like lunchtime at Russo's. I'd prepared espresso; Matt had brought Italian snack food—garlic bread sticks and almond biscotti.

"I couldn't decide," he said, waving one bag in each hand, as if he were weighing the items on an analytic balance. "What do you think? Which of the two staples of life? A, bread, or

B, biscotti?'' When I hesitated, he dropped the bags, came over to me, and added a third choice. ''Or maybe C?''

We chose C, and saved the food for later.

MUCH LATER, when we were ready for serious police work, I summarized my interview with John, focusing on the last bit of information I'd gleaned—that Yolanda was doing research that required access to old newspapers.

''What could Yolanda have been looking for?'' Matt asked. ''Your boron controversy?''

My boron controversy? I supposed it was mine. ''That was my first thought. But that would be pretty early—although there was research in the field, the first commercial reactor didn't come on line until 1954. And, besides, why would anyone look at *Journal* files when the lab library is one of the best resources in the country for technical information?''

''Maybe there was some other upset involving boron? And maybe she wasn't looking for scientific data, but some sort of community angle—you know, the-city-is-in-danger-from-the-lab kind of thing. The *Journal* would be more likely to report it than the lab.''

''But why would John keep something about boron from me? He probably thinks I know every scientific blip in history anyway.''

''True. But you're still convinced he knows what she was investigating?''

I nodded. ''I'm afraid so.''

We'd moved from the kitchen to my blue-gray corduroy sofa, farther from the temptation to continue snacking on bread sticks and biscotti, but closer to the box of Sees candy on my coffee table. Elaine had taken it as her personal responsibility to make sure I always had California chocolates on hand. I bit into a bordeaux.

''So, it could be something that would incriminate him.'' Matt held up his hand to stave off my negative reaction. ''Even though he's not guilty.''

''Or something that would hurt the memory of Yolanda.''

"What about the library expansion? Could that have figured in a motive?"

I shrugged my shoulders. "We need to talk to the church lawyer. Frances Worthen."

Matt gave me a sidelong look. "We? You mean we can recommend it to Parker and Berger, don't you?"

"Of course."

"Speaking of whom…I did learn a few things from them, mostly alibis of people she worked with. All pretty solid."

"How about her boss, Tony Taruffi? Do you remember his alibi?" I'd told Matt about the alleged Taruffi-Fiore affair. I was hoping for "Tony was home alone and no one saw him." No such luck.

"He was at some gala at the Warner Center, with an out-of-town business associate from Washington." I tried to form a picture of Tony Taruffi and Garth Allen among Boston's elite at a lavish event. It didn't quite gel, but I supposed it was easily verifiable.

"We'll have to keep digging," Matt said.

Digging. As in burying Yolanda. I thought about the disposition of her body, which I'd learned from Frank before I left the Galiganis.

"It's out of my hands," he'd said. "A national mortuary service contracted with Cavallo's to prepare her for transportation to Detroit. Because of John's—John's interests, I couldn't even do the embalming."

I'd tried to pay only half attention as Frank described the rules for sending decedents out of state. In a plain cardboard box it turns out, with the body packed in tightly enough and tied down with a couple of straps so it doesn't slip around.

"It makes shipping less expensive. Some families want a casket on this end, and it costs a fortune. It's the difference between about six hundred dollars, and twenty-five hundred dollars."

Once Frank got started on business talk, it was hard to stop him—at least this conversation was bloodless. I imagined Yolanda in a plain brown wrapper, being handled like any other package on a commercial airliner. More exactly, I pictured a corpse next to my new green luggage on my last trip across country.

"They have to arrive a couple of hours before the regular baggage is loaded, and it's usually stored separately if there's room," Frank said, as if I'd expressed my squeamish thoughts out loud.

"Are you OK?" Matt's voice and light touch brought me back to my living room. "This is all going to work out, Gloria."

I smiled. "Thanks, and I'm much better than I would be if you weren't here."

I thought how lucky I was that, without saying it in so many words, Matt was with me on this mission to find the real murderer of Yolanda Fiore. He knew what the Galigani family meant to me, and he'd known Frank since he started at the Revere Police Department in the early sixties.

"I still remember Frank forcing me to witness an autopsy in the ME's lab when I was a rookie," Matt had told me on an early date. "He said I'd be a better detective later, and he was right."

We were about finished information sharing when my phone rang. "Elaine," I said, knowing the call could only be from someone who lived where it was three hours earlier.

Since Rose had more important things on her mind than my love life, I'd left a message on Elaine's machine, a vague reference to a dilemma about my relationship with Matt. Not urgent, I'd said, but Elaine was likely to respond as if it were. Elaine's relationship history was rocky—more like a series of avalanches—but she had insights beyond the scope of my experience.

She didn't waste time. "What's the scoop with Matt? He proposed, right? And you're all upset? I knew there was *something* going on the last time we talked. Tell me, tell me."

I didn't have many friends, but the two I had knew me very well. "It's nice to hear from you." I used a tone that said I wasn't able to talk freely. At least not about that topic.

"Is everything all right?"

"Of course. Matt's here, and we're working on this case I told you about."

I pictured Elaine, a technical editor at the Berkeley lab, in her home-from-a-date clothes. The best dresser in our circle at the lab, she'd be wearing an eye-catching summer ensemble that set off her blond-gray hair. The rest of us, whose wardrobes were more like Marie Curie's lab/wedding outfit, called her "Radcliffe" or "Smith," to tease her about her debutante look.

"So, you can't talk. I'm dying here, Gloria. Am I right? Did he propose? Just say yes or no, or scream or something."

I laughed. "I'm not sure."

"You're not sure?" Elaine laughed as hard as I'd ever heard her.

"Fine, Elaine, I'll call you later." I didn't do much better at a serious tone, and by the time we hung up, I figured Elaine was as frustrated as I was.

But at least she didn't have to deal with what came next.

Matt's response.

"I suppose you told Elaine about my clumsy proposal the other night," he said. I felt my face redden. Molecules from my last Sees nougat took over my mouth, leaving me unable to swallow. My distress was not lost on Matt. "I'm not trying to rush anything, Gloria."

I swallowed. "I know."

"A decision by the Fourth of July will be fine." A wide grin. "Just kidding."

His disarming smile nearly prompted me to make an immediate decision. Jump on his lap and yell, YES, I told myself. But in the next moment, I panicked—he reached into his back pants pocket and pulled out a small box. A ring-sized box.

He handed me the box. "Now might be a good time to give you this."

My eyes widened, my eyebrows went up without my specific instructions. My stomach muscles tightened.

"Matt…"

"Just open it."

I lifted the muted blue velvet cover. Inside, on a bed of ivory silk, was a beautiful piece of jewelry—a pin, about three centimeters square, a replica of an element of the periodic table. The background was pale green, the border gold, the letter B in the center, in gold.

B, the chemical symbol for boron.

"Where in the world did you find this?" I stared at the details—in the upper left corner, the atomic number, 5; in the upper right, the atomic weight, 10.81.

"I have my sources," Matt said, obviously pleased at my reaction. He moved closer, held me.

My head was full of questions, all of them addressed to myself. Why can't I make this decision? Why am I afraid of this? And the big question: What is wrong with me?

I don't know how long we sat on the couch, but when I woke up at four in the morning, Matt was gone. He'd propped my head on a pillow and covered me with a light afghan. A note, written in red felt tip, was on the coffee table. I read Matt's neat printing:

GLORIA, I GOT BEEPED. GLAD IT DIDN'T WAKE YOU. TAKE YOUR TIME. YOU'RE WORTH WAITING FOR. I LOVE YOU.

I smiled, pulled the cover over me, and went back to sleep.

SIXTEEN

I CLEARED MY HEAD on Wednesday morning by taking a long walk. Down Revere Street, past St. Anthony's Church, all the way to Revere Beach Boulevard—about a mile, and then another mile along the water's edge. At one time the one-block-wide strip of land between Ocean Avenue and the Boulevard was crammed with rides, food stands, nightclubs. And arcades where you could put a penny in a slot and a fine oak cabinet-cum-vending machine would feed you a sepia-tone photo of Rock Hudson or Joan Crawford.

Now high-rise apartment buildings and a smattering of tiny parks took their place. Although it had been decades since I or anyone else had bitten into a candied apple from Uncle Eddie's Apple Dandy stand, the smell of warm caramel and the sounds of creaking machinery and tinny music stayed in my head. I had the beach to myself this early morning, except for a few other lone walkers who were no more in the mood to chat than I was.

But the mild surf, bright sun, and long memories were not conducive to the work I'd cut out for myself, and I finally headed home.

IN MY ROCKER, with a second cup of coffee, I reviewed the motives I'd concocted for Yolanda's murder. The classic reason for murder—the jealousy of a lover—fit both Tony Taruffi, if Councilman Byrne was right about an affair, and Derek Byrne. And, unfortunately, John Galigani. Moreover, if Yolanda were as promiscuous as it appeared, there could be countless other lovers I had no way of knowing about. Matt had promised to bring up this matter with Parker and Berger.

Another possibility was that the motive was connected to the library expansion documents. I imagined Yolanda checking old newspaper files, investigating land claims, and thereby posing a threat to one side or the other. That notion generated a list of suspects, including Frances Worthen, attorney for the Church, and Derek Byrne again. But the most passionate about the project seemed to be Director Leonard *pro* and Councilman Byrne *con*.

Finally, if a boron controversy figured into Yolanda's death, Taruffi was a candidate, giving him two reasons to dispense with her.

Three murder theories—love, territory, and science—as far apart as they could be. My head ached.

When the phone rang, I snatched it up quickly, happy to leave my confused mental charts and lists. Councilman Byrne's deep, lilting voice surprised me.

"Gloria, I wanted to tell you how much I enjoyed our lunch yesterday. Delightful."

Surely he didn't mean the chicken, or the tense repartee about the library.

"Yes, it was a nice event" was all I could put together on such short notice.

"You know, I was thinking about our conversation, about this and that, and I know you didn't ask, but—" The councilman paused for a laugh, of the heh-heh type. "It occurred to me you might want to know more about me."

I shook my head in confusion, happy we weren't face-to-face. Was this an old man wanting attention? I held my breath as I considered the possibility that he wanted to date me.

"I—uh." I was doing worse and worse with this conversation, but fortunately the councilman didn't need much feedback. He continued.

"I never gave you my alibi for the night poor Miss Fiore—I suppose it's Ms. Fiore—was killed."

"I—uh."

"Oh, I know you didn't ask, but I have great respect for what you're trying to do, and I want to make the record complete."

"Did the police—"

"No, no. The police didn't question me. Why would they?" I heard a note of anxiety in the old man's voice.

"No reason. I—"

"Well, here's where I was. I belong to an informal club, over in Everett. We play cards, pinochle usually, every Thursday. And there I was last week, until well after midnight. Just a group of retired mayors, councilmen, judges, and the like."

So, important alibi witnesses, was the message.

"I see." I used my best play-along voice.

"Now of course, I don't know exactly when the young lady died, but I know my boy left at eleven, so it had to be after that."

Another plug for his son's innocence. Maybe that's what this phone call was about. "Of course."

"And although I was alone from about one in the morning, I think if you check with the boys they'll tell you I was in no condition to overpower a healthy young woman. In fact, I did overindulge myself." Another heh-heh laugh, leading me to wonder if he was inebriated at this very moment. "I had to be driven home by old Rafftery. He'll tell you as much. Not that I want this spread around, but, as I say, but for your own peace of mind."

"I appreciate your telling me, Councilman."

"You're a godsend, Gloria. Good night."

I hung up, confused, but happy I hadn't been hit on. Not that I had anything against septuagenarians, but my love life was already complicated enough.

I NEEDED TO FOCUS on one line of inquiry at a time for this investigation. Boron would be the easiest road to take for now, and I'd be researching two things at once—a motive for murder, and my project with Erin Wong's class. It never took long for me to convince myself that the answer—any answer—lay in science.

The day had turned cloudy. Rain was in the forecast, a welcome change. I turned off my air-conditioning, opened windows, and went on-line to visit the commercial nuclear power industry. After only a short time, I realized the task of building a reactor, even a tiny one, would be daunting.

I called Erin Wong.

"What if we construct a model waste pool instead of a reactor?" I asked her.

"Oh, no," she said, disappointment in her voice. "It sounds like a toilet. Oops, sorry, I'm becoming my students."

I laughed. "It's all right. I know how it sounds."

"On the other hand, maybe the kids would rather work with garbage. Can we call it a nuclear garbage pool?"

I laughed again, amazed at how quickly she could translate into the language of her students. "Good idea. Why not? It is a kind of, uh, toilet."

"Tell me more."

Music to my ears. "As the fuel in the rods gets used up—it's called *spent*—it's not useful as a source of fission. But it's still highly radioactive, so it has to be placed in an environment that will contain the radioactivity."

"And this environment is the waste pool."

"Right. I can forward some Web sites to you so you'll see what they look like. A life-size spent fuel storage pool runs about twelve by twelve and forty feet deep," I told Erin. I clicked on my calculator and keyed in the numbers. "If we use a scale of one inch to one foot, like a typical dollhouse, the thickness of the walls would have to be about five inches."

I described the picture on the screen in front of me. I'd found a good photo of a hot cell technician maneuvering fuel assemblies—long, cylindrical containers—into the pool of liquid. According to the caption, in spite of her wearing an elaborate protective suit with two sets of gloves, the woman's body was surveyed for radiation five times an hour.

"Wow. Fascinating. I think this will work."

For the first time in days, I felt relaxed. Nothing like a little science talk and arithmetic to ease stress. I sat back and pictured the classroom activity. Erin's high school students were probably too old to enjoy a purely construction project, but I didn't think they'd mind a few such tasks, such as painting Styrofoam to look like concrete with a stainless-steel lining.

I went on, telling Erin about other components we'd have to model. Although I was determined to leave enough to the students' imagination, I couldn't resist having a store of backup ideas. An old milk crate might work for the rack at the bottom of the pool, the fuel rods could be fashioned from clay. Blue food coloring in the water would simulate boron and other moderating solutions.

"Some of my advanced students will want to know the physics of the waste problem," Erin said.

"Nothing would please me more. We can place signs around the pool, with supplementary information. They can do the research themselves for the text." I saw the placards already, with interesting icons and neat lines of type. THE TEMPERATURE OF THE POOL WATER IS ABOUT THIRTY-FIVE DEGREES CENTIGRADE, on one card. ONE-THIRD OF REACTOR FUEL IS REPLACED EACH YEAR, ADDING THAT MANY RODS TO THE WASTE POOL, on another.

"This all sounds terrific. I'm really grateful you'd give us your time. We're on for next Wednesday, right?"

"I'll be there around one."

After I hung up with Erin, I continued to search nuclear sites, coming upon an Internet article on the Yucca Mountain waste disposal project—two hundred thirty square miles in the western part of Nevada, controlled by a number of federal agencies. It had been at least ten years since the site had been proposed as a feasible repository. I thought about having Erin's students study the 1982 Nuclear Waste Policy Act, which established the procedures for comparing and selecting potential sites. Waste from seventy-two commercial reactor sites and five Department of Energy sites had been waiting for safe burial for decades—the first commercial plant went on-line in Pennsylvania. It was certainly time to move the waste from the pools around the country to safe, underground burial.

But that was my personal political opinion, which I would try not to insert into the classroom discussion.

Before I had a chance to become overly annoyed at the illogic of government policy, my phone rang.

"Are you alone?" Elaine asked.

"Yes, unfortunately." It amazed me how quickly I'd gotten used to having someone around on a consistent basis. Over the course of a year—not very fast by the standards of Generation X, but supersonic speed for most of my peer group—Matt and I had gone from weekend-only dating, to once-in-the-middle-of-the-week, to almost every evening.

Elaine laughed. "That's how I feel. I'm between men again. But at least that means we can talk. Spill it, Gloria."

I let out a long, noisy breath. "I don't know what to think."

"Try focusing on feeling, not thinking." Heresy, for a scientist. "Now, tell me everything. The exact words." I could hear a sipping noise and pictured Elaine reclining on her floral chintz sofa, with a delicate china cup of peppermint tea. Under the spell of that image, I carried the phone to my espresso maker and switched it on.

"He gave me a pin," I said.

"A pin?"

My new boron pin was on the counter, still in its ring box. I picked up the velvet case and snapped it open. "The pin is a little square. You know, the way the elements are displayed on a periodic table chart. And it has a gold B for boron in the middle. And..."

It was Elaine's turn to sigh loudly. "Terrific, Gloria, more science jewelry. Just what you need. I think that means you're engaged."

I laughed, and gave Elaine a report on Matt's invitation, or what seemed like an invitation.

"Not an invitation, a proposal. It's called a proposal."

"I need your help, Elaine. What's wrong with me?" I poured a cup of espresso, preparing myself for her answer.

"He said he wants you to move all your clothes and furniture to his place, and you're wondering if he's ready to commit?"

"He said 'maybe'…"

"Gloria." Her voice was firm, the voice you use when a child is being stubborn. "OK, let's review. We know you love him. You've told me, and you've told him and he's told you, right?"

"Right." I gulped. The way Elaine put it, it sounded very serious, very final.

"So let's run through the usual reasons people don't jump at the chance to take that next step. Number one, fear of commitment. That's obvious. Number two, you think you're unworthy of him or you don't deserve happiness. This could be a holdover from growing up with your mother telling you that. Number three, it might not work and one of you will get hurt."

I felt like a case study assignment for Psych 101 students. I'd thought my fears were unique, but it turned out my first three were from a textbook list.

The fourth, I knew, was more unique, and I was ready to share it with Elaine. I'd barely articulated it to myself.

"I think it might be Al," I told her, hesitation in my voice, nervousness throughout my body. I thought of my fiancé as I knew him more than thirty years ago.

The last time I'd seen Al Gravese—short and dark, with a low hairline, like a younger version of Matt Gennaro—was on a Friday before Christmas, three months before our planned wedding. He'd dropped by the flat I shared with my father after my mother died.

"I'm not going to be able to take you to the show," he'd said, in his gravelly voice, also not too different from Matt's. He was wearing a dark blue tie I'd given him for his mid-November birthday. "I got some business." In his uneducated pronunciation, it sounded like, "I gut some bidness."

I never knew the nature of Al's business, but I remembered being thrilled by his secret life, as if that gave me status I didn't otherwise have. I was so proud of the way he lavished gifts on my father and me. My mother had died by then. Al showered us with fine leather goods, silk robes, gold cuff links and earrings. "Go have a good time at the track," he'd tell my father, peeling off bills from the roll he always carried.

I shook away the memory, happy I was no longer young and foolish. At least not young.

It took Elaine less time than I expected to figure out what I meant. I assumed she'd think I was confessing to loyalty to Al's memory. But she was smarter than that. "So, if you get engaged to Matt, or whatever it is he wants to do, he might *die?*" The line between us crackled, and I wished it were a call-waiting signal for one of us. I felt Elaine had reached into my soul and pulled out something I hadn't dared look at.

"You're good," I said, when I recovered.

"You're easy, Gloria. I wish I could be this insightful with my own relationships. Now, let's work on this. Didn't you tell me you found out exactly how Al died?"

"I did."

"It was a hit, wasn't it? The car crash was set up by his enemies."

"I love your television language, but yes, it was deliberate."

"Not exactly your fault, was it?"

"No." I took a sip of my espresso and shifted on my rocker.

"It's not like he contracted some disease by having sex with you."

"Elaine!" I said.

She laughed at the mock horror in my voice. "You've got to get used to the S word, Gloria. And you've got to realize Matt is not Al and you are not the Gloria of 1963."

She had a point. Several points.

COMPARED TO MY conversation with Elaine, turning back to thoughts of murder seemed easy. I lined up everyone I'd talked to in connection with the case, placing them behind my mental two-way mirror. Which one looked like a killer? In my limited experience, there was no way to tell. They came in all sizes, ages, and genders.

One of Matt's friends, who taught in an administration of

justice program, had written a new book on murderers. "This looks like something you'd enjoy," he'd told me. About as romantic a present as my boron pin, but I loved them both.

I took it from the shelf and flipped through the pages. Are killers chillingly aberrant monsters, the author asked, or are they a part, however perverse, of something in our culture as a whole? The jacket copy was provoking. Only recently, it said, have scholars begun to focus intensely on murder as a window on society and a revealing subject for social historians. In the days of the Puritans, murderers were seen as chief sinners in a community of sinners. Their fall was a warning to everyone. In today's society, the killer is often seen as an alien monster whose crimes reflect his separation from the rest of us.

Insider or outsider? The topic was almost as interesting as the measurement problem in quantum mechanics.

The digression on the nature of killers didn't get me very far, so I turned to the victim. What did I know about her? Born in Detroit, living in Revere five years, many boyfriends, an activist, fired from the lab. My information about her outlook on life had come from John Galigani, whose behavior would seem suspicious to anyone but those who loved him.

Before I had to consider the many points against John, my phone rang again.

"Gloria, I can't believe I didn't think of this," Andrea said, her breathing labored as usual. "The lab's Open House. It's this coming weekend, and it's a perfect way for you to walk all around the site and, you know, investigate."

Indeed it was.

SEVENTEEN

I'D DREADED FAMILY DAYS, as we called them at my Berkeley lab, and not only because it meant an extra cleanup effort. We were also required to secure all levels of sensitive information, think up clever ways of explaining our programs to the families and friends of colleagues, and maintain a cheery countenance and positive attitude toward our place of employment. And this throughout two long weekend days.

Tutoring Matt and the RPD was rewarding, as was explaining scientific concepts to Peter Mastrone's captive audience of high school students, but I didn't enjoy entertaining little Josh and Stacey, or Grandpa Ned, who never stayed around long enough to learn anything. The children just wanted a balloon and a hot dog from the special vendors brought in for the event, and the grandparents looked at their watches every two minutes.

I never dreamed how much fun Open House could be from the other side—as a visitor. On Saturday morning, Matt and I were escorted by lab-employee-in-good-standing Andrea Cabrini. Her green badge sat high on her wide chest, hanging on a flat black shoelace. As I expected, she gushed over my boron pin.

"Wow. Did you have that made up special?"

I looked at Matt and smiled. "Matt found it, and he won't say where."

"Wow," Andrea said again, looking back and forth between the boron pin and Matt. I had the feeling she wanted one of each. I also felt very lucky.

We walked past the requisite souvenir booths—T-shirts, pens, water bottles, balloons, all in maroon and gold with the lab logo. The Charger Street lab was technically a division of the Massachusetts University Department of Physics, which had its main campus in Boston. But hardly anyone remembered the connection unless they read the fine print on their paychecks, a lost art in the days of electronic funds transfer.

"Where do we start?" Matt asked, looking at the program and map, specially prepared for the Open House.

In normal circumstances, I'd have been eager to visit one of the extraordinary installations I'd read about. The Charger Street lab had developed world-class precision engineering tools, for example, plus other intriguing projects—decoding the human genome, optical switching, supercomputers, biocounterterrorism, seismography.

But today the overriding circumstance for me was the Yolanda Fiore investigation and John Galigani's alleged role in her murder.

"Let's see the Reactor Safety Program is showing," I said.

ONLY TEN IN THE MORNING, and the temperature was already near ninety degrees. Relative humidity not much less, I guessed, waving my program in front of my face. The respite from the brief rainstorm two days earlier had faded from my memory, replaced by stickiness and discomfort. Rose had told me if I could survive the first summer back in Revere, I was a true native. I'd passed the test—I'd begun my second round of seasons—but the credential didn't make it any more comfortable.

We took advantage of the lab's taxi service, a regular feature of any large national laboratory I'd ever visited, and rode one of the outsized, air-conditioned, white vans to a large, old building on the north side of the facility. Since the Reactor Safety Program generated mainly reports and white papers, the staff had offices in what used to be military barracks. The "real" buildings, the ones with amenities such as foundations and indoor plumbing, were reserved for programs that used mainframe computers and other sensitive equipment.

We entered a faded green wooden structure, one sprawling story high, housing all the projects related to commercial nuclear reactors. The scientists and engineers in this building had served for many years as technical consultants to the congressional oversight committees that regulated nuclear energy.

On display in the lobby was a large model. For a minute I thought I'd landed back in the Revere Public Library, but this was a replica of a pressurized water reactor, a PWR in the trade. I was beginning to see my life as a series of miniature representations. If only I could shrink to their size, I might learn what was going on in the real world.

The PWR model dominated the lobby area, at least three times the size of dollhouses I'd seen on my rare, reluctant trips to toy stores.

More colorful than the real thing, the model reactor had a row of buttons along the front panel—push a button and a particular area lit up. The three main sections were color-coded. The auxiliary building, which housed the control room, fuel handling and storage equipment, and emergency systems, was crayon green. The rounded cement containment section was fiery red. Not a good idea, I thought, unless the designers wanted the visiting public to think *meltdown*. The last building, which housed the turbines, condensers, and the generator to produce the electricity, was California-sky-blue.

We were early enough to have beaten the rush of little Joshes, Staceys, and Grandpa Neds, so Andrea and I took turns pushing buttons. We watched the water pressurizer turn bright orange, the control rods purple, the reactor core a sunshine yellow.

"There's the steam generator," Andrea said.

"And the heat exchanger."

"And the pump."

"And the exit line to the turbine."

No lacy curtains, floral dining-room chairs, Victorian lamps, miniature pets—here was a dollhouse I would have liked as a kid.

Matt stood by, grinning, as if he were watching children in a toy store. He finally made a contribution to our animated chatter.

"Look at the little people," he said, pointing to the tiny plastic figures that represented plant workers.

"How come there aren't any women?" I asked, making a note to have equal numbers of male and female workers in my model waste pool for Erin Wong's class.

While I pictured little women in radiation suits and hard hats, Tony Taruffi's voice intruded.

"A great oversight," he said. "Maybe you could make a female inspector for us." Garth Allen was by his side, in a seersucker suit, a fashion statement I hadn't seen since I was in high school.

"I'll do that." I smiled, and introduced the men to Matt.

"The real police?" Allen's graying eyebrows went up. "Is this another official call?"

"Not at all," Matt said, with a disarming grin. "I'm here to learn about nuclear physics." With a little coaching from me, Matt had overcome the tendency of many lay people to say "noo'-*cue*-lar" instead of "noo'-*clee*-ar."

"Are you impressed by our model? There's a lot more action." Taruffi pushed a button on the side of the structure, and a puff of pretend steam came out of the bright red containment building. From inside the model, a deep, broadcast-quality male voice announced: *Millions of atoms of uranium 235 hit each other and break apart in a chain reaction. The process, called fission, creates heat, which turns the water to steam.* The cloud of lavender vapor traveled from the heat exchanger down an elaborate system of pipes until it reached the turbine shaft. *The steam drives the turbines and electricity is generated.*

Not bad, though I would have added a mention of the neutrons released, which are the actual bombarding particles that sustain the chain reaction.

"So fission is just an elaborate way to boil water," Matt said. My best pupil, I thought, as the rest of us nodded.

"Right," Andrea said. "In other plants you're burning coal, oil, or natural gas to make the steam, and the rest of the process is the same." She waved her chubby arms. "More or less."

My mind was as busy as the intricate layers of pipes, valves, wires, and pumps in the PWR model. How was I going to segue from nuclear reactor mechanisms to Yolanda Fiore? I needed to know if she and Taruffi had had an affair, for one thing, and if our waste pools ever suffered from insufficient boron, for another. Matt's presence made the task even more daunting. I found it difficult to be fraudulent or overbearing in his presence, one of the few inconveniences our relationship posed.

A plan took shape in my head, but I'd need Andrea's co-operation, on the level of extrasensory perception. I looked at her and rolled my eyes toward Matt. He'd become engaged in a conversation with Taruffi and Allen about the lab director whose daughter was on the police force. After several blinks, winks, and facial contortions on my part, Andrea picked up my message.

"Excuse me," she said to the group of three men. "Matt, I'd like to show you where I spend a lot of my time, out in the machine shop."

"If you don't mind, I'll stay here," I said. "I'm doing a project with the high school science club, and I'd like to discuss it with Tony and Garth."

Matt looked at me, screwed up his mouth to his most crooked grin, and shook his head slightly. It wasn't a "don't do it" message, I told myself, just an "I know what you're doing" one.

"I'm constructing a model waste pool," I told Tony and Garth when Andrea and Matt left the lobby.

"Interesting," they said, one after the other.

I explained my connection to Erin Wong at Revere High. "I want to lead the students through a project with more than just technical ramifications. And nuclear power has many issue surrounding it—social, economic, environmental, *safety*.''

''Of course, there's where we're number one,'' Garth said.

Taruffi looked like he'd rather be grilled by the real police who'd left the area.

''I remember your description,'' I said, not wanting a repea of Garth's speech on the many redundant systems used fo spent fuel safety at U.S. reactor sites. I scratched my head jus beyond my eyebrows. ''Did we discuss Yolanda's concern about the amount of boron in the pool?''

''We did.'' He raised his index finger, pointed it at me ''And I have some additional information. Put it together fo you after our last discussion. If you're going to be here anothe five minutes, I'll run back to my office and get it.''

''I'll be here. I have some things I need to talk to Tony about, anyway.''

Tony rolled his eyes, only slightly, but enough to convey hi annoyance to all of us just before Garth left.

I started off with a request I knew Tony would be happy to honor. I opened my arms to encompass the model PWR. ''I'd love to borrow this for my class.''

Tony's face brightened, his posture relaxed. This was hi forte—spreading goodwill to the community. Even better, the community schools. ''By all means. We have a little-known lending program that I wish more teachers would take advan tage of.'' So you can keep the funds coming for outreach ac tivities, and keep your job, I thought, ungenerously. ''We'l send it to the school, and even set it all up for you. All you have to do is pay for return shipping.''

''Perfect.'' I guessed my own budget could handle the charges if the science budget at Revere High could not.

''We also offer a scientist or engineer for an hour or two to explain the physics, but I guess you'd be doing that yoursel in this case.''

I nodded. We chatted about the importance of science edu cation, how more technical staff should volunteer for such pro grams, and the wonderful teacher workshops sponsored by the

American Nuclear Society. Tony and I were on such good terms at that moment—he must have thought the only "things" I wanted to discuss had to do with borrowing his little reactor— I almost hated to disrupt the atmosphere.

Almost.

"By the way, was I the last person to hear about your close relationship to Yolanda Fiore?" I asked him. I did my best to make *close relationship* sound like *affair*, at the same time attempting a coy smile. Not my best talent.

Tony's expression turned sour. He clenched his fists, which he then immediately stuffed into the pockets of his pale blue summer jacket. I imagined he'd learned that control device in a class with a title like "How to Deal with Difficult People." His bushy eyebrows seemed closer together than ever.

"I assume you don't expect an answer to that question?"

"Too much to hope for?"

A heavy sigh, through gritted teeth. "I don't appreciate where you're headed with this."

I didn't hear a *no*. I ran through the responses I'd expect if my suggestion had been way off—a laugh, a quizzical look, an unequivocal denial. Gloria, the relationship expert, became convinced on the spot that Tony and Yolanda had indeed had an affair, in spite of John Galigani's inability to believe it.

"And where is it you think I'm headed?" I asked.

Tony glared at me. "Get another hobby," he said. In the next second, Garth Allen rejoined us, and I was spared more venom from Tony, except for one parting shot. He picked up a diminutive hard-hatted figure holding a miniature clipboard. Taruffi's eyes had narrowed, and were trained on me. "Do you want to borrow a little plastic inspector also?" he asked.

I was surprised he hadn't aimed the tiny yellow bulldozer at me. It was hard not to turn away, but I kept my gaze and my voice steady. "No, I'll take care of that myself."

EIGHTEEN

IF ONLY THE Revere Public Library would have an Open House, I thought. Or if only I'd paid more attention to the people Rose introduced me to at the holiday fund-raiser.

On Monday morning I climbed the library steps, black leather briefcase at my side, ready to spend the whole morning if that's what it took to meet the suspects on my list. I couldn't imagine what the library had to do with Yolanda's murder, but it was the crime scene, its assistant director was the victim's boyfriend, and there was a controversy over its next incarnation. Not to mention a similar death in the same spot ten years earlier. Four strikes. Worth looking into.

I'd taken my own reading material—my boron notes and the articles Garth Allen had given me. I expected the RPL's nuclear physics holdings to be slim, and wondered if I could use that as an excuse to talk to the director or her assistant. I imagined myself whining about the city library's not owning enough nuclear reactor material, when a mile or so away the Charger Street lab held a premier collection.

Whenever I thought of my discourse with Tony Taruffi, his parting phrase, "get another hobby," rang in my ears. Very close to "take up sewing," which the threatening note to me had advised. Not the exact words, but the same idea. The same author?

I remembered how certain John had been that Yolanda would not have had an affair with her boss. Now I had to ponder whether he'd known all along, and lied to me. And what if the Yolanda-Tony affair had occurred while she was with John? In spite of his brother Robert's remark—that "everyone and John used to date"—John was a one-woman-at-a-time guy, bound to be unhappy if his partner was unfaithful. I felt reasonably certain of this, because John had written to me frequently, more than either Mary Catherine or Robert. Maybe because writers in general write more letters, too.

I shook away the thought that John denied knowing about the affair to cover up his motive to kill her. The only other explanation was that he didn't know Yolanda very well. For now, I'd go with that.

I'd hoped to bump into Dorothy Leonard at the library, but instead I ran into the Catholic Church. This time their attorney, Frances Worthen, looked anything but a lawyer. No power suit, no briefcase, just a large manila envelope in her hand. She wore a long sundress, a flowery yellow and pink design with spaghetti straps, the kind of outfit meant to be worn only by women as young, tall, and slender as she. As if she needed the extra height, her shiny brown sandals had three-inch-high square heels that reminded me of the blocks my mechanic used to hoist my Cadillac.

I wondered briefly about her nationality, a habit I seemed to have reverted to once I returned to Revere and my ethnic roots. Her name sounded WASPish, but she had long dark hair, thick and curly, and olive skin. Surely such a new-millennium-looking woman wouldn't have adopted her husband's family name?

She was on her way out of the building. As we shuffled back and forth—who should pass through the door first?—I tried an old trick.

"Ms. Worthen. How nice to see you again," I said, slipping easily into the deception. I was counting on a lawyer's likely resistance to admitting a lapse of memory. As I hoped, she pretended to remember me, probably excusing herself mentally. Easy to forget this nondescript senior citizen who covered her arms even in the New England summer weather. "Dr. Lamerino," I added, in a tone that implied she already knew that.

The title, which I seldom used professionally, often came in handy at times like this, when it was irrelevant.

Worthen shifted the envelope to her left hand and extended her right. "Yes, of course. How are you?" she asked, a broad, vacant smile taking over her thin face.

I shook her hand and rushed to capitalize on the moment. "I've been meaning to call you. Do you have time for a cup of coffee?" She looked at her watch. Bad sign. "Or maybe we could chat inside for a moment. I promise I won't take long."

Her smile was replaced by a confused look. Still, I could tell she wouldn't risk brushing me off, no matter how unimportant I might look. Who knew? I did call myself Doctor. I might be a potential client, or politically well connected, the friend of a VIP. It seemed I'd spent six years in graduate school for the privilege of misrepresenting myself.

"Sure," she said, an enormous question mark in her voice.

I led her to seats at a table near the circulation desk, in front of the science bookshelves. Not nearly a big enough collection, I noted. I'd chosen deliberately, to take advantage of a large metal fan—a temporary replacement for the failed air-conditioning system—for both its cooling and its background noise, in case something exciting and confidential came up.

Between the front door and the reading room, I'd reinvented myself and was ready with my opening. "Since I've just moved back to Revere, I'm very interested in picking up pieces of history I've missed." I pointed to the model of the library-to-be, in the center of the entryway. "For example, I'd like to know more about this expansion project."

Worthen breathed heavily, the beginning of an annoyed look crossing her fine features. Maybe I hadn't chosen wisely. Maybe I should have assumed my other disguise as a police representative.

"They have a proposed six-million-dollar budget. They've chosen the architect. It will take a year and a half to complete," she said, in a bored, singsong voice ticking off points on her fingers. "During that time the inventory would be moved to temporary quarters. Probably the old Immaculate Conception rectory. I'm sure Mrs. Leonard has some brochure you can look at.'' Worthen waved her hand, as if to dismiss the discussion as unworthy of her position in life, and stood to leave.

I couldn't let her get away. I stood up next to her. ''Why is the project controversial?''

Worthen stiffened, her rich dark hair lifting with the breeze from the fan. ''You must know I'm not at liberty to discuss an ongoing negotiation.''

''Of course, I do understand. I'm just curious. I can't imagine why the Catholic Church would spend its time and money on what seems like a spurious cause.'' I glanced at the manila folder she clasped to her breast. ''Unless there's some documentation for the alleged burial site?''

The next voice I heard came from behind us. I hadn't seen Derek Byrne descend the stairs from his office.

''As a matter of fact, that's *our* documentation, confirming there's *no* sacred ground out there.'' Derek tilted his head in the direction of the back of the building. ''These papers have just come to light, and are not even filed yet with the city. Frances is taking them away to have her own experts look at them.''

Worthen frowned. ''Why are you—''

''Every citizen has a right to know. It will eventually be public record, Fran.''

In spite of his combative words, Derek's tone was light. When he put his hand on Worthen's shoulder, I couldn't decide whether it was a flirtatious or a condescending gesture. But when his eyes met hers, I settled on flirting. Bordering on intimacy.

I wondered if there were a romantic relationship here, but realized how unqualified I was to judge. I could hardly evaluate my own love life. I remembered overhearing their argument the week before. I'd noticed no sign of affection between Derek and ''Fran'' at that time. Yolanda with her boss. Derek with the opposing attorney. Maybe the Yolanda-Derek connection was a very open relationship, a contemporary brand of commitment.

I latched on to the possibility that the two people in front of me were lovers—it gave me another motive to assign to Derek Byrne. The scenario: Derek and Frances Worthen are an item, behind Yolanda's back. Yolanda finds out and puts up a fuss, deciding goose and gander should have different standards. They argue, and Derek accidentally hits her on the head with the coat rack.

I put it aside as a last-resort fantasy.

"Dr. Lamerino is investigating Yolanda's murder," Derek told Worthen. He'd lowered his voice, but his tone was surprisingly neutral, given that he was the boyfriend of record of a recent murder victim.

Worthen looked at me with new respect. "You're with the police?"

If I had a bite-size biscotti for every time I'd been asked that question in the last year, I thought, I'd never be hungry again.

"I work with the department on science-related investigations." My standard response, and not exactly a lie, even though I didn't have a contract for this one and no science-related connection had developed.

"So they think Yolanda was killed by someone at the lab?" Worthen seemed relieved, as though she might otherwise have been a suspect. Which, in my book, she was. On the spot I created a subplot where Worthen fakes documentation of a burial site, to stop the expansion project. Yolanda finds out and... It had possibilities. I wondered how much Derek and Worthen knew about John Galigani's alleged involvement. If Dorothy Leonard knew, they must also, I guessed.

"You must know I'm not at liberty to discuss an ongoing investigation," I said, with a winklike smile at Worthen. She relaxed her shoulders, grinned, and rewarded me with a touché blush. Mission accomplished. "But I can tell you that, at the moment, no one has been ruled out." I pointed to the library expansion model. "For all we know, this could be the motive."

I had no idea what I was saying, whether I might even be committing a crime—obstructing justice, fraud, what did I know?—but it furthered my agenda, so I pushed that kind of concern to the back of my mind.

"Well, I don't see how our little business disagreement can have anything to do with a murder." Worthen seemed to be genuinely considering the possibility as she said the words. "I personally hardly knew Yolanda, and she certainly wasn't involved in our transactions."

"No, she wasn't," Derek said. "And in fact, this argument about the property goes back many years, way before Yolanda moved to Revere."

"It goes back at least to my husband," Dorothy Leonard said, walking down the stairs from the mezzanine. Just what I wanted. A full house of library suspects. "Councilman Byrne successfully stonewalled the project ten years ago. My husband almost got it through. If he hadn't died…well." She threw up her hands in a resigned gesture, then turned to me. "We seem to be seeing a lot of each other, Dr. Lamerino." I heard no pleasure in the tone.

"I came for a library card."

That drew a laugh all around, and I hoped it wasn't because my illiteracy was legendary.

"You seem determined to become involved in our negotiation." It was impossible to tell Leonard's true feelings about this as she addressed me. Annoyance? Resignation? Delight, as with a precocious child?

"This time my father's bringing out the big guns," Derek said. Another friendly smile at Worthen.

"And this time we have documentation," Leonard said. Shoulders back, at full height, she was as tall as Derek.

Worthen shrugged. "It's the councilman who's driving this again," she said. "We—the Church—weren't that serious until he took up our cause and demanded we follow through. And he's a big donor."

Worthen looked at me and put her hand to her mouth, wishing, I was sure, that she hadn't forgotten I was there. For me, I wished I could be present when the Holy Father became aware of a young female attorney who glibly used the papal

We, including herself in a reference to the Archdiocese of Boston.

A few minutes later, Derek and I were alone, the two women having proceeded separately to whatever their destinations had been before I interrupted them.

"I see the lions are gone," I said, noticing the clear area against the side wall.

Derek smiled and gestured toward the loft, the mezzanine opposite the one that housed the administrative offices. "They finally made it up where they belong—with the other material we're keeping for the Historical Society. Can you believe delivery people these days? They pull up here, ten o'clock at night, and say that's it. Their shift is over. No way are they going to carry the lions up one more flight of stairs."

"They look pretty heavy."

"Cast bronze, from Thailand. They weigh about three hundred pounds each, and I'm supposed to take care of them myself?" Derek looked as though he were reliving his annoying experience. "I finally got them to come back this morning, before we opened."

"So the delivery people left the lions in the middle of the lobby at ten o'clock?" I was sure Derek wondered why I wanted these details, but I had John on my mind...John and his alleged timeline.

Derek nodded. "Yolanda was here when they arrived. She heard the truck pull up and called me on the interoffice phone."

"And this was on the night she was...?"

Another nod. "I was working upstairs while Yolanda was in the basement using the computer. After the delivery guys drove off, I hung around awhile longer, and left myself about eleven."

"Did anyone else come, in between the delivery of the lions and the time you left the building?"

"No. We were closed of course. Why all this interest in the lions? Do they have something to do with Yolanda's murder?"

"No, no. Just curious. It has nothing to do with the case."

I hoped I was right.

How could John have seen lions that were delivered after he says he left the scene? The timeline ran through my mind as I walked to my car. I saw it as clearly as if it were written on the fluffy white clouds that hung over Beach Street.

8:30 p.m.
John drops Yolanda off at the library, Derek lets her in.

10 p.m.
Patience and Fortitude are delivered, left in the lobby. (Delivered by whom? Should I check out the delivery service for a possible suspect?)

11 p.m.
Derek leaves the library. Yolanda is alive, according to him.

?
John, back in the library with Yolanda, sees Patience and Fortitude in the lobby.

For my own sanity, I had to add two other lines.

?
John leaves the library, Yolanda is still alive.

?
Killer arrives.

I looked to the left, in the general direction of the police station, wondering where Matt was. I hadn't seen him since the Open House at the lab on Saturday. There had been a murder/suicide at the edge of town, near the Lynn border, and he was busy, I reminded myself. "No science in this one," he'd said. I hoped that was the only reason he hadn't called.

I'd parked around the corner on Sewall Street. The first thing I noticed was how my Cadillac was listing to the right, toward the curb, as if a tire was flat.

But I was wrong.

Two tires were flat.

Bad luck, I thought. Until I looked closely. I saw the angry slash marks, the rubber pulling away from the rims, the exposed inner linings. Someone had taken a knife to my tires, on this lovely tree-lined street. A teenager? There was no longer a high school nearby, no easy targets of blame.

I walked quickly toward the busier Beach Street, taking my cell phone from my purse at the same time. I realized I was alone, the only pedestrian on the street, the few parked cars empty.

Or at least, I hoped they were empty.

NINETEEN

I SAT IN MY LIVING ROOM, carless until Ching-Liang at Florello's garage finished outfitting my Cadillac with two new tires. Unless I wanted to borrow one of the shiny black hearses in the Galigani Mortuary garage, which I didn't.

I tried to process the recent attacks on me and my property, more like pranks, as if some thirteen-year-old were after me. A nasty note, like one that might be passed in homeroom. An alarm set off, but no entry. And now slashed tires. Or was this just a string of bad luck, a coincidence of minor misfortunes? I didn't really think so.

The realization that I might be the target of a murderer dawned on me as I paced my small living room, hugging my arms, trying to concentrate. In an odd twist of memory, I recalled the stain on Councilman Byrne's jacket at the luncheon. A spot of car grease? I shivered. Was I in a time warp?—Byrne gets a smudge on clothing first, before he slashes my tires? And the note—that had also seemed backward, a warning possibly written before Yolanda was murdered.

Strange things happened in the world of quantum theory, the realm of leptons and quarks and ten-dimensional string theory, but not in the real world of Cadillacs and cappuccinos. Tunneling through energy barriers and even time reversal were allowed if they occurred in the very, very small timescale of quantum physics—but the Yolanda Fiore murder case was as big as everyday life in Revere, Massachusetts.

Still, I wished I could get a look at the councilman's stationery.

Stuck at home until a call came from the auto shop, I retreated to my boron reading, a good distraction. No great insights, except I was able to convince myself that although Yolanda had investigated waste-handling practices, she hadn't been able to come up with a plausible transgression. That made Yolanda annoying, but not threatening, to the likes of Garth Allen, and it eliminated all but a personal motive for her boss, Tony Taruffi, to kill her.

It was time to reinterview John Galigani. I had to determine how much he knew about the research project that sent Yolanda to the old *Journal* files.

And there was the matter of the inconsistent timeline for John, Patience, and Fortitude.

"YES, I DID GO BACK," John whispered into the phone. It had taken three tries to get through busy signals at the Galiganis', and five minutes of conversation for John to come up with the truth.

"John." It came out two syllables. I hadn't planned the carping tone, but I was piqued that he'd lied to me.

"I'm sorry, Gloria. But I knew it would sound fishy." *It's* lying *that's fishy,* I wanted to tell him. I heard his heavy sigh, then his weak voice. "I finished up my article at home, E-mailed it off to Arnie at the office, then drove back to the library."

"Because…?"

"I wanted to end on a conciliatory note. When I got there, I didn't see Derek's Jag. He has this black '89 XJ6 that you'd know anywhere. It's very cool, even though he says it has bad brakes and you need two hands and a knee to open the door."

"You sound fond of Derek, or at least his car."

"I like him. It wasn't his fault Yolanda dumped me for him." I wished the police could hear this John Galigani, so mild-mannered, not even holding a grudge against his competition. "So, I called Yolanda on her cell phone that night. She let me in—it was about eleven-twenty, eleven-thirty. That's when we had the Patience and Fortitude conversation.

That story about the lions was true, it's just that it happened later than I told you. I figured no one would believe me. She was alive when I left her, Gloria."

John's voice was strained. I pictured him chewing his lower lip the way his mother did when she was upset. His reasoning was understandable in my mind, although he'd obstructed justice, withheld information that would help narrow down the time of Yolanda's death, and lied to all of us. I feared my empathy was coming from our close friendship, rather than from a reasoned assessment of his behavior.

I had one other question before I'd give him a "you have to tell the police" speech.

"What was she working on, John? I have a feeling you know what Yolanda was researching in those old *Journal* files."

Silence on the other end. "John—"

"OK, OK." I could hear a long sigh of resignation. "It was about her grandfather. I guess he'd been in jail, here in Revere, years ago, and she wanted to look into it. Evidently he skipped bail or something and went back to Italy. The story was, he stole his wife's jewelry and sold it to finance the trip out of the country. Yolanda had this idea that he wouldn't have done that, so she thought she'd try to clear his name."

"Why was he in jail in the first place? And what made her think he wouldn't have jumped bail? Did he—"

"I don't know. Really, this time I don't know. But I have the feeling that's why she left Detroit and came back to Revere in the first place. Why it took her so long to work on the project seriously, I don't know. And I don't know if she had any evidence. It might have been just a reporter-thing."

"A reporter-thing?"

"Yeah, reporters always want to investigate. We're looking for that big story, the one that will win the Pulitzer. You know, all the president's men, etc. And if you think there's something worth exploring in your own family, you're going to want to pursue it all the more, whether you have evidence or not."

My mind raced, making connections, adjusting to the new information. "Why didn't you tell me before?" Carping again.

"This could be very important, John. What if her grandfather was mixed up with something, some criminal behavior that's still going on in Revere. Maybe Yolanda found out and that's why she was murdered."

I'm not a good phone person. I need to see people to have a meaningful conversation of any length. Either that, or I require immediate advances in video-phone technology. I wanted to read John's face, the set of his chin. Instead, the only expression I could see was my own, a frustrated countenance reflected in the glass frame of the San Francisco poster in my living room. I carried the phone to the window and gazed at the empty space where I usually parked my Cadillac during the day. I wished for its miraculous reappearance so I could drive to the Galiganis' and look John in the eye.

"I doubt her grandfather's problems had anything to do with Yolanda's life today," John said. "It was a long, long time ago."

"How long?"

"Well, probably in the 1940s since those were the years she wanted files for."

I did the math—1995 minus 1940. More than half a century ago. Still...

"Did you give her the old files?"

"No, I hadn't gotten around to it. I guess I was stalling, trying to bribe her. You know, use the files to get back together. That's another thing we argued over the night she..."

This part I didn't want to hear. What about Carolyn Verrico, who was expecting to go to Bermuda with him? I hated the idea that John was courting one woman while trying to rekindle a relationship with another. I thought I knew him, but realized it was foolish to expect a young man to share his sexual philosophy with his parents' best friend, no matter how often they corresponded. Better not to pursue that line, but I still wasn't through.

"I'm not sure I understand why you wouldn't at least have told the police about the research, John."

"I didn't see any point in bringing it up. Why should I

tarnish her memory, her family's memory, by dredging that up? The family obviously moved to Detroit to get away from whatever it was, why would I force whoever's left to revisit it? Her grandmother is in her nineties.''

I shook my head at him, though he couldn't see me.

"And you really don't know why her grandfather was in jail?"

"No, honest." His voice had the ring of a Boy Scout, and I saw John's right hand raised, the way it was in a photo of him, in his little green uniform, on my bookshelf.

This time I believed him.

I NEEDED TO KNOW what happened in the 1940s. I knew about Pearl Harbor, World War II, and the first sustained nuclear chain reaction, but what happened in Revere? Since John no longer had access to *Journal* files, and I didn't have any other contacts there, I went on-line to my favorite search engines.

I'd been browsing only a short time when my doorbell rang, and a better resource arrived at my door.

"I know you don't have a car," Rose said, "so I brought some goodies."

God forbid I should be without goodies for half a day. I relieved Rose of half her burden, which consisted of two pink bakery boxes and two plastic bags filled with fruit, crackers, cheese, sparkling cider for me, wine for her.

"This is wonderful," I said. "Thank you. It's good to see you out and about."

Rose wore a matching pale green skirt and sleeveless blouse, and beige sandals with the stylish square heels I'd seen on the young attorney, Frances Worthen.

"Well, it's about time I did some work down there." She pointed in the direction of her office, one floor below my apartment. "Martha has been very good, working overtime through all this, but I have to take care of some things."

"Lucky me," I said, opening the pink boxes, sending sweet smells through the kitchen. Almond. Candied fruit. Mascarpone.

Rose smiled. "Not only that, John won't eat, although he's looking better this last hour, since he talked to you on the phone." *That's a surprise.* "And Frank's in class. I need someone to feed."

"Frank's taking a class? After all these years in the business?"

She nodded. "He needs to, to keep up his license. Five credits every year. So he works the sessions in during the summer when business is slow."

As long as I'd known the Galiganis, the funeral business still held mysteries for me. How can there be seasons for dying? "Does that mean people die in cold weather more than hot?" I asked Rose.

She shrugged. "It seems so. We average about thirty-five cases a month in winter, twenty-five in summer. Of course, there's the holiday season that accounts for some increase, when there are more suicides. I remember one Christmas Day when Frank had eight clients." She shook her head, and I knew she was saying quick prayers for all of them. "Anyway, lately he's had classes in pathogens—blood borne, airborne, whatever. Today he's in a disease class, and—are you OK with this, Gloria?"

Did I want to know more? I nodded, wanting to give my friend wide latitude in her good mood. "What about the disease class?"

"Well, Frank explained it to me. Suppose you lift a sheet off a corpse that had a disease? You have to know what you're dealing with and take the proper precautions."

"Thanks for the explanation." That wasn't so bad.

We sorted out the food and drink, and within a few minutes a late but delicious lunch was spread out on my coffee table. "I need your help," I told her, once my mouth recovered from a large chunk of pepper jack cheese. "I need some information about Revere in the 1940s."

Rose, who never filled her mouth with large chunks, but always nibbled instead, sat up straighter on the rocker. "Is this about John? I overheard a little of your conversation, something about Yolanda's grandfather, but I didn't want to pry."

I raised my eyebrows.

Rose gave me a charming smile. "I know, that's hard to believe, but I'm trying very hard to be patient and wait until I'm called on, if you know what I mean."

"I really appreciate that, Rose. And now we need your help, your vast store of Revere lore, your—"

She waved her hands in front of her, waist high. "I'm on it. What do you need to know?"

"Whatever you can dig up about that period. Crimes, especially. Who was in jail, scandals in the city, that kind of thing."

Rose put her plate down. I wished I could lose interest in food so quickly. She screwed up her nose, squinted her eyes in concentration. "The 1940s. That would be about the time of that moonshine liquor tragedy I told you about. The one where Councilman Byrne's family was wiped out, in a manner of speaking."

Now we were getting somewhere. "Do you remember the names of people who were arrested?" I was hoping for a Fiore among them.

Rose squeezed her eyes shut again, as if she were trying to read small print from a computer monitor in front of her face. Her active, well-organized memory bank. "Well, there were a lot of stills in those days. Especially around the Malden Street area, and farther back on Washington Street. Some individuals, and some families, in business together. Let's see, the Della Rosas, the Vecchis, the Radocchias, the Petrinis…"

"Rose, you were only a little girl at the time, just like me. How do you know this stuff?"

She raised her perfectly plucked eyebrows. "I've lived here all my life, Gloria."

The things you miss when you leave home. "Anyone else?"

"And, of course, there were the Scottos, the ones involved in the Byrne calamity. I told you about him. Sabatino, I think his first name was. Yes, Sabatino Scotto. He escaped to Italy while he was out on bail."

Escaped to Italy. Yolanda Fiore's grandfather escaped to Italy. If I'd been paying attention, I would have put it all together. I slapped my forehead. "Why don't I listen to you, Rose?"

She smiled and rocked way back on the glider. "I'll never know."

I buckled down, sorting through the pieces. "Did you tell me the Scotto family moved to Chicago after Sabatino fled to Italy?"

Rose nodded vigorously. "Chicago. Or somewhere out west."

"Could it have been Detroit?"

She stood up. "I see where you're going with this, Gloria. Yes, it definitely could have been Detroit. And some Scotto or other could have married a Fiore."

We looked at each other, our faces happier than they'd been in a long time.

It felt very good to have a hug from my best friend.

TWENTY

IT HAD BEEN a long time since I'd needed an excuse to call Matt, but at the moment I was happy to have one. I phoned him immediately after Rose left to pursue her genealogy research, but I didn't reach him until nearly seven o'clock that evening.

"We might have a lead," I told him when he finally answered the page.

"We...?"

I explained the workings of Rose's mind and how we'd come up with a possible Scotto-Fiore-Byrne connection. "So either man had a strong motive to kill Yolanda," I said, wrapping things up neatly. "The father or the son—Councilman Byrne or Derek Byrne."

"Or both, I assume, using your logic."

I didn't like the way he said *logic,* as if there weren't any to my argument. "Or both," I said, holding my ground.

"Just so I'm clear, even if it *was* her grandfather who wreaked havoc on the Byrne family, why would they take it out on Yolanda?"

I hadn't thought that far ahead, but *revenge* wasn't unheard of in family lore. I said as much, citing as many movies as I could think of in the godfather genre.

"I don't mean to be hard on you and Rose, but that's flimsy." Hearing no comment on my part, Matt continued. "Or maybe we should discuss this further, in person."

I hadn't told Matt about the tire incident, and didn't relish the thought of exposing my vulnerability. I kept it simple. "My car is in the shop."

"I know. Michelle Chan saw it in Florello's lot. Anything you want to tell me about that?"

The city of Revere seemed to have shrunk since my school days, its multicultural network in high gear. "I assume Michelle or Ching-Liang filled you in."

"Two slashed tires. Should I be worried?"

"It was just a prank." I hoped my voice stayed at a normal pitch.

"Glad to hear it."

"So, are you coming over?" I asked, part flirting, part challenging.

"I'm already over."

For a moment, I was confused. Then I heard the blare of a car horn. I went to the window. Matt was leaning against his car, across Tuttle Street. It was still light enough for me to make out his crooked grin.

"HERE'S ANOTHER ANGLE," I said when Matt refused to get enthused about Yolanda's possibly being a Scotto on her mother's side. Happily, he *had* been enthusiastic about seeing me, delaying our work session for more than an hour. "Dorothy Leonard claims to have documentation that the property behind the library is not consecrated ground, that it has always been city land, and never a cemetery."

"And?"

I sighed. "You're making me do all the work. What if that's what Yolanda was researching, not her family history? And what if she found out something that favored one side or the other in the controversy over the expansion? Leonard seems determined to get this project under way, probably in part because it was her late husband's dream. Suppose Leonard forged the documents and Yolanda found out about it. That would give Leonard a motive to kill her. And Councilman Byrne is equally determined to stop the plan, so if Yolanda found the documents were not forged…never mind, that doesn't work as well.''

''And why would Yolanda be interested in this?''

''It's a reporter-thing.''

My phone rang, letting me off the hook before I had to justify John Galigani's phrase.

''Is it too late?'' Rose asked, sounding wide awake.

''Not at all. It's not even nine o'clock.'' And even if it were midnight, I wouldn't have been able to curb Rose's excitement. ''And Matt's here.''

''Oh. Then should I wait till tomorrow? I have this chart to show you. The family trees.''

''Already? Bring it over, by all means.'' I assumed she wasn't calling from below my window.

''They're connected, Gloria. Yolanda was a Scotto. I'll be right over. For once I'm glad I'm not interrupting anything.''

IT HADN'T TAKEN LONG for Rose to reconstruct the genealogy of the Fiore and Scotto families, as far back as we needed them. She arrived at my apartment, chart in hand.

''How did you do this so quickly?'' Matt asked her.

''As I always tell Gloria—''

''I know, you've lived here all your life,'' I said. ''You know everyone. And everyone's grandfather. What a memory.''

She shrugged. ''A good enough memory. Plus, Frank helped. Plus, plus, I made a few calls.''

Though it weighed on my mind, I didn't ask why John still hadn't participated. Evidently he'd suspended his reporter-thing persona, not applying it on his own behalf. No one else brought it up either.

The three of us bent over Rose's trees. She'd used paper from a newsprint pad and thick markers to generate the histories of two families.

The couple at the top left were Sabatino Scotto and Celia Pallavo, both born in Italy, and married there in the late 1920s. The couple then came to the United States, traveling directly from Ellis Island to Revere, under the sponsorship of relatives who had preceded them. They had four children: Vincent, Michael, Mary, and Clara. Rose had followed the convention of genealogy charts to put rectangles around males, and ellipses around females.

At the top right, a new tree started with Corrado Fiore and ? Miliotti—Rose apologized for not being able to determine Signorina Miliotti's first name—born in Italy, married in Detroit, Michigan, around 1930. This couple had three or four children, one of them named Luigi. Rose explained that she didn't have as many sources for the Detroit family.

After Sabatino Scotto escaped to Italy, the remaining Scottos moved away from Revere, to Detroit, where their youngest daughter, Clara, met and married Luigi Fiore.

Rose had drawn a red line connecting Clara Scotto and Luigi Fiore. Under them were two large ellipses: Yolanda Fiore, and her sister Gabriella.

"This is nice work, Rose," Matt said. "I'm going to have to get you a police consultant contract."

She laughed. "For genealogy-related cases?"

I shook my head. "And all this without the benefit of the Internet," I said.

I heard a *humph* from both Matt and Rose.

We took off from the chart. Sabatino Scotto, his family settled in Revere, goes into the moonshine business. Like many, he continues the operation long after the end of Prohibition. The councilman's parents, who are among his customers, drink from a bad batch. One is blinded, the other dies.

Sabatino would have been a man in his thirties at the time of his trial, Councilman Byrne a teenager. Old enough to want to do something to avenge his family.

"And then, all these years later, he gets his chance. The granddaughter of the man he'd always wanted to kill comes into town." Rose was into this saga.

"Very Italian," Matt said.

Rose and I growled, and gave him looks that told him it was a good thing he was Italian himself.

"We could have figured this out a long time ago, if only I'd been more careful about which city the Scottos had moved to," Rose said.

"Don't blame yourself. All the cities out west look alike," I said. "Chicago, Detroit, Des Moines, San Francisco—"

Rose nodded, oblivious to my attempted joke. "So, what's next? I'm starting to see why Gloria likes police work." She looked at Matt. "Besides you, of course."

Blushes all around.

"All I can do is give this to Parker and Berger," Matt said, picking up the newsprint. "See if they want to requestion Derek Byrne, find out if he knew Yolanda was a Scotto, or if he even knew what the Scottos did to his family fifty years ago. As for the councilman—" Matt shook his head. "It'll be up to the department whether to talk to him, too."

"You mean he might be exempt, just because he's a city official?" I asked.

Rose sat back, appearing to know the answer.

Matt shook his head, but only slightly. "I'm not saying that, exactly. Just that it takes more than this to question someone like that, officially."

I had "unofficially" in mind, as soon as I had my car back.

BEFORE ROSE LEFT, Matt volunteered to dig into the old police files on the Scotto case. This cheered her up a bit, but she left considerably less thrilled than when she arrived. Still, it was clear that Rose was happy to be part of the investigation— much more appropriate to her personality than sitting around waiting for others to clear her son's name. And if any case was especially suited to her skills and experience, it was one involving the history of Revere.

"I THINK IT'S TIME," Matt said when we were alone again.

A nervous wave went through my body, so strong that I was amazed I stayed firmly seated.

"You're right," I said in a weak voice, resigned to a conversation about our future living arrangements. Matt stood, and I expected him to join me on the couch. Instead, he walked past me, to my computer.

"It's about time I learned how to use this thing. Let's see if the Internet is all it's cracked up to be. Shall we start with Prohibition?"

"The Internet! You want to learn the Internet." I hoped my exuberance didn't give me away. No confrontation about our relationship. No ultimatums. Just an Internet lesson. I let out a deep breath and smiled.

"What did you think I meant?"

"Let's go on-line," I said.

I pulled up a second chair and sat to the side of the computer, placing Matt directly in front of the monitor, a new fifteen-inch flat-screen model that I'd bought with my last check from the RPD.

I led him through the steps to access a search engine, where he typed in PROHIBITION. "Whoa," he said, jerking his head back when he got more than half a million hits. "What's this? The prohibition of chemical weapons, homosexuality, and marijuana, and the home page of the National Prohibition Party." Matt's first lesson in narrowing a search.

EIGHTEENTH AMENDMENT got better results. Ratified on January 16, 1919, effective one year later, and the law for thirteen years. Matt read from the screen. "The National Prohibition Act covered alcohol, brandy, whiskey, rum, gin, beer, ale, porter, and wine, plus spirituous, vinous, malt or fermented liquor, liquids and compounds, whether medicated, proprietary, patented or not, containing one-half of one percent or more of alcohol."

"Thorough, if unenforceable."

We scanned through a mountain of interesting information, Matt's right hand gaining agility with every click and move across the mouse pad. We looked at lists of biographies—of rumrunner Bill "The Real" McCoy, Al Capone, Eliot Ness, Bugsy Moran, Carrie Nation, and "Machine Gun" Jack

McGurn. Matt paused over the details of the 1929 St. Valentine's Day Massacre.

"This is great stuff," he said, still adjusting his head to find the best focal distance. "High drama."

I was thrilled that he'd taken to one of my own interests. For me, the Internet provided fascinating reading, far beyond the attractions of the fiction section of a library.

"Listen to this," he said, reading from a commentary by a local reporter. "'The thirteen years of the noble experiment were seen by some as our greatest attempt at being a moral nation, and others as an enormous failure that only fueled organized crime, immoral behavior, and disrespect for the law.'"

"Interesting. You see why I love to surf."

"Mmm."

Not a ringing endorsement, but I had time to work on him.

We bounced from site to site, and although I knew Internet statistics were not the most reliable, I got hooked on the numbers the sites offered. In 1929 alone, it was estimated that Americans brewed nearly 700 million gallons of beer in their homes, and between 1925 and 1929, 678 million gallons of homemade wine were drunk.

"Why would anyone take a chance like that—drinking unregulated booze?" Matt asked.

"We're not the ones to ask, I guess."

Matt and I were both teetotalers. At so many social functions, I was asked if I had religious or moral objections to the consumption of alcohol, and I guessed some people didn't believe me when I said I just didn't like it. Not the smell, not the taste, not the texture of any drink I'd tried. On a regular basis, Matt and I heard, "You don't know what you're missing. You should try a good wine."

We'd smile, and shake our heads, neither of us inclined to add another fattening, potentially unhealthy habit to our list. And even more expensive by the ounce than cappuccino.

We tried to think of an analogy to the bootleggers' business. What if cannoli were outlawed?

"Would we find ourselves sneaking around with mascarpone

not approved by the FDA, baking shells in the middle of the night?" A silly moment, wonderful to share.

A reference to San Ramon, California, a city very close to Berkeley, where I'd lived, caught my eye. Inspectors from the DA's office patrolling a canyon staged successful raids over the course of several months. They determined where the stills were by the absence of frost on barn roofs—heat generated by a gasoline-fired still would keep a roof frost-free.

I loved it when science came to the aid of law.

We learned that while speakeasies earned a lot of press, most bootleggers lived in the communities where they made and sold alcohol, so they were not thought of as criminals but as "Uncle Sal," the family friend, bringing the makings of a party. I wondered if the Byrne family of Revere had welcomed Sabatino Scotto as their deliveryman on a regular basis, like the milkman, the iceman, and the insurance man who came to collect the monthly premium.

Apparently, for people like Scotto and his customers, the convenience of backyard stills and homemade hootch was too strong to end with the Twenty-first Amendment, which repealed Prohibition in 1933. I was surprised at the many references to the *current* cases of illicit liquor production and sale.

"Look at this," Matt said. "If we want to, we can make moonshine ourselves, right from these recipes."

I nodded. "There are at least as many as I have for lasagna."

The first step in one recipe was *go to the woods and find a good place to hide your still, near a good source of water.*

Quite a hobby.

Matt stood up to stretch. "Midnight," he said, checking my clock on the living-room wall, one of the world's most accurate, receiving its signal from Fort Collins, Colorado. "This stuff can keep you up all night."

I nodded. I felt I would have made more progress if I'd done the Internet search alone, but I wouldn't have had as much fun. But how did this help with the Fiore murder case? As a way of understanding the era, and perhaps Yolanda's murderer, I decided. That is if they were related at all. Another complete circle of reasoning that got me no further in helping John Galigani.

Before he left, Matt showed me tickets for "Cooling Off," a jazz group he liked.

"Fourth of July weekend? Sounds wonderful," I said.

I hoped by then John Galigani would be a free man. Maybe when that happened, I'd feel free to concentrate on my own future. As a permanent resident of Revere. As a police consultant.

As a police wife? Maybe Tony's wife, the wedding coordinator, could help me plan the event.

I choked on a piece of almond from the biscotti Matt and I had been nibbling on.

"Are you all right?" he asked.

"I'm fine."

TWENTY-ONE

A CALL FROM ROSE GALIGANI on Tuesday morning saved me from going back to the Internet for doctoral-level research on moonshine. There wasn't too much more I could do anyway, until I saw whether Matt had uncovered any useful information from the old department files.

"This police work is all-consuming, Gloria. I have so many things I want to look up and find out and interview."

I smiled—I'd learned a long time ago to enjoy Rose's unique syntax.

"I don't know what to do next," she said. "How can you tell which clue to follow? Now I see why you get into this."

"And I'm so glad to have you as a partner," I said. Police talk among girlfriends. "Did you come up with anything else since last night?"

"Just Miliotti's first name—it's Rose, if you can believe it. But I have an idea about those papers concerning the library property. If you can get a copy of the documents, I can have them checked out."

"How?"

"I know people," she said, her voice deep and serious before it erupted in a laugh. "There's this guy in Chelsea—we use him when we have an issue about documents—death certificates, immigration papers, you'd be surprised what we have to deal with some"

"Rose, I meant *how* am I supposed to get a copy of the documents?"

"Well, I can't do everything, Gloria."

THERE WAS A POSSIBILITY that John, as a member of the press, would have easier access than I would to a copy of the ownership documents. But I remembered Derek Byrne's saying the papers were recently discovered by the Historical Society and hadn't even been filed with the city records office yet.

John was also the one who could get me into the *Journal* records on the Scotto trial, but he still hadn't offered to help. It worried me that John was being very passive about his own case. I dared not ask Rose if she'd noticed or if she knew why. I needed a little more time—or John's exoneration—before I'd feel on completely solid footing after our falling out. I made a note to ask John about it, after I figured out the right way to phrase it. I couldn't remember when I'd had such trouble communicating with the Galigani family.

As I saw it, there were two ways I might acquire a copy of the land use documents—from either the pro- or the con-expansion side. Either way, I'd have to lead the person to believe I could help, perhaps by implying I had a way to prove the papers true or false, depending on whom I approached. Would it be Derek Byrne, Dorothy Leonard, or Frances Worthen? Or maybe I'll interview the cardinal. I laughed at my own joke.

Of the three serious options, Derek seemed likely to be the most easily won over. I couldn't say why, but I considered the two women impenetrable. I was willing to absorb some of the blame for that feeling, but I suspected also that women who reached high levels of power needed to cultivate a certain mettle that ate away at their approachability, perhaps more than men did.

And if I talked to Derek again, I might find out how much he knew about his grandparents' tragedy, and about Yolanda Fiore, whose mother was née Scotto.

THE LIBRARY WAS becoming a familiar place, inside and out. This time I parked my car, with its two new tires, on a busier street, surveying the area before unbuckling my seat belt. Circling the building was an old stone wall, topped with a row of gray stones that had been ground into sharp points. I was sure they were meant to form a decorative edge, but I saw them as a row of weapons, ready to impale their next victim. Perhaps my tires. Perhaps me.

In the hot morning sun, I shivered as I looked up and down the street. Silly. It was all clear.

I SAW DEREK BYRNE immediately, at the circulation desk at the front of the main floor. His long, thin body was draped over the counter. In a light blue suit and a tie that matched the countertop, he looked cool and comfortable, at ease with his staff and surroundings. The small air-conditioning unit stuck in the window casing was working again.

Glancing around, I could see clearly that more space was needed. Bookcases were squeezed into every corner of the large, open area, some of them fine dark wood, others a lighter wood, others dull gray or bright blue metal. Rows of shelving blocked parts of the tall, narrow windows.

Derek seemed glad to see me. He pushed himself away from the counter and buttoned his jacket as he approached, as if out of respect for an older woman. I knew I'd been wise to choose him over Frances Worthen and Dorothy Leonard.

"I'm here on business. I hope you don't mind," I said after a few words of greeting. I didn't want to mislead him about the purpose of my visit. "As you can imagine, I'm still working on Yolanda Fiore's…case."

His pleasant, lightly freckled smile collapsed. "I've been over this so many times, Dr. Lamerino. I don't know what else I can tell you." He seemed genuinely sorry not to be able to offer more. I had to nudge myself into remembering the strong motive he had for murdering Yolanda. Whatever Sergeant Matt Gennaro thought, Italians didn't have the lock on revenge killing.

"You might be able to help me get to know Yolanda better. If you could just answer a few questions." He gave the slightest nod. Not a wholehearted *yes,* but not a *no* either. "How did you meet, for example?"

Derek pointed to a set of round-back chairs tucked into a light-wood circular table, and we took seats about a third of a circumference away from each other. "We met at a Chamber of Commerce dinner last year—Yolanda wasn't even supposed to be there. She was filling in for her boss, who was sick."

"Anthony Taruffi?"

He nodded. "We ended up sitting next to each other, whispered through all the speeches, and then went dancing afterward."

"And that was a year ago?"

"Yeah, about a year." Right after she left John Galigani, I figured. Unless they overlapped. "Yolanda hated that kind of function, and I kept teasing her about it. I like those events, strangely enough. You get to meet people you might be working with later."

I remembered Rose's comment about how Dorothy Leonard was promoted over Derek. "Very politically astute of you. I'm sure that makes you a good director, uh, assistant director."

Derek laughed. Even I knew immediately what a poor attempt that had been at subtlety. "And, if you'll forgive me, you're not very political, Dr. Lamerino. Yes, Dorothy was named director even though I've been here in one capacity or another for more than ten years. They pulled her from the City Council. But it's all part of the game, and she's a good manager. Dorothy's wanted this for a long time, probably since Irv died."

"Her husband."

"Right. I worked under him for a short time. Good man, too."

Back to Yolanda. I cleared my throat. "How long was it before you found out who Yolanda's grandfather was?"

Derek raised his eyebrows. The muscles around his jaw tensed. I thought I saw an internal debate about whether or not to lie. After a moment, his face relaxed and I assumed truth won out. "That wasn't common knowledge, believe it or not. But my father had her checked out. He automatically suspected everyone who moved here from anywhere in the Midwest, especially Detroit. He always claimed the Scottos would be back."

I smiled. "I guess Revere is a hard place to leave for good."

"Apparently." Derek seemed to understand the reference to my own return, and smiled back. "But Dad didn't tell anyone about Yolanda, as far as I know, and I certainly didn't."

"How about vice versa? Did Yolanda talk to him about it—maybe apologize for the family in some way?"

He shrugged his shoulders. "I'm not sure. It was always tense between them, the few times we were all together. But I figured it was just that memory, no matter how long ago, my father couldn't drop it. Yolanda and I never discussed it, except one time—when I told her my father knew who she was." Derek looked around the nearly empty reading room, as if to keep Yolanda Fiore's secret safe from the one or two older people reading newspapers in the corner. I noted that both of Yolanda's men were of one mind in their attempts to protect her family's reputation.

"He couldn't have been happy about your relationship." Here I was, going far beyond what was my business, but Derek didn't seem to mind.

"Hardly. But there wasn't anything he could do about it. However…" Derek stopped, his countenance changing. I couldn't tell if his thoughts brought him sadness, embarrassment, confusion, or a bit of all of them. "To tell you the truth, we wouldn't have lasted much longer anyway."

"You were going to break up?"

"More than likely. And it had nothing to do with my father, although I think he suspected it was coming to an end. It was just…we were two different people with different ideas about commitment."

I nodded and murmured a syllable of understanding, as if I knew exactly what he meant. Sympathetic, worldly wise Aunt Gloria. "Well, I know about her affair with her boss."

Another eyebrow-raising, correct guess. "For one," Derek said.

My turn for raised eyebrows. A new picture of Yolanda

Fiore was forming in my mind. I wondered how much Detectives Gennaro, Parker, and Berger knew about Yolanda's paramours. When a victim has had many intimate partners, that's usually the starting point for the police investigation. I made a note to review this with Matt. Not only was it more appropriate for the police to pursue this line of questioning, but I was getting distracted from my primary mission.

"Derek, I'd like to have a copy of the documents you gave Frances Worthen, showing land ownership and use."

He frowned. "I don't know…as I told you last time, Yolanda wasn't concerned about the expansion project, either way. I don't see what it could have to do with her death."

"You're probably right, but I feel compelled to follow every possible lead, until we know exactly what she was working on when she, uh, was on the Internet downstairs." I'd never had such a hard time saying the word "murder" or its derivatives. It might have been Derek's ocean-blue eyes, looking so sad and vulnerable. I reminded myself how those eyes had looked when Frances Worthen was around—"flirty and available" came to mind. I pressed my case. "And I may be able to help. I have some contacts that might bolster your cause."

So far he was not impressed, maintaining a dubious, uncooperative look. At the same moment, one of his staff—an older woman with upswept hair reminiscent of the fifties—left her spot behind the circulation desk and headed for us. I wondered if he'd planned the interruption as I did sometimes, prepping a secretary to call me out of a meeting after a certain span of time.

No time to fool around. "Derek, it's probably better for you to give me a copy of those papers than be officially required to produce them at a later time." I didn't know what I was talking about, but I must have sounded convincing, because Derek gave the fifties woman instructions, and ten minutes later I walked out the door with the documents.

As I descended the steps to the sidewalk, I looked over my shoulder for Dorothy Leonard to come and snatch my briefcase from my hand. Or for the tire slasher. Seeing neither, I allowed myself a silent whoop of victory.

TWENTY-TWO

ON THE WAY HOME, I reviewed the interview, primarily to fix it in my memory, since I hadn't taken any notes. What struck me was that Derek had so many motives, from betrayed lover to avenging grandson, with important, controversial documents in between. And Matt had admitted that Derek's alibi was no better than John Galigani's. Both men had claimed to be home alone by midnight on the night of the murder. Finally, Derek was certainly strong and tall enough to have overpowered Yolanda.

Derek Byrne—means, motives, opportunity. Almost too easy.

I turned my attention to Derek's father. Councilman Byrne's parents weren't exactly innocent victims of Sabatino Scotto. They must have known the risks. Unfortunate as it was, the Byrnes weren't the first to suffer the tragic consequences of drinking alcohol from a backyard still. I imagined, however, that these facts might not have curbed the young Brendan Byrne's deep resentment of the Scottos. And a desire to kill them? That was the question.

Derek had told me his father knew he was about to break up with Yolanda. Would that give the councilman more or less motive to kill her? Would it be easier to murder your son's ex-girlfriend than the one he's still seeing? Or, since she'd no longer be in line to give his family an heir with dreaded Scotto genes, would that ease the tension? I wished I knew the criminal mind better. Or at all.

It wasn't any easier to understand Yolanda's life. A picture emerged of her flitting from one man to another. Derek. John. Taruffi? Derek had implied there were others. I shook my head in dismay.

A glance at my briefcase, on the passenger seat like a silent, comforting friend, gave me hope. The land-use documents were tucked into a side pocket. At least I'd made some progress, and Rose would be pleased.

I CAME HOME TO a bright orange six on my answering machine, representing nearly my entire complement of friends and relatives.

Andrea called to thank me for dinner. She wanted to get together to review the outline she'd prepared for her first class with Peter Mastrone. Three months ahead of schedule, a woman after my own well-organized heart.

My Worcester cousin, Mary Ann, welcomed me back from my vacation in California. She had a way of sounding like my old-school aunts and uncles who could appear positive, then make you feel guilty a nanosecond later. "I'm sure you would have called me eventually," Mary Ann said in a sweet voice.

The call from Rose sounded like an encrypted message setting up a hit. "My man in Chelsea is ready to accept the package," she said. "Let's arrange a pickup and drop-off time."

I'd taken the legal documents from my briefcase and flipped through them while I listened to my messages. I was immediately intimidated by their official look—very wide margins, numbered lines, the seal of the City of Revere, a generous sprinkling of heretofores and henceforths, one or two Latin phrases per page, and strange alphanumeric strings, like 710CMR7.65(2)(d)(iii)(a). I flipped past the pages of text to the drawings, noting the scale on one of the close-ups—1" 3/32", it read. I never understood why engineers wouldn't adopt the metric system, but that was the least of my problems as I tried to interpret the sheaf of papers.

Three of the drawings looked like a child's rendition of the library building from different angles, with trees no better drawn than I could do. There were also aerial views of the interior and exterior, showing parking spaces for more than one hundred cars.

I was glad someone else was responsible for authenticating the papers. How would you ever know? Probably some very high technology analysis made it easier to distinguish real from fake documentation. But then I tended to attribute all progress to the advance of technical knowledge.

From Erin Wong's message I learned that Tony Taruffi was ready to deliver the model reactor to the high school. I wasn't quite prepared for the project, but I knew that another meeting with him would be to my advantage, as far as information-gathering. It gave me secret pleasure that I intimidated him. Not something I was proud of.

I made a callback list. Andrea. Mary Ann. Rose. Erin.

Elaine Cody's call was also in code. "Let me know how the project is going. Any milestones? Have you set a deadline yet?" I wondered how Matt would feel about being referred to as "a project."

Matt's call was last. Could he come by with the old police files on the Scotto trial?

"Please do," I said, returning his call first.

But Rose beat Matt to my apartment, not waiting for me to call her back.

"I can't linger," Rose said. "I have an appointment with Cappie at three. Do you have the goods?" She winked, and pulled an imaginary cloak across her face.

I handed over the papers, stuffed into a manila envelope at the last minute, at her request.

"In case they're watching," she said.

I thought her attitude was a little extreme for someone who hadn't even had her tires slashed.

AN HOUR OR SO LATER, after a suitably long greeting, I briefed Matt on my meeting with Derek. I emphasized his comments on Yolanda's active, polygamous love life.

"Parker and Berger are working that angle. Don't worry," he said.

But I did. I wanted my old life back, the one where Rose and Frank and Matt and I played canasta every week, and all the Galigani children were safe and happy and untouched by serious crime.

Matt read to me from the police file on the old Scotto case.

"Listen to what they found in Scotto's backyard, up on Malden Street. And I quote: two fifty-gallon stills in operation, condenser cisterns, coils, five-ply burners, gasoline pressure tanks, tanks full of mash, tanks full of water ready to set, and five-hundred-gallon reserve tanks above the still for pumping the mash. There were hoses, receiving kegs to catch the whiskey when it came out of the stills, filter barrels, sacks of barley, caramel coloring for the brandy, ten-pound packages of yeast, sugar. Plus hydrometers, test tubes, and a row of two-burner stoves, coal-oil lanterns—it goes on and on."

"Wouldn't it have been hard to hide all that paraphernalia?"

Matt nodded. "It makes you think the police knew all this was there, but didn't bother to do anything about it until someone died."

"I'm certainly glad that doesn't go on these days," I said.

"Right."

We smiled at our mutual, clever sarcasm.

Matt and I took turns with the arrest report, the fingerprint form, evidence inventory, and a set of articles from the *Journal*. We fell into our comfortable routine for working a case together, alternately reading to ourselves, mumbling aloud when something caught our eye, asking a question, throwing out a theory. And, of course, nibbling on Sees nuts and chews from Elaine.

"Involuntary manslaughter," I said. "Remind me what that is."

"Recklessly causing death under circumstances manifesting extreme indifference to human life."

"Not that you know it by heart."

He gave me a smile and we said together, "It's what I do."

"It's easy to see how 'recklessly' fits," I said. "These amateurs with no knowledge of chemistry put together makeshift equipment to purify poisonous, denatured, industrial grade alcohol. They use lead and zinc in the construction of the stills and storage vats. And under the conditions of extreme heat, the poisons are distilled right into the alcohol.''

"Now who sounds like a textbook?''

I shrugged. "Misuse of science, even chemistry, galls me. I just saw an op-ed piece in one of the old *Journal* clippings in this pile. They cited cases of brain damage and insanity that resulted from drinking moonshine. Byrne's mother, Grace, was blinded and his father, Brendan Sr., died, as sure as if Scotto had administered the poison directly.''

"The newspapers were pretty tough on him. At least there's that consolation.''

"True. It's a wonder he was let out on bail. Not to mention he was a perfect candidate for maximum flight risk.''

"He was a U.S. citizen, though,'' Matt reminded me. "And it depends on who was on the bench that day.''

"You mean, maybe one of his customers?''

"Exactly,'' Matt said.

"Here's a description of Scotto. Five feet one and a half inches tall, one hundred sixty-five pounds—''

"Chunky,'' Matt said, sucking in his stomach.

I nodded and tucked in my own. "Brown eyes, dark hair parted in the middle. Sounds like my Uncle Jimmy, except for the tattoo. Scotto had a bunch of grapes on his arm. I would have expected a heart or a—''

"Grapes, grapes.'' Matt's muttered interruption was accompanied by his rapid shuffling through papers scattered on my coffee table. "Where did I see something about a bunch of grapes?'' He picked up a typewritten form, so yellow and brittle with age that pieces of it fell onto his lap. "Here it is, on Mrs. Scotto's list of jewelry stolen from her bedroom vanity. One of the most expensive pieces was a pendant with sapphires and emeralds arranged like a bunch of grapes.''

"A family symbol, I guess.'' I put down my folders and leaned across to look at the photograph clipped to the report, one of a set that cataloged Celia Scotto's extensive jewelry collection. Diamond earrings, a cross set with rubies, elaborate necklaces and brooches. Nothing so frivolous as my boron pin.

"That's strange," I said. "You think she'd cover for her husband and not confirm the reports that he stole her treasures and ran. I wonder why she turned him in?"

More shuffling while Matt found the report he was looking for. "She didn't. Look at the timing on this. A week before he disappeared, while Scotto was still at home, out on bail, she reported a robbery."

"Someone else stole the jewelry?"

"Or they were setting up a cover story together."

"It seems we're learning something new every minute on this case, even though it's been closed for fifty-five years." But did any of it matter? I wondered if Matt had the same doubts about researching an interesting, but potentially useless, period in Revere's history. I didn't want to break our rhythm by asking, and we'd almost finished with the material he'd brought.

We'd gone through several day's worth of the *Revere Journal,* the *Chelsea Record,* and the *Winthrop Sun Transcript.* I didn't know there were so many separate small-town publications. We had only one more envelope to go—more articles and photographs from the *Journal* published during the days following Mr. Byrne's death and Scotto's arrest. The longest piece included a snapshot of a crowd in front of City Hall, taken before the bail hearing, protesting the potential release of Sabatino Scotto. We could make out signs that included every derogatory term we'd ever heard for Italian-Americans: PUT GINNEYS WHERE THE MOON DON'T SHINE. SPECIAL JAILS FOR WOPS. KILL DAGO MURDERERS. PUT SCOTTO'S BODY ON A BOAT TO ITALY. "Just like a reporter to focus on the most inflammatory responses," I said. Then I thought of another reporter, John Galigani, and blushed at my stereotyping.

"What have we here?" Matt asked. He pointed to a young man, isolated from the group, leaning on a lamppost on Broadway. A sullen, troubled look marked his long, narrow face. It was a close shot, and even with the grainy, old newsprint you could tell his eyes were a light, penetrating hue. The caption read, YOUNG BRENDAN BYRNE, VICTIMS' SON, RECOMMENDS NO MERCY FOR SCOTTO.

"Hmmm." The syllable came out of both our mouths, and we sat back, as if we both had enough to think about for a while.

TWENTY-THREE

ROSE RACED US UP Broadway through rush-hour traffic, under the overpass, and into Chelsea.

"Cappie's ready," she'd said, unannounced, standing on my threshold at eight o'clock on Wednesday morning.

For the second time in two days, she'd skipped the phone call that usually preceded her visits. Even if she was only one floor below my apartment in the Galigani Mortuary, Rose would use the intercom first if she felt like coming up for a coffee break.

"You never know, Gloria. You could be entertaining," she'd say with a wink that meant, *I can only hope.*

Apparently her son's predicament had caused her to change her habits. Including her driving habits, I noted with alarm, as she whipped around an enormous Stop & Shop truck.

I'd expected to find Rose's man, Cappie, between a check-cashing office and a bail bondsman, all establishments with bars on the windows and doors, so I was surprised when we pulled up to a new two-story office building with attractive landscaping. I brushed past pink roses, pansies, and orange and yellow flowers I couldn't name. Day lilies, Rose informed me. Her look said she'd expect anyone who could recite the elements in the periodic table to know the name of a simple flower.

Cappie, I learned, was short for Caporale. Christopher Caporale was an expert in a field I didn't even know was a field, authenticating documents. He had a boyish face, though I could tell from his posture and his gait that he was my age or older.

His brown eyes seemed extra wide, as if he needed all the lens aperture he could get to inspect the fine print on documents.

His office was a treat to behold—more like a lab. Cappie's table had graduated cylinders with brushes, styluses, and out-of-the-ordinary pens. Neat shelves with beakers and microscopes in all sizes, lighted magnifiers, lenses, calipers, filters, diffraction gratings, stacks of cotton swabs. A row of liquids in many hues—a viscous blue, thin reds and purples, a yellowish suspension in a gel. Something about the arrangement reminded me of Frank Galigani's embalming prep room with its jellies and creams, and wax—for filling in deep wounds, Frank had told me gratuitously.

Instead of New Age posters like the ones that papered Tony Taruffi's walls, an enormous periodic table adorned the space behind Cappie's workbench. One side of the room was dedicated to a state-of-the-art computer system with the largest scanner I'd ever seen. I felt at home.

"I'm glad to finally meet you, Dr. Lamerino," he said, drawing my attention away from the photo of a hunk of titanium that filled the 22 block of the chart.

He led us to a corner with a round table and upholstered chairs—his conference area, kept neat for visitors like Rose and me, I guessed.

I ran my eyes over a column of framed certificates, lined up vertically next to the window. Cappie was named as a member of the National Association of Document Examiners, a state-certified document examiner, an instructor to police personnel in eighteen states, a lecturer in statement analysis. And he'd done a stint with the Democratic Party, investigating voter fraud. As long as his credentials were authentic, we were in good hands.

"Did Rose ever tell you about the forgery ring she and Frank were in?" Cappie asked me, pouring coffee from a black-ringed dewar.

I looked at my friend, my eyes wide. "Forgery?" We'd taken seats around a table that was clear except for the manila envelope with the documents I'd received from Derek Byrne.

"I told you about it, Gloria," Rose said. She nudged my arm as if to jog my memory. "It was about ten years ago, maybe more. A block of five hundred blank death certificates was stolen from the old Revere General Hospital, which of course isn't there anymore."

"I got the police to work with Rose and Frank." Cappie sounded like a proud mentor. "The Galiganis pretended to want to buy some certificates, and they roped in the guys."

"We really didn't have much to do with it," Rose said. "The police just used our name and the mortuary to lure the crooks, but they wouldn't let us be in the building."

I had only a vague recollection of the police taking over the Galigani Mortuary, an incident well before the Revere Police Department and Sergeant Matt Gennaro had piqued my interest in matters of law enforcement. I found myself wishing I'd been there for the bust.

"Matt wasn't involved," Rose said, as if I'd asked. "The police put the word out through their informers, and then they were waiting in Frank's office when the guys came. They used undercover people that sort of looked like me and Frank. One of them was Rusty Nigro's daughter, if you remember her, just in case anyone had seen us. It was pretty exciting, even if we didn't get to see it go down. That's it, isn't it, Cappie? Go down?"

Cappie smiled. "You've got it, Rose."

"I can see why blank death certificates might have some value to a criminal, but why would a funeral director want to buy them?" I asked.

Cappie pushed up the sleeves of his light denim shirt, revealing smooth-skinned, nearly hairless arms. His face, too, seemed to be preadolescent, as if he hadn't needed his first shave yet.

"Remember, it's usually the undertaker who obtains the death certificate from the hospital or nursing home or whatever, and files it with the Board of Health. They can't get a burial permit until then. Also, the certificates have the official seal on them, so all someone has to do is fill in the form, and the person is dead.'' Cappie snapped his fingers, snuffing out a life. "Say, it's a criminal—he can come back as someone else.''

"You never know what's valuable,'' I said, amazed at this world I'd never lived in.

Cappie nodded. "Even with all this new Internet stuff, there's still a lot of checkpoints that require paper. There's a big market for blank birth certificates, too. And immigration forms, marriage licenses, military discharge papers—you name it.'' He ticked off the desirables on long, graceful fingers that seem out of proportion to his short, stubby body, as if they'd been specially designed for fine penmanship. "People use the blanks to steal an identity or create a new one, or—and this is big business—to claim benefits like VA and social security.''

"Imagine,'' Rose said. She shook her head in distaste at an invisible criminal seated in our midst.

"And don't think there aren't some funeral directors out there, among others, who wouldn't blink an eye at helping someone do this, if the price was right,'' Cappie added.

Rose's face took on a sad expression. The way mine did whenever I learned of a scientist who wasn't a pillar of integrity.

Cappie spread the contents of our envelope over his table. "Yep, there's still a lot of paper crime. Speaking of which…'' He tapped our documents with his index finger.

"Paper crime?'' I asked, my body responding with an excited twinge.

"I'll say. These papers have been altered, no question. Where did you say you got them?''

I explained what little Derek had told me of the papers having been found among material the library was storing for the Historical Society.

"It's no surprise that they haven't been filed. It's a pretty crude job of doctoring, I must say. Let me show you.''

Cappie smoothed out one of the folded line drawings of the land bordered on three sides by Lowe Street, Library Street, and Beach Street. On the fourth, the south side, was the new

Immaculate Conception Church, its parking lot butting up against the library lot. He'd selected the one with a simple outline of the library building, showing not much more than the shape of the building and its position on the lot.

"See this number right here. It says the existing lot is 26,572 square feet. Well, that's enough to include the proposed extension. Pretty handy, isn't it? But with my EUV machine—never mind what that is—and a few years' experience, I can show you a dotted line that's been erased."

Rose and I leaned on the table, on either side of Cappie. We both squinted, as if we could make our eyes as keen and probing as a licensed document examiner's equipment. I had to admit it was difficult to see the line under Cappie's stylus, but my eagerness to believe it was there added a dimension. I expect it was the same for Rose, and we both made appropriate *Eureka* noises.

Cappie set aside his thick lens and stylus. "I was able to determine the original numbers, at least approximately. It's my belief that the lot below the deleted line is only a little more than twenty thousand square feet, and above the line is another six thousand or so square feet."

I sat back and took a breath. "And they've made it look as though the whole lot was one piece, all of which has belonged to the library from the beginning."

Cappie nodded. "Or at least as far back as has ever been recorded. They erased the two numbers, and put in the total. I didn't even try to date the ink on the new number, because the rest is so obvious."

"What are the chances that someone would be taken in by this?" I asked.

"If you ask me, it's a piece of cake to figure this out. Ordinarily I'd have to scan in the document and use some fancy image-processing software to detect writing that might have been erased. But I didn't need anything that sophisticated for this, just that instrument in the corner." Cappie pointed to what looked like an elaborate microscope with appendages of light sources and calibrated staging areas. "It uses infrared light and filters to differentiate inks and papers and bring out hidden material. It's pretty standard equipment.''

"So the Church's experts will probably also know these documents are forged?'' Rose asked.

Cappie seemed to nod and shake his head at the same time. "I'd like you to think I'm a genius, but I can't imagine anyone but an amateur being fooled by this. It's as if they weren't really serious about it.''

"Well, we can't thank you enough, Cappie,'' Rose said. "You're the best.''

Cappie brushed away her compliment. "Nah, the right light plus a few chemicals and a touch of photographic artistry. That's all you need to do this job.''

"Right,'' Rose said, winking elaborately. She discreetly placed an envelope where the documents had been. I guessed they'd agreed ahead of time on a fee for services.

I wasn't quite finished with our expert. "If it's such an amateur job, then why do you think they bothered to do this at all?''

Cappie shrugged. "They probably hired this out, and being unacquainted with the criminal element, they got gypped,'' Cappie said.

I tried to imagine the meticulous Dorothy Leonard getting "gypped.''

Cappie continued. "Maybe it's a stall, while they get some other paperwork through. Some deadline they had to meet, and this buys them time.'' A slight grin formed on Cappie's blemish-free face. "Or maybe they're just stupid. Criminals usually are, you know. Did you hear the one about the bank robber who slipped a GIVE ME ALL YOUR MONEY note to the teller written on the back of one of his own deposit slips?''

It was an old story, but we all laughed. I remembered similar stories from Matt. But I didn't for a minute think Derek Byrne and Dorothy Leonard were stupid.

Now that we had the facts on the documents, I struggled to tie the crime to Yolanda's murder. Neither John nor Derek thought she cared at all about the expansion, but it was possibly that she discovered the fraud and decided to cash in on it. Anyone capable of dumping John Galigani could do anything, in my biased view.

Rose had begun to pace, her rhythm interrupted by obstacles common to a laboratory environment—a small centrifuge, power supplies, tanks of chemicals. I had the feeling our project was minuscule on the scale of things Cappie usually handled, and that he did it so quickly as a favor to the Galiganis.

"But assuming it was the library director and/or the assistant director—they're intelligent people," Rose said.

"Doesn't mean they don't do stupid things in a time of crisis," Cappie said.

"I hope that's it," Rose said. "Otherwise, if they weren't serious, they also wouldn't be likely to kill someone to keep from being exposed."

"Good point," I said.

And bad for John's case, I thought.

ON THE WAY TO HER CAR, Rose and I linked arms. We walked in silence, until I inadvertently shared my thoughts. "I wonder if John knows about the forged documents?" I mumbled the words to myself, then caught my breath when I realized I'd spoken aloud. "Rose, I didn't mean to imply that John…"

"Don't worry, Gloria, I'm not going to snap at you. I hope I never do that again."

My jaws relaxed. I could see the deep shades of fatigue around Rose's eyes, the untended pallor of her cheeks. "It was perfectly understandable. You're doing very well considering all that's happened."

Rose shrugged. "Not really, but thanks for saying that. And I don't know why John hasn't offered to help—like on TV when reporters or cops are accused of a crime they go out on their own investigating, and then duke it out with the real guilty one. I don't know whether to be glad or sad he's not doing that. He sits around the house playing with his laptop all day."

I nodded. "People react differently." Gloria, the insightful friend to the rescue.

"Frank is the really calm one, of course. Who knows where we'd all be if it weren't for him? You know that's one of the reasons he wanted to go into mortuary science, besides for the chemistry and, you know, biology. He knew it was partly a counseling job. He's so good at it."

I'd let her ramble on, barely listening. I was busy trying to determine if the information we'd just learned had anything to do with Yolanda's murder. I should be pleased about the result, since it seemed to narrow down the list of likely perpetrators. Why else had we chased a forgery? Just because it was there? Were we getting sidetracked?

Rather than pursue that depressing line of reasoning, I made a chart in the air over Cappie's day lilies. Until this meeting, I'd have bet on either of the Byrnes as Yolanda's killer, principally over the moonshine tragedy. I wrote *Brendan* and *Derek Byrne* on my retina. With the new information from Cappie, the top candidates were *Derek Byrne* and *Dorothy Leonard*, whose project was furthered with the fake documents. It wasn't too hard to keep track. Derek's name overlapped both lists. I wondered if real law enforcement personnel used pseudo-Venn diagrams to solve murders, and how often they worked.

Rose chattered on. I tuned in in time to hear, "…and where would we be without you, Gloria?"

I squeezed her arm and blinked back a tear, happy to have my friend back.

TWENTY-FOUR

"ANY PROGRESS?" Elaine asked. I'd rushed into my living room to take her call. Rose had dropped me off after a leisurely breakfast at our favorite bakery across from City Hall.

"We just came back from a meeting with a document specialist," I said. "Those land ownership papers I told you about were definitely doctored. So it looks like—"

"Gloria, I'm not talking about the case."

"Oh." Matt and me. Not that I'd forgotten. I was nearly ready to tell Matt my decision. I thought of the hundreds of photographic plates I'd developed in my spectroscopy research. The thin glass plates needed to soak for a critical number of minutes in the developer fluid before they'd be ready to be lifted out and dropped into the fixer solution. I saw my answer through the murky liquid, the words taking shape, becoming more clear each second. "We've all been pretty busy," I told Elaine.

A deep sigh from California. I pictured Elaine in her orange-fabric cubicle at Berkeley University Laboratory—BUL, as we fondly referred to it. She'd be sitting in front of a monitor ringed with yellow adhesive notes, dressed in a classy summer outfit while engineers and scientists came and went all around her in cutoffs and T-shirts.

"I wish I were closer."

"What would you do?" I asked her.

"Trick you two into a candlelight dinner with soft music and—"

"Neither of us likes candlelight. We can't see well in low light and, besides, candles are a fire hazard."

"OK, I give up. Tell me about the murder case."

I briefed Elaine on the newest information, even before I'd had a chance to tell Matt, I realized.

"So, your victim could have uncovered this fraud, or she could have just been there in the library and overheard something about the forgery."

"It looks that way."

"Nothing to do with all that moonshine research you've been doing?"

"I guess not."

Beep. A call-waiting signal.

"That's me," Elaine said. "I'd better get back to work. Think romance!"

I laughed and hung up. And went back to thoughts of murder.

BY NOON, I'd outlined a plan of action. Step one—talk to Matt about Cappie's analysis—was thwarted when I had to leave a message on his machine. Step two—confront Dorothy Leonard—met an impediment when my phone rang.

"Gloria!" The alarm in Rose's voice sent ripples of panic through my body. "John…" was the next word I heard clearly.

"What's happened to John?" I imagined her son in the hospital, having collapsed from tension, or in a coma after being attacked by Yolanda's killer. Or…

"He's gone."

Gone, as in abducted? I had to remind myself John was no longer a child who could be scooped up in front of the post office while his mother did an errand. Gone, as in dead? I dared not ask, let alone think it for more than a moment.

To my relief, Frank's slightly calmer voice came over the line. "John left the house, and probably the city, since his overnight bag is gone. There's a note. I'll read it to you. 'Away for a while. Don't worry. I have to do my job. It's best if you don't know any more.'" Frank paused, then sighed heavily. "That's it, Gloria. I can't imagine where he'd go. Or why."

I could, but I didn't say so.

MY HEAD WAS SPINNING with new thoughts, new information, new questions. I wanted to spend the rest of the day tracking John down. I had a pretty good idea where he'd headed. But I'd agreed to go to the high school to meet Erin Wong and Tony Taruffi to set up the model nuclear reactor. I had seriously neglected my reactor pool project in favor of document fraud and moonshine. At this point I'd be better off making a still with Erin's students instead of a boron-laced waste pool.

I'd also committed to have dinner with Andrea to go over her presentation to Peter's class. And I knew my cousin Mary Ann was sitting in her pristine Worcester living room, fingering the antimacassars, waiting for me to call. Meanwhile I mentally edited a long speech I couldn't wait to give to Dorothy Leonard and Derek Byrne.

In retirement I was becoming better at multitasking than I'd ever been as a professional physicist. I took my cell phone from its charging base and set out to do at least two things at once—head for the high school and make some calls on the way. I'd read that some states were about to outlaw using handheld phones while driving—DWP, driving while phoning?—but so far I would be legal in Massachusetts.

I punched in my cousin's number. I wasn't proud of my reason for calling her first—I knew Mary Ann made the novena to Our Lady of Perpetual Help every Wednesday afternoon, so she wouldn't be home. At a little after one o'clock, she'd just be standing as the priest came in from the sacristy to lead the prayers. The perfect time to call and leave a message.

"This is cousin Gloria," I said. "I just got back to Revere and wanted to say hello. I'll call again and set a date to come and visit. Hope you're well."

A fine way to treat a seventy-something-year-old relative, I thought. But I was relieved that my tactic worked.

My next call was to Matt, who, happily, was not at a novena.

"The documents were doctored," I said, negotiating a left from Broadway onto Mountain Avenue, toward Revere High. The new Revere High, I called it, though it was almost twenty years old.

"I heard," Matt said.

"And John—"

"I heard."

"Then I guess we're all caught up."

Matt laughed. "Frank called me a few minutes ago."

"I think I know where John is."

"Detroit."

Why was I amazed that Matt would also be able to figure it out? John wasn't playing games on his laptop all this time, apathetic to his own predicament. He was using white pages and search engines and the services of e-ticketing agencies. He was doing what reporters do. Investigating.

"The displaced Scotto family," I said. "Especially the grandmother."

"That's what I think. She'd be, what, maybe early nineties now. Some chance she's still alive, and that she'd remember something that would help John figure out who killed Yolanda."

"And there's the funeral. He'd want to go to Yolanda's funeral."

"Now you're ahead of me on that one. How'd you think of that?"

"Think about where I live."

He laughed. "Residential hazard."

"John's not in trouble, is he?" I asked. "It's not illegal for him to leave the state since he hasn't been charged with anything, right?"

I heard a sigh from Matt. I wondered which street he was on. For all we knew we were passing each other on Beach Street, on our cell phones, both guilty of DWP. I pulled up to the high school, still on the phone, waiting for Matt's answer.

"No, it's not against the law, but it does make him look more suspect."

Not the answer I wanted, so I assumed the role of defense attorney. "If he were guilty, wouldn't he go to Brazil or some beach in Bermuda? Why would he go to Detroit?"

"Of course, we don't know where he is. He might be in Brazil. Or maybe he's in Detroit to apologize to the family, or to eliminate them also."

"Matt!"

"You asked. I don't believe that, Gloria, but if you ask what might a cop think, I'm telling you."

"Is that what Berger and Parker think?"

"I'm not sure they know. I'm giving John another hour or two lead time, which I shouldn't, then I'll call them. I'm hoping Frank will do it."

"I can't see Frank or Rose figuring out where he is. They're not exactly tuned in to reason right now, and anyway, they wouldn't be breaking the law if they don't inform the police their innocent son has left their sight for a day."

"Are we fighting?"

I took a breath and laughed, slightly. "We might be. My fault. I'm sorry. I don't want to fight."

"I don't either. I love you, Gloria."

That was enough to cause the phone to slip from my hand.

THE HIGH SCHOOL Rose Zarelli, Frank Galigani, and I attended, one of the many beautiful redbrick buildings in Revere, had burned down in the seventies, replaced with a modern structure a few blocks away on what used to be the Mountain Avenue quarry. With its straight lines and beige stucco exterior the new Revere High looked more like it belonged in a California valley town than among the established brick buildings of the East Coast.

One of my goals was to reach Erin's second-floor office without running into Peter Mastrone who'd been teaching Italian and American history there since he graduated from college in the late fifties. It didn't quite work out that way, but I was spared a long conversation by the arrival of the lab's model

PWR in an enormous wooden crate, large enough for Patience, Fortitude, and a tiger or two.

"Erin told me you'd be coming this afternoon. You're late, of course. And besides, if I'd known sooner we could have had lunch," Peter said, following me and two men in black support belts who were pushing the crate, on a large dolly, down the hall. Only my cousin Mary Ann could rival Peter in his ability to make an invitation sound like a rebuke. Peter's arms were full of student notebooks I recognized as containing his standard homework assignments.

Within a few minutes, Erin's office was crowded with Peter, Tony Taruffi, me, and the two deliverymen, all waiting for further instructions. She dispatched everyone efficiently, getting rid of Peter without seeming to aggravate him as I usually did.

"Call me," he said, picking a splinter from his button-down shirt. I was sorry I missed his brush with a PWR crate, and I wished Peter didn't always bring out the petty side of my personality.

I'd talked on the phone to Erin Wong and E-mailed her often, but had never met her. I was surprised at how tall she was, for an Asian woman anyway, at least five four or five. She had the same brand of luxurious black hair as Officer Michelle Chan.

The unveiling of the PWR took place in the large science hall in the east wing of the building where four of Erin's students met us. She'd invited two boys and two girls—one Asian, two Caucasians, and one African-American, a reflection of the new ethnic makeup of the city. My classmates had been primarily Italian or Jewish, both of Mediterranean origin, and therefore hard to distinguish. With similar hair color and nose profiles, Sol Finkelstein didn't look that different from Sal Fanciulli.

There was no diversity in the students' wardrobes, however—they all wore predominantly black, except for the girls' pastel tank tops. The boys' pants hung wide and low on their hips, the crotches around their knees. No tartan plaid skirts or neat button-down shirts. I wondered what these students would think about the way my classmate, Johnny Pacioli, was ushered to the principal's office for wearing ''dungarees'' to class one day.

Tony Taruffi, presiding over today's event, didn't miss the opportunity to make a little speech about the benevolence of the Charger Street lab, making this loan possible through its outreach program. His collar barely stretched around his thick neck, forcing his paisley tie to sit on his chest at an awkward angle.

When young Jamel asked him about the tritium leak reported in the *Journal* a week or so ago, Tony responded in true PR style.

''The situation was under the control of the scientists and engineers. At no time was there any threat to the laboratory employees, the public, or the environment,'' he said, straight-faced.

I'd hoped Jamel and his friends would pursue the question, if only to make Tony squirm, but they seemed ready to play with the model reactor instead. They took turns pushing buttons and exclaiming over the verisimilitude of the steam and the lavender vapor from the heat exchanger. I'd specifically asked Tony not to bring the documentation on the various functions and systems so the students could do the research themselves.

I hadn't done very much prep work for this meeting, counting on years of working in the field to carry me through until the first real class. But I had managed to collect photos of waste pools and reactor environments to get the students started in their construction project.

It didn't take four bright, energetic teenagers long to figure out a way to put lights on extended, adjustable coils for lowering into the tank.

We ended the session with soft drinks in the faculty lounge where I'd met Peter several times during my visits to his classes. We treated the students to soft drinks from the vending machine, but Erin had the good sense to make real coffee for the adults, using individual filter holders and ground-on-the-spot coffee beans.

"This is going to be very cool," Jamel said.

Nods from Mi-Weh and David, and a yawn from Charlotte, the only blond in the room.

"Aren't you excited about this project?" I asked Charlotte, immediately regretting that I'd embarrassed her.

She covered her mouth and drew in her breath. "I'm sorry. I didn't get much sleep last night. Our band won the regional competition and the prize was a trip to the ice-skating show at Warner Center. We didn't even get back to the parking lot until one this morning."

Congratulations from all, plus an extra word from Tony, still keeping his role as master of ceremonies. I hoped he wasn't planning to come to the regular project sessions. We'd scheduled daily meetings for the rest of the week to get things started.

"Well, good for you," he said, in what I heard as a condescending tone. Or maybe it was the only tone in his repertoire. "You know, as long as Warner Center has been there, I've never been in it. I go by it a lot when I go to the North End to my favorite pizza spots. What's it like inside?"

"Like, huge. They have this special sound system, and..."

Charlotte went on about the acoustics and other cutting-edge features of the Warner Center, but my mind was back on what Tony had said—or, more precisely, admitted.

I remembered Matt's telling me about Tony's alibi for the night of Yolanda's murder. He had special tickets to a Warner Center event. When asked to produce the stubs, he'd said they were in Austria with his companion of the evening, or else in a Viennese trash heap. He'd added that this person held a high office in the IAEA, the agency that oversaw nuclear power worldwide.

The first time I met Taruffi, he'd said, "I heard about you," or something to that effect, so he could have sent me the note.

It all fit.

I wasn't so good at multitasking that I could process this

new twist and still pay attention to the conversation. I looked at my watch and stood abruptly. "Oh, dear," I said. "I didn't realize what time it was. I'm going to be late for another appointment."

I gathered my purse and briefcase and acknowledged good-byes from around the table. As I turned to go, I inadvertently caught Tony Taruffi's eye.

"We'll see you soon," he said pleasantly. But the expression on his face said he expected the next meeting to be anything but pleasant.

TWENTY-FIVE

I HURRIED TO MY CAR, parked at a side door near the intersection of Mountain Avenue and School Street. I looked over my shoulder constantly, or as often as I could without tripping. I expected to hear Tony's footsteps on the driveway, to have him pop out of the bushes, or pole vault over to me from the fields at the back of the building. One thing I was sure of, Tony knew I'd caught the discrepancy in his two stories about Warner Center.

All that moonshine research for nothing, I thought. And the same for the whole project with the property documents. And John, probably in Detroit, tracking down a dead end. Now it seemed it was a science-related case. Or at least a lab-related case, having to do with illicit romance in the PR department, or boron, or both.

Would Tony follow me? Should I drive straight to the police station? When my cell phone rang, I was driving south on School Street, headed for Matt's office. I startled and checked all my mirrors, as if Tony would be calling my car to announce his stalking. I calmed myself by focusing on other reasons he might have had for concocting a phony alibi—a compromising liaison with whoever replaced Yolanda, for example.

My car was unbearably hot and I was perspiring, both from running and from fright. I pushed the air-conditioning lever all the way to high and took a breath. As far as I knew, Tony didn't even know my cell phone number. I clicked the phone on, took another breath, and relaxed when I heard Dorothy Leonard's voice.

In keeping with my new trend to multitask, I'd stepped out for a minute while Erin was brewing coffee, and called Dorothy Leonard's office.

"I got your message," she said.

Coincidentally, I was at the bend where School Street runs into Beach Street, a stone's throw from the library. I assessed my situation: fleeing one suspect, contemplating arriving into the arms of another. But surely a public library was safe. I pushed away a little voice in the back of my head. Not for Irving Leonard or Yolanda Fiore, it said.

I focused on the still-unresolved matter of faked documents. "I'd like to stop by and talk to you for a few minutes," I said. "I have something important I'd like to discuss."

A long sigh. "I thought you would."

Aha! I thought. Dorothy Leonard is about to confess. She's been waiting all along for me to focus on her.

But I realized this was at least my third *aha* of the Fiore case, and I still hadn't made any progress helping bring in the murderer.

SITTING BELOW her marvelous Revere Beach Boulevard prints, Dorothy Leonard seemed quite at ease for someone who had just confessed to forgery. I wouldn't have been surprised if she took out a manicure kit and redid her long nails, a deep coral that matched both her sleeveless linen dress and her lipstick. Her nonchalant attitude put a damper on my theory that she'd be motivated to kill the person who discovered her treachery.

"You're a step ahead of Frances Worthen, who, I expect, will come back with the same finding. As soon as I got your message I called the lawyers and withdrew the papers from the record." She arranged the fashionable gray streak in her dark hair. "So, technically, I've committed no crime." Dorothy made a tent of her fingers and gazed over my head. "I knew the documents didn't have much chance of making the grade— I've dealt with Cappie myself in the past, authenticating manuscripts and so forth—but I needed to buy time. Another twenty-four hours would have done it."

Stonewalling—one of Cappie's guesses. I'd have to tell Rose Cappie was indeed an expert in the field. "What happens in twenty-four hours?"

"June fifteenth is the drop-dead date for filing objections, counterpapers, and so on. I thought if I could just stall things past that date…" She spread her hands in a gesture of resignation. "It was worth a try."

Her expression turned so sad, as if she'd lost the Director of the Year award, that I almost felt guilty for spoiling her plan.

"Weren't you taking a big risk? If you'd been found out after the decision…"

She nodded. "It wasn't that smart, I know. I told myself it wasn't really a crime since we're so sure there was no burial ground there. The way the police plant evidence when they know they've found the right person."

I frowned at her matter-of-fact comment on police work. "I don't think—"

She held up her hand. "I didn't mean Matt, of course. But we just needed a bit more documentation, and all I did was change some numbers, to add a few square feet. I've had a little experience myself with document examination."

Not enough to make Cappie proud of her, I mused. Dorothy continued her argument, as if she were in front of a jury, instead of someone who stumbled onto the plan and no longer had a reason to expose her.

"Look at what we do have," she said, partly to the wall behind me. "Even without any funny business—all our zoning and building permits are in order, back to 1902. It would have taken a special zoning permit to establish a cemetery in the first place, and if there were one, it would have shown up. The city offices have no record of any such document. Plus, at least half a dozen books have been written about the history of Revere by local authors, and none have mentioned a cemetery in that location."

A convincing defense. And more words than I'd ever heard Dorothy Leonard speak at one time. "Then why bother tampering with the papers?" I asked her.

She shrugged. "Just an extra precaution. I was hoping to impress the Catholic Church."

We smiled, co-conspirators, sharing an in-joke at the expense of Bernard Cardinal Law.

"Does Derek know about this?" I asked her. Interesting as all this was, I still had a killer to find. Maybe Derek took this pseudo-crime more seriously, I thought.

She shook her head. "Derek doesn't know anything about this. He's sweet, and naive. He really thinks these papers fell into our hands at just the right time."

"And he still doesn't know?"

"Not unless you've told him. And I think we'll win this anyway. Fortunately for us, the Church is not a great keeper of secular records. About all they have is obituaries from old newspapers and parish bulletins with a vague reference to burial in that general vicinity. But the announcements could just as easily have been directing the faithful to the old Rumney Marsh cemetery."

"You're the one who really wants this project to go through aren't you?"

Dorothy's eyes misted over, as she nodded slowly. "I couldn't stand the idea that this would fail again. It was Irving's dream."

"What made it fail when he was director? Surely Councilman Byrne couldn't have stopped it by himself."

"Byrne wields a lot of power. He convinced the rest of the Council that the money should be used for a new cultural center. Which, by the way, has never been built."

"It almost sounds like he had a personal vendetta against your husband. As if he wanted to stop the expansion just to be nasty to Mr. Leonard. Who was appointed when he died?"

Dorothy raised her eyebrows in mock surprise. "Joe Reilly, the councilman's friend, wouldn't you know. Someone who had no interest in expanding the library. Actually no interest in the library." Dorothy smiled. "But if Byrne's intention was to foil the Leonards' careers, he got an even bigger surprise when I was appointed last year."

Revere politics were coming together for me. "You were promoted over his son. That must have been hard for him."

A vigorous nod. "Indeed, although I do like Derek. I think another factor in the councilman's contrariness here is that he'd rather have this undertaking come later and be credited to his son. In spite of the political haggling, the people of Revere want this project to succeed. And, not only did his son *not* get this job, but a *woman* did. Dear old Brendan has a problem with females in authority, as you may have noticed." Dorothy sat back in her chair and swiveled a few degrees. A broad smile took over her face. "Poor old man. He had the nerve to tell me to join a sewing circle."

I gulped. "What an interesting metaphor." I smiled, to match Dorothy's expression, hoping my distress—to me it seemed visible—would come across as amusement at the councilman's choice of words.

The image of the note I'd received, on formal, off-white stationery, floated between us. TAKE UP SEWING. First the note, then Tony Taruffi's comment to me, now Councilman Byrne's advice to Dorothy Leonard.

Dorothy seemed not to notice my discomfort as I tried to figure out whether Taruffi or Byrne had sent me the note, or whether all the men in Revere had suddenly gone macho. In line with her talkative mood, Dorothy gave me an account of her husband's vision for the library, and of his untimely death at forty-six. Or perhaps she simply allowed me to be there while she reminisced.

"Irving was working late—it was a Friday night. He was often here late on Friday so he could take the rest of the weekend off. The custodian found him early Saturday morning, at the foot of the stairs."

"So you weren't here at the time?"

She trained her eyes on me, giving me a soft, amused look. "I wondered when you were going to get around to that. I was in East Hartford, Connecticut, visiting our daughter, Sarah, at her school. But what you really want to know is my alibi for the night Yolanda was murdered. Coincidentally, I was also at

Sarah's that night, ten years later. Sarah now lives in Malden, with her family. I was baby-sitting my young grandson.''

I felt my face flush, embarrassed at my awkward probing. ''I—''

''No, no, it's all right, I know you're close to John Galigani's parents, and it's always hard when one's child is in trouble. I remember how it was when Irving died. His father was a doctor, you know, to make it even worse. Medical people always expect to be able to save their loved ones from death of any kind, of course. My father-in-law was devastated.''

Dorothy's eyes drifted off again. I felt like an eavesdropper on a discussion she'd had with herself many times in the last ten years.

''Apparently Irving had been carrying a large crate of folders and lost his footing at the top of the stairs. The crate and all the contents were strewn over the bottom landing. It was very strange, since I remember the folders were an odd collection of files he wouldn't ordinarily be concerned with. Files I thought his staff would handle. And Mrs. Tremel who worked for him back then said the same thing. She said Irving had marked the crate for long-term storage.'' Dorothy frowned and wagged her head, as if to scold Irving Leonard for the foolish error that cost him his life and denied her many more happy years with him.

She turned back to me and to the present. ''Yes, I want this project to succeed, Gloria, for Irving. I want it badly enough to tell a fib here and there, but I would never kill another human being.''

In spite of her perfect figure and elegant presence—what other grandmother could wear a linen dress in the summer and end up with only the most discreet set of wrinkles?—I believed her.

ONLY MY MOTHER'S TOUGH training about keeping commitments prevented me from canceling dinner with Andrea. I had serious mental reorganizing to do, charts to create, notes to update, not to mention tracking John Galigani. I'd hoped for a message from him, his parents, or Matt, but no new information had entered my apartment electronically while I'd been gone. And no more threatening messages, either, I was happy to say.

I had barely enough time to set out the lasagna pan when the doorbell rang at six o'clock.

"I brought the salad, and some bread, and a few cookies," Andrea said, though I'd agreed only to the salad.

Andrea was always excited to be in my flat, looking through my books and admiring the California prints on the walls. This evening she brought unprecedented energy and enthusiasm, thanks to her scheduled appearances in Peter Mastrone's classroom.

"I've been driving by the high school during my lunch hour," she told me. "I wanted to see what the kids were like these days. I parked along Mountain Avenue yesterday, and School Street today, so no one would think I was a pedophile or anything."

It was just like Andrea Cabrini to raise the concept of teacher preparation to a new high. "That was a good idea. What did you learn?"

"There were so many Asian students. I was surprised. I went to high school in West Adams and we didn't have much variety out there. So, I changed the plan for my first subject."

"Not Jenny Bramley?"

She shook her head. "What do you think of my using C. S. Wu instead?"

I nodded and smiled at her. "The woman who did the experiments at Columbia. One of my favorites."

"Yeah, I've been reading up on it. Two men, Lee and Yang, were the theorists and they got the Nobel Prize in 1957, the first scientists of Chinese birth to win it. But Wu should have been acknowledged, too." Andrea shook her pudgy finger at me, as if I were the Nobel committee, skipping over a female whose experimental results were crucial to the milestone—the overthrow of parity that changed the way physicists looked at symmetry in the universe.

"I think Wu is an excellent choice, Andrea. And I agree

she's gotten too little credit and recognition. You've done a lot of work very quickly.''

She sighed. "My evenings are pretty free. I'm really grateful to you for giving me this assignment."

"It works out well for me, too," I said. I didn't bother sharing with her how relieved I was not to have a regular commitment to Peter. "What else did you pick up on your stakeout at the high school?"

"Well, this is going to sound crazy to you, but not all the kids are skinny, you know. I was worried about that. I—"

My own chubby heart went out to her. "You don't have to apologize, Andrea. I understand that feeling."

"I was wondering if you could help me choose something to wear. I know you hate to shop, but maybe if I bought a nice outfit, I'd feel a little more…qualified."

I pictured myself spending precious time at the mall, picking through dresses and suits and fancy shoes. Then, in a matter of seconds I edited the scene, and Rose Galigani stepped in to take my place.

"You need a personal shopper, Andrea, and I know just the person."

AFTER DINNER and a run-through of Andrea's transparencies— I talked her into cutting the number in half, to ten instead of twenty—I walked out with her.

"I have to pull my car into the garage," I explained. "When I came home earlier, a delivery truck was blocking my driveway." I smiled at the notion that the bottled water phenomenon had arrived on Tuttle Street.

"I don't know how you manage that big car," Andrea said, unlocking the door of her normal-size sedan.

"I've had practice," I told her.

I'd left my Cadillac at the curb at the end of the dead-end street. I stepped carefully in the dark, along the crumbling sidewalk, where the roots of large, old elms had shattered the cement. Smells of various ethnic dinners hung in the still, humid air. I detected the aroma of at least one Asian dish, and another that was close to my own lasagna.

Ten o'clock—still a good two hours before I'd run out of energy.

My feet were healing surprisingly well, considering how neglectful I'd been of the California doctor's instructions—soak for fifteen minutes twice a day, sprinkle with medicated powder, rest. I wondered who had time to bother. My list of things to do was long enough without adding *pamper feet*. I reviewed the list as I passed neat old houses and tiny front lawns: check the Internet white pages for Fiores in Detroit, tell Matt—finally—about the note in my desk, since the subject of sewing kept coming up, do a little boron review before meeting with Erin Wong's students again.

The next item had to do with Tony Taruffi's alibi, and the next thing I saw was Tony Taruffi appearing before me, coming from behind the last tree on Tuttle Street.

TWENTY-SIX

I FUMBLED WITH my key chain, stuck in the pocket of my knit pants, trying to locate the little red panic button that had served me well during another Tuttle Street ambush. I chided myself for not having it ready ahead of time, before heading down a dark, quiet, dead-end street. The shadow of St. Anthony's Church, behind me on Revere Street, was doing nothing to protect me.

"Time to chat, Gloria," Tony said, grabbing my arm. He felt as strong as he looked, with his upper arm muscles straining the ribbing on his short-sleeved shirt.

Chat, I thought, taking a breath against the painful pounding in my chest. At least he hadn't said, *the jig's up,* or something else with a ring of finality. It was too dark to see the expression on his face, but his voice was relatively calm, and his hold on my arm was lighter than I'd expected, given the method he'd chosen to initiate a conversation.

I opened my mouth, probably to scream, although I wasn't responding logically. Tony put his hand up. He'd walked me a few steps to a spot illuminated by a streetlight and I could see his look was one of panic, not aggression.

"Look, I didn't mean to frighten you." He glanced down at where he held my arm, and frowned. "Sorry," he said.

He let go, and I briefly considered running away. I knew I could never outrun him, however, even in my most athletic shoes.

"I suppose this is about your alibi." Brilliant, I told myself.

Not only do I not attempt to escape, but I remind a maybe-killer why he should attack me.

Tony nodded, a sheepish look taking over his face, making me slightly more comfortable about my safety. "I'm a married man," he told me. "I have a family, and I have a responsible job. I'm in the public eye. I have to be careful."

"You mean you have to be careful you don't get caught?"

Tony screwed up his mouth. "This is not really your business, Gloria. But yes, I was with a woman, not my wife, and I'd rather not have to tell the police."

Although we both whispered, our voices seemed loud, as if they were being amplified, the stagnant air acting as an efficient transistor. A few lights glowed from the windows, mostly moving TV images.

"So you want me to convey your innocence to the RPD?"

"Something like that."

I shook my head. Not that I'd had any direct experience with adultery, but I remembered reading that men who cheat on their wives do it often. "So you did have an affair with Yolanda Fiore," I said, hoping to get something useful from this unpleasantness.

"What does that have to do with anything?"

"Did she dump you? Is that why you fired her?"

I took a moment to congratulate myself on good police procedure. My linear, one-track training in science had been hard to overcome, but I'd finally learned to *not* answer a question, and proceed instead with my own agenda. Tony was born to that kind of rhetoric, however, and proved a tough opponent.

"I was with another woman the night Yolanda was murdered," he said.

The broken-record technique. I tried to stay focused. "I see, so you dumped Yolanda for this other woman—what was her name?"

"Nice try."

I grinned. "And then you fired her."

"You're making this very hard for me."

"Thank you." I indulged myself in a fantasy, where Sergeant Matt Gennaro was standing in the shadows, one elm tree over, watching my performance and applauding. This image was preferable to reality, in which I knew he'd be upset at my careless disregard for my own safety.

"I fired Yolanda because she was using the lab computer system for personal research. I admit I was looking for an excuse. She was not what you would call a company person. But you can check the employment records. Her termination papers are there. I'm sure you can use your pseudo-police status."

I ignored the sarcasm. "Do you know what the research was about?"

"Genealogy. It's a big thing now, you know. Everyone is writing memoirs. They find a great-great-grandfather who was the first man in Suffolk County to make gloves with five fingers and they think it's some exciting, groundbreaking, big deal."

"Did you ever see evidence of that—a chart on the screen or something?"

"I sure did. It wasn't hard to sneak up on her—she only had a cubicle, you know." *Unlike me, a supervisor,* was the unspoken boast. Recalling the fishbowl that was Tony's office, I was amazed he clung to status symbols. "She even E-mailed Italy, for God's sake."

"It doesn't cost any more to E-mail Italy," I reminded him.

"Yeah, well, it's just the idea."

"I assume you knew all this through the lab's computer security program?"

Tony nodded. "Right. They have software now that can intercept every keystroke. I had a hunch, since every time I approached her at her computer, she'd zip over to the desktop or a lab file. As if I were an idiot. So I had her targeted. Had her E-mail and Web use intercepted. Once they confirmed my suspicions, I fired her." Tony snapped his fingers, snuffing out a career.

"You fired her, then you killed her." This last attempt was only halfhearted, more to aggravate him than because I believed the accusation. I hated Tony's smug expression, but I was losing my confidence in him as a murderer.

He made an unpleasant snorting noise, and I had a peek into what his snoring might be like. "Give me a break here, Gloria. Firing is one thing, killing is another."

A good point. With that, Tony sprinted away. I had the disturbing realization that my suspects were dropping off, like extruded metal dripping from a precision-engineered needle.

MY OUTDOOR INTERVIEW with Tony Taruffi had taken less than a half hour, but a lot had been going on in my apartment. I opened my door to a ringing phone and a message on my machine. I picked up the phone, with the awful thought that it might be time for another threat or prank. I prepared myself for heavy breathing, but heard instead an upbeat voice.

"Gloria, this is Brendan Byrne. I hope I didn't wake you."

"No. In fact, I'm just arriving home." More or less.

"I want to thank you and your dear friend for your excellent work in uncovering the document fraud."

That was fast, I thought. Apparently Councilman Byrne was on someone's short list for breaking news. "Thanks for your kind words. I had very little to do with it."

"Now, don't be modest. And, by the way, I'm sure you've been informed that my son was in no way connected with that devilish scheme."

"Yes, Mrs. Leonard said as much. May I ask how you found out about our tests so quickly?"

He laughed. "There aren't that many lawyers in Revere, Gloria. They're all connected." I remembered Dorothy Leonard's comment about calling her lawyer immediately after she heard my message. She might as well have called the councilman directly.

"Well, I'm glad we could be of help."

"Who knew to what depths Dorothy Leonard would stoop for that project of hers? Of course, I had my suspicions."

I took a breath, annoyed. Perhaps it was the irritation, perhaps because he was keeping me from answering the message I hoped was from Matt—for whatever reason, I goaded the councilman. "Mrs. Leonard seems to think it won't matter. She says they have enough documentation without the fraudulent property papers."

"Not on her life."

His voice had turned angry, the genial old man gone from the telephone connection. I counted three Brendan Byrnes. One, the young man, off to the side of the crowd at City Hall, seeking revenge for his parents' cruel fate. Two, the doddering old Irishman who treated himself to pinochle with the boys, and a hangover once a week. And three, the crafty councilman, protecting his son at every turn, opposing him only on the library project.

"That's strong language, Councilman. How come the failure of this project—one that your son is in favor of—means so much to you?"

A pause, during which I envisioned the councilman calming himself, running his long fingers through his thick white hair. "The property is holy, Dr. Lamerino." My title, delivered in a patronizing manner. "Is it so hard for you to believe a person in public life can be motivated simply by religious considerations?"

"As a matter of fact, yes."

"Then we have nothing more talk about, do we?"

"I guess not. Good night, Councilman."

I hung up the phone, curious at my own reaction, more than his. He wasn't the first man to treat me condescendingly. I wondered if the councilman had also phoned Rose to thank her personally, and if it had ended so badly. I decided it was too late for me to call and check. Rose was an early riser and might even be taking medication to help her sleep. The morning was soon enough.

But maybe it was time to check the old man's alibi.

ALTHOUGH I HADN'T BEEN physically hurt in any way, I was exhausted from the tension of the past four days, and ready to put my head on Matt's broad chest and tell all. The threatening note to me, the matching envelope in Yolanda's trash, the blaring intrusion alarm, the slashed tires, the ambush by Taruffi, the nasty end to my conversation with Councilman Byrne. And I wanted a sympathetic ear to hear me whine about the futility of research on moonshine and faked documents. Plus the dead end on boric acid. And, to borrow an expression from Rose Galigani, *plus-plus* her son John, an absconded suspect.

How handy that Matt had called during the mental gymnastics between Tony and me.

I played his message. "It's after ten o'clock. Where are you? Any lasagna left over? I'm on my cell."

Multitasking once again, with one hand I used the speaker phone to return Matt's call, and with the other carved out a generous slice of lasagna.

WHO KNOWS WHAT chain of associations prompted my next move?—from lasagna to Italian to Tony Taruffi to E-mails to Italy, perhaps. I picked up the phone and punched in Tony's home phone number. When he'd scribbled it on the back of his business card earlier in the day, in case I had a question about the lab's model PWR, I never thought I'd use it.

"This is Gloria," I began, speaking to Tony's answering machine.

"Hi, Gloria." Not a hopeful tone as Tony intercepted the message. I smiled at the idea that Tony might be worried about what I'd do with my new information. I'd left it ambiguous—whether I'd reveal his false alibi, alert his wife as to his latest adultery, or forget about the whole incident.

"I'm ready to deal," I said. I wasted little time since Matt, the person with the real power to make deals, was due any minute. "Does the lab's computer security staff have copies of Yolanda's Web use and E-mails?"

"Sure, but why do you care? I know you want to clear John Galigani. He's out of town right?"

"How do you know that?"

"Small town." Tony laughed. "Nah, really, I'm buddies with the *Journal* people. Don't forget my job is to network with the media." Only Tony could make an innocuous phrase like *networking with the media* sound morally questionable.

"Anyway, I told you, these E-mails were just about personal, family stuff."

"And how do you know *that?*"

"Because I needed to cover my—myself, so I made copies for my files."

My heart soared. "Then we have a deal."

MATT AND I HAD settled on my sofa while the lasagna heated. The smell of melting cheese was almost as comforting as Matt's gentle caress.

"It's not that any one of these incidents was terrifying," I told him, my head against his chest. "But I have to admit, taken all together, they make me nervous."

He kissed my forehead. "They should make you nervous. I'm glad you told me. I wish there were something we could use in all this." Matt picked up the note, the only tangible symbol of what was causing my distress. "I'll at least take this and see what I can do with it. You never know…watermarks, fingerprints…" He trailed off, without much enthusiasm.

Matt's reasonable response surprised me. I remembered clearly one evening when he stood in my apartment and tore up a contract I had with the RPD. He'd felt number one, I'd overstepped the bounds of my agreement, and number two, I'd placed myself in physical danger.

Of course this time there was no contract, but still…

"You're not mad?"

He shook his head. "It's not useful for me to be mad. I have to trust you. I can't spend the rest of my life worried about you, so I've built this little compartment where you're a cop, and I don't worry any more than I would about my partner."

I sat up. "This is the first I've heard of it. Thanks."

He pulled me back and ruffled my hair. The timer on my microwave oven sounded, but it was a long time before we paid any attention to it.

TWENTY-SEVEN

I WAS AT MY computer early on Thursday morning, determined to show up at Revere High School fully prepared for class, just as I'd always done in my days as a student. Whether out of fear of repercussion from my mother, or love of learning, or a little of both, I'd always done my homework.

Using a simple graphics package, I made a few rough sketches of the components we'd need for the waste pool. Full scale, the fuel pellets of uranium are about three-quarters of an inch in diameter, about five-eighths of an inch long. They're inserted, one on top of the other, into twelve-foot-long, slender metal tubes, usually stainless steel. When filled, pressurized, and sealed, the tubes become known as fuel rods, which are then bundled together to make up the core. I'd leave it up to the students to scale down the sizes to fit our model.

While I worked, the Fiore case swam around in my head. E-mails to Italy, Prohibition, nuclear waste, false documents. On Monday night I'd dreamed the entire library had imploded, like the fuel pellet in a laser fusion target chamber, caving in on itself. A maelstrom of books whirled around the interior of the building, finally funneling down the lethal stairway. Thousands of hardcover biographies, paperback novels, over-size art books, atlases, and reference volumes tumbled headlong, knocking over the coat rack on their way to the basement.

I knew I had either too many clues or none at all.

And one more memory, a happy one, flitted among the murderous thoughts in my brain. Matt had stayed the night. He'd delivered my morning coffee with two mini-biscotti before going home to change his clothes and report to work. Did I want to wake up that way every morning? Yes, was at the tip of my tongue.

I remembered the first time Matt and I met. Rose had set up the meeting, supposedly for purely business purposes. Rose had heard the Revere Police Department was looking for scientists who could help as expert witnesses and as technical consultants for a variety of criminal investigations.

"His name's Matt Gennaro," she'd said. "Wife died ten years ago. Her heart. No children. We've known him for years. Family was from Everett, but they're all gone now, except for a sister on the Cape."

"They have two thousand scientists down the street," I'd said. "The Charger Street lab is overflowing with candidates for this job."

Rose shook her head. "Not ones like you. The lab scientists have a vested interest when the crime takes place on their property or if it involves one of their own. You're a godsend, coming in from out of town like this."

"I'll think about it."

"Just come and meet this guy, Gloria," Rose had said. "You don't have to date him."

I'd caved in to Rose's prodding, warning her it might not work out.

And I'd warned Matt also. "I've never done anything like that before," I'd told him at that first meeting. "What if I ruin your case?"

He'd smiled. "Don't worry. It doesn't hinge on you. We just want your expertise. We'll prepare you for what questions to expect, and you answer truthfully."

Another smile, no doubt meant to calm me, but in fact it charmed me.

I liked his kind eyes, his comfortable body. Since none of my uncles had weighed in at less than two hundred pounds or so, Matt looked just right to me. Not so fit that I couldn't imagine myself resting my head on his chest.

AFTER MATT LEFT on Thursday morning, I was able to work until about eight o'clock before my apartment came alive with calls and a visit.

Rose was first, and frantic.

"Where do you think he is, Gloria?"

"Try not to worry about it, Rose. He'll probably call you as soon as he has something." I'd decided not to tell Rose about my guess, shared by Matt, that John had gone to Detroit. I understood Rose's concern, but for my part, I felt John was safer in the Midwest. The murderer is in Revere, I told myself.

"*Has* something? You mean you think John's working on the case? I suppose that would be good, wouldn't it?"

"It might be."

"I thought about calling all his friends, but what would I say—*is my son the fugitive there?*"

"Strictly speaking, he's not a fugitive." I was happy to eliminate at least one of my friend's troubles. Matt had told me no one on the RPD seemed concerned about the missing John Galigani.

"Probably because of his parents," he'd said. "They're not worried about finding him if they want him."

I'd carried the phone to the window, and now I noticed the hearse pulling into the delivery area at the back of the building. "Here comes another client," I said to Rose, in an effort to get her talking about something she loved—the Galigani Mortuary business. "It's pretty busy here these days."

"It certainly is. Did you see the Indian woman, Mrs. Patira, in A? Frank had to paint that red dot on her forehead."

I'd often tried to set Rose straight on this issue—I did not make regular visits to the decedents who rested temporarily on the first floor of my residence—but she clearly didn't get it.

"Gosh, I missed the dot," I said, but the subtlety was lost on Rose.

"There's also a small red line on her scalp, that you can hardly see, but it signifies that she was a widow. And she'll be buried facedown. Isn't that interesting?"

I'd asked for this. "Fascinating."

"She had a little boy, too, only eight years old. Very sad. They let him see her in the casket, and he lashed out at Robert, as if he's the one that took his mother away. So Robert talked to him for a long time. He's very good with kids. So is John…"

Oh-oh. "Are you coming in to work today?"

"I'm here."

"You're downstairs? Why didn't you come up?"

"I thought you might still have company…you know, he sometimes drives an unmarked that's unfamiliar to me."

He. We hung up on a laugh, and a date for a coffee break at ten o'clock.

MATT'S CALL WAS BRIEF, since we'd been apart only an hour or so. He'd agreed to have Berger and his temporary partner, Ian Parker, check into Councilman Byrne's alibi.

"They're not too happy about it, but they'll do it. It won't be a pleasant reception. Some of those guys Byrne hangs around with are the elders of Revere."

"That doesn't put them above the law."

"Right."

Another laugh-filled hang-up.

When I turned away from the window, I saw an envelope on the floor in front of my door. A large brown manila envelope had been slid under it during the two or three minutes I was on the phone with Matt.

I was correct in my guess that Tony Taruffi had acted quickly. A note was clipped to the envelope—a piece of pale blue stationery, with cramped handwriting. *Enclosed material you requested. Didn't want to wake you. T^2*

T-squared, for his initials. Tony probably thought it was the way to my heart, but I'd never liked cute uses of mathematical or scientific notation.

Once again I abandoned boron for Yolanda Fiore or, more correctly, for John Galigani. I pulled out a sheaf of eight-and-a-half-by-eleven sheets—pages and pages of E-mails in a tiny font. Another collection of sheets clipped together contained the Web-use statistics for the two weeks before Yolanda was fired. A gold mine. The end that justified the means—promising Tony Taruffi I wouldn't reveal his infidelity. It will come out soon enough, I told myself, and probably his wife already knew.

I flipped through, estimating fifty pages of E-mails, some with replies and replies to replies in italics. I wished I had Yolanda's original E-mails instead of T²'s copies—I was sure she'd have highlighted the important parts. These copies were hard to read, with double and triple brackets before every line. And how do I know Tony gave me all of them? I wondered, but then settled down to plow through the small print.

The E-mails were addressed to cousins, aunts, uncles, and friends. Each time, Yolanda began by identifying herself—

I'm Yolanda Fiore, in Revere, Massachusetts, USA. I found you through the Internet and wonder if you can help me. In 1940, my grandfather, Sabatino Scotto, was involved in a crime...

The first replies covered a range, from no information, to a referral to another person, in another town—a Rapone, perhaps, or a DiGiglio. But after a week of searching, Yolanda met some Italian relatives.

Cousin Maria Ambrosio said she went through scrapbooks and photo albums to see if she could find a mention of Sabatino Scotto. MAYBE HE CHANGED HIS NAME, Yolanda wrote back. NO ONE ARRIVES IN OUR HOUSEHOLD DURING THE DATES YOU GIVE ME, came the answer.

As I read, I added branches to Rose's genealogy tree. The oldest relative still alive in Italy was Celia Pallavo's sister, Yolanda's great-aunt on her mother's side, Gia Pizzimenti. Gia was not well, it seemed, but mentally alert. She remembered the scandal and even offered to harbor Sabatino, God forgive her, but he never arrived. Gia's message was sent through one of her grandchildren, whose English was admirable—

Cara Iolandina. My name Luisa. My grandma Gia was the sister of your grandma, Celia. Gia says they wait for Sabatino many weeks. He never come. Celia in America was broken heart, but she never give up. She keep writing to ask has he come, because he take her jewels. Supposed to bring them to us for paying, and she say he never cheat like that.

So Matt was right—Celia reported her jewelry stolen as a cover for her husband. I wondered how Yolanda felt when she learned her grandfather really did intend to skip bail.

By the time I finished reading the E-mails, I felt I'd read a Mario Puzo novel. I'd never read his fiction, but I'd seen the movie versions. I wondered if the stories in his books were as compelling as the tale I'd fleshed out through Yolanda Fiore's E-mails. Maybe I'd check one out as soon as I had a library card.

I ARRIVED AT the high school only minutes before our three o'clock meeting. The all-black-clad students were busy with Erin, who was in a flowery peach sundress.

"Do you think we can enter this project in the science fair?" Jamel asked.

"I don't see why not. Ms. Wong and I will have to discuss the rules."

"Really? Cool." This from Charlotte, with nods from Mi-Weh and David.

Charlotte, Revere High's star clarinetist in the school band, and the one who inadvertently busted Tony Taruffi's alibi, had an ingenious idea. "I still have all my Legos," she said. "I think I can rig up a system for lowering and raising the assemblies in and out of the rack in the pool."

More *reallys* and *cools*. I was happy teenagers weren't above using the play systems of their youth, in spite of the forbidding outfits they assembled.

I'd brought a video disk produced at my Berkeley lab, so

they could see the life-size operations of a waste pool. A rich baritone voice came on, the spokesperson for an unidentified government agency: "Our Energy Department says only one of thousands of canisters that hold the waste will fail while it is still 'juvenile,' that is less than a thousand years old."

The students didn't miss a chance for ridicule. "That's a long time to be adolescent," Charlotte said.

I paused the disk at a close-up of the pool and the technicians, all in cumbersome white suits and head coverings. The robotlike figures used long poles to manipulate the fuel assemblies, the tops of which were several feet below the surface of the water.

"Do we have this straight? The waste is in the pools because we think if we bury it, radioactive atoms might get into the water table?" Mi-Weh asked.

"Right," I said.

"So we have, like, tons of radioactive waste sitting above the ground where it can spill over or, like, anyone can fall in?"

"Sort of," I said.

"Wow," Jamel said, moving closer to the screen. He ran his pen down the display, showing how deep the pool was. He scratched his neatly shaved dark head. "I'll bet you could put a body down there, and no one would find it for, like, fifty years."

Fifty years. "I guess that seems like an eternity to you. More than three times your lifetime."

The students and their twenty-something teacher laughed.

Fifty years. Fifty-five years.

I stood up abruptly. "Excuse me. I have an important errand I just remembered."

What if a body had been buried not in a boric acid waste pool, but behind a building for fifty-five years?

That was the question I asked myself all the way to the police station.

TWENTY-EIGHT

MATT LEANED BACK in his old gray office chair. The aging springs and patched-up vinyl seat gave out sounds halfway between creaking and groaning.

"There are a lot of gaps here, Gloria."

None that I could see. I'd laid it out for him, and in my mind it all fit. Yolanda Fiore, the reporter, doing what reporters do, investigates the disappearance of her grandfather. She determines that Sabatino Scotto never got to Italy. The young Brendan Byrne murdered him and buried him in the lot behind the library. Yolanda figured it out, and he had to kill her, too. And, of course, that was the reason Byrne had to stop the excavation for the library expansion, lest his crime be exposed.

"First, we can't prove Scotto didn't go to Italy. We only know the people Yolanda contacted denied seeing him there." Not what I wanted to hear. I'd been so relieved to find Matt in his office, it hadn't occurred to me that he'd dispute my theory of a double homicide, with the killings fifty-five years apart.

"It was a pretty exhaustive search of several families. The Pallavos, the Avallones—"

"OK, but they have every reason to lie, to preserve a family secret, and to hide their own crime."

"Do you think harboring a fugitive is a crime in Italy?"

Matt laughed. "Maybe not." He was not to be distracted very long, however. "Say Byrne did murder Scotto—and at this point I think you're picking on him because he's the only one we've been looking at who was an adult in 1940—if we dug up a body, how would we know it was Scotto? Maybe it was a legitimate burial, like the Church is saying we'll find there. What makes it a murder victim?"

"We use DNA."

"Scotto's DNA is not on file. Where would we get data to make the comparison?"

"We could match to Yolanda, and show it's her family."

"We just happen to think of trying to match to Yolanda?"

"No, she just happens to have determined that her grandfather didn't go to Italy. So she's suspicious when a body is dug up. And let's not forget revenge. Byrne finally has a chance for justice."

"In his mind."

"Of course. She's a Scotto, and at least one Scotto will pay, if not the right one."

A nod, but not a concession. "OK for now. Let's start down another track. Why would Byrne think anyone would point the finger at him?"

"Well, Byrne would be worried that we can make a match to Yolanda, and everyone knows he had motive to kill Scotto."

"Didn't you tell me…" Matt flipped through his small notebook, but I knew the gesture was for show, teasing me. "Let's see, your interview with Dorothy Leonard. Here it is. The library expansion project is likely to go through anyway?"

"Yes, but with Yolanda out of the way, it's less likely anyone will care about some bones that are dug up. As you pointed out, they could just say it might be Horatio Alger."

"Who's that?"

"I forget."

Matt's big grin and obvious approval of me, combined with the sight of my photograph on his desk, gave me a cozy feeling, inappropriate for the gravity of the matter at hand.

Matt refocused quickly. "You haven't told me what ties Byrne to this crime, to make him worried enough to murder Yolanda."

Finally, one I was ready for. "He threw the murder weapon into the grave and it has his fingerprints on it."

"Hmmm."

I folded my arms across my chest. *So there.* "And Byrne worked for the city government, so his prints are on file."

"Hmmm. Then we wouldn't need Yolanda at all would we? So why would getting rid of her end Byrne's troubles?"

This time the *hmmm* was mine, and followed by a very soft "I don't know."

"What was that?"

"Let's go have an early dinner. My treat."

AT SEVEN O'CLOCK, having left Matt at the curb, I walked past Mrs. Patira in Parlor A and Mr. Rinaldo in Parlor B and climbed the stairs to my apartment. Matt had a meeting with a community service group and would be over later.

I plopped down on my glide rocker, too full of the chicken piccata special to concentrate. I made the mistake of reviewing all I'd done in the less than two weeks that I'd been back from my California vacation, which had been anything but restful. I picked up the Web-use sheets from Yolanda's computer, and fell asleep.

I WAS JOLTED AWAKE by my ringing phone, in the middle of a strange dream no doubt prompted by Matt's attack on my double homicide theory and my own circular reasoning. I couldn't remember the details of the images, but I knew a spiral staircase was involved.

"Gloria, it's John." His voice seemed to come from my dream.

I rubbed my eyes and hoisted myself to a sitting position. John who? I almost asked, never one to make the transition from sleep to wakefulness very easily.

"Where are you?" I asked instead. "Your mother is worried sick…and that's no way to greet you, is it? How are you?"

"I'm OK. I'm at a pay phone."

"I don't think anyone is taping this conversation, John."

"Sorry. I'm in Detroit. You probably figured that out. I really wanted to be at Yolanda's funeral. I'd met her sister, Gabriella, once when she visited Yolanda in Revere. No one here knows the details of the murder investigation, that I'm—''

His voice cracked, almost imperceptibly, and I felt a catch in my throat. ''I'm glad you went, John.''

''Really?''

''Really.'' Speaking as your Aunt Gloria, of course, not as an adviser to the RPD, nor even as your mother's best friend.

''Let me tell you, it has been very interesting. Yolanda's grandmother, Sabatino's wife, is still alive. Mrs. Pallavo. Ninety-five, but very sharp. Reads the newspaper every day, does the crossword puzzle.'' Either John was adopting his mother's habits, or he was building his case for a credible witness in Yolanda's grandmother. ''Mrs. Pallavo says Sabatino would never have disappeared like that. They had a plan all worked out. A way to get messages back and forth, everything. And she never heard from him.''

''And she sounded believable to you?''

''Yeah. I'm convinced that Sabatino Scotto never got to Italy. Not only that, but Yolanda grew up with this story. Her grandmother has been urging her for years to look into it. I'm sure that's why she came to Revere, but maybe that's even why Yolanda became a reporter in the first place. It's as if she was meant to find the truth.''

And to die for it, I thought.

I gave John a few details of my own that corroborated his findings. I might also have misled him slightly, with a tiny exaggeration about how good our case was against the councilman. The coast is clear, was my message.

''Are you coming home soon?''

''Oh, and get this,'' John said, skirting the issue of his truancy. ''Here's a small-world story that reporters love—after Sabatino disappeared, Celia became very ill from depression. Irving Leonard's father was the doctor who treated her. She says he was very good to her, the only one who believed her, and she wanted to be remembered to him. I had to tell her he died ten years ago. I think he's the only one in Revere that she remembers. She's blotted out the ones who turned against her, I guess.''

"This is all interesting, John. We can talk more when you get home.''

He laughed. "Yeah, OK. I get it. I'll take an early flight tomorrow. Will you tell my mother? I didn't want her to get all hysterical.''

"Too late.''

He laughed. "I know, I have a lot to make up to my parents.''

"They'll just be happy to have you back. And it would really be better if you called yourself.''

"I'll think about it. Thanks, Gloria.''

I put down the phone and smiled, as if I believed the story I'd given John.

I PICKED UP the printouts Tony had delivered, amused at the image of him, behaving like an overanxious defense attorney, determined to produce enough paperwork to keep me busy and off the track of talking to his wife or the police.

The computer security administration at the Charger Street lab had done a thorough vetting on Yolanda, tracking her Web use over two weeks. They'd been so successful that she was fired at the end of the period. I thought back to my occasional nonwork-related browsing—mainly to frivolous interactive science sites—at BUL in California, and wondered who'd been looking over my shoulders electronically.

I reviewed the list of Web sites Yolanda had visited, many of which I recognized from my search for information on Prohibition. I pulled down my locator menu and typed in the first unfamiliar URL.

The address brought me to an article about the recent surge of moonshine, especially in the southeastern part of the country. A group of history-minded citizens in West Virginia had filed a petition to erect a museum to commemorate the heyday of the wood alcohol business, in what they called the moonshine capital of the world. The plan was to sell a safer version of hootch, billed as "boutique liquor."

I tried to imagine what Brendan Byrne or Yolanda Fiore might think about celebrating a "business" that cost lives and the destruction of families.

Another URL listed local Web sites and links to the library project. I should have realized the expansion proposal would have its own site. Didn't even every day-care center have one nowadays? I clicked through links that took me to the past, to the library's history, landing on one labeled OBITUARIES. A dark, formal look-and-feel took over my screen. A black banner, with long-stemmed calla lilies along the length of the page. The year, 1985. The deceased, Irving Leonard.

Mr. Irving Leonard, 46, director of the Revere Public Library, died in a tragic accident at the library on Friday. Mr. Leonard was the beloved husband of Dorothy, and father of Sarah, 21. Private burial will be followed by a public commemoration at Revere City Hall on Tuesday, 2 p.m. Besides his wife and child, Mr. Leonard is survived by his father, the retired Dr. David Leonard. Donations may be sent in Dr. Leonard's name to the National Library Fund, Washington, D.C.

The next page—if Web frames could be called pages—had the text of speeches and eulogies delivered at the City Hall service. I had no way of knowing which links Yolanda had searched, but I scanned all of them, as I felt she must have done. Eventually, I found a link I was sure Yolanda paused over—the text of a lengthy address by Brendan Byrne, an active Council member at the time. He'd peppered his testimony with anecdotes about his friend Irving.

No one worked harder than Irving. And, sadly, it was that devotion to duty that caused his untimely death. Imagine a guy with a lovely wife waiting at home working late on a Friday night, with one last chore he doesn't want to leave for his weekend staff. So he picks up a broken, old crate marked for cold storage and...well, that was Irving. Nothing was beneath him, he'd do anything to make the Revere Public Library, and all our lives, the better for his presence.

Another *aha* escaped my lips. But I had one more connection to make before the *aha* would survive the scrutiny of Sergeant Matt Gennaro.

I checked the clock on the wall above my desk. Not even ten-thirty. Still early enough to call Dorothy Leonard. This judgment by one who'd recently had a nap. I quickly flipped through the recent additions to my telephone and address book, and found her home number.

"No, it's not too late, Gloria. What can I do for you?" Not an enthusiastic tone in her voice, but who could blame her? I'd uncovered her document scheme, and come very close to accusing her of murdering either her husband or Yolanda Fiore or both.

"I need to know if Yolanda Fiore called you during the two weeks or so before she was murdered." I heard a grunting sound that said *oh-oh*. I hastened to reassure her. "I'm not still...investigating you, believe me. But this is very important. Did Yolanda have any questions for you about the circumstances of your husband's death?"

A sigh, remembering. "She did, as a matter of fact." I fought not to fill the silence that followed. Misleading the witness was not out of the question for me. Fortunately, not necessary as Dorothy continued. "She wanted to know something about that crate. Was it written anywhere what the crate was like. That it was old and broken and marked for storage, that kind of thing."

"Was it?"

"Not that I recall. It was kind of a joke between Irving and his staff. The basement where they stored things was so cold, they called it, well, cold storage. But no, it never appeared in any public record that I know of.''

''And you told Yolanda this?''

''Of course. I didn't know how she'd found out about it, and she wouldn't tell me even why she cared.''

I wasn't surprised that the grieving Dorothy Leonard missed the slip by Councilman Byrne at her husband's service, nor that police detectives wouldn't be paying attention either. He was an elder of the city, after all, even then.

I was about to hang up when another question came to my mind, a nagging connection from my phone call with John.

''Do you remember your father-in-law talking about a Mrs. Celia Scotto who would have been his patient in the forties?''

''Oh, you mean the Scottos who were involved in the moonshine tragedy?''

''Yes, are you familiar with the case?''

''Not specifically, except of course that it involved Derek's family, but I do remember Irving bringing it up once or twice. He got interested in it for some reason. Why are you asking?''

I realized Dorothy probably had no knowledge of Yolanda Fiore's connection to Sabatino Scotto. ''Nothing you need to worry about. Thank you very much for your time.''

I hung up and sat back on my rocker.

I'd been wrong. It wasn't a double homicide. It was a triple homicide. Scotto in 1940, Leonard in 1985, and Fiore in 1995.

TWENTY-NINE

MATT WAS DUE any minute—I had just enough time to lay out my story.

I bookmarked the relevant Web sites on my computer. To put order to the tangled threads in my brain, I opened a new document and made a timeline.

1940 —Eighteen-year-old Brendan Byrne intercepts Sabatino Scotto on the way to the airport, murders him, buries body behind the library. (Jewelry still missing, likely on Scotto's person.)

1984-5 —1. Library expansion proposed; exposure of grave threatened. 2. Irving Leonard discovers Byrne's secret. (How? Through his father, the doctor who treated Sabatino's wife—Irving decides to investigate, Byrne's vehement opposition to project alerts him and he figures it out? Possible!)

1985 —Byrne murders Leonard; throws crate down stairs after body to fake accident.

1995 (before?)—Yolanda Fiore investigates grandfather's disappearance, and also the library expansion controversy (why?), which leads her back in time to Byrne's incriminating gaffe at the Irving Leonard memorial service.

June, 1995 —1. Yolanda confronts Byrne? (Is discovered by him in the library? No, not a random meeting at eleven o'clock at night.) 2. Byrne murders Yolanda.

A few questions to ask Byrne when he was arrested, I thought smugly, but no serious gaps in my theory this time. I was ready for Matt.

I thought my high school class deserved some attention since it was Jamel's observation about bodies buried in a waste pool that inspired me to think about Scotto's body beneath the library lawn. I searched the Internet for the latest map of the active nuclear power plant units in the world, but I was too agitated to concentrate on anything other than my triple homicide theory. In the end, I decided to take a shower and lie down until Matt arrived.

I WOKE UP to the smell of coffee, the sound of sparrows, and the sight of Matt, dressed for work, standing by my bed. It was Friday morning.

"I was going to apologize for not showing up last night, but I see you didn't notice. The meeting went very late and I was completely exhausted."

So was I, I thought. I almost suggested how nice it would be if we could fall asleep exhausted, together. Instead, I asked, "What time is it?"

"By my imprecise analog wristwatch, nine o'clock."

I'd slept almost ten hours, a new record for me. I felt rested for the first time in a while. Who knew what I could accomplish with this much energy—too bad the case was solved.

Matt had made coffee and toasted fresh bagels he'd picked up. Two plain for him, one cinnamon raisin for me. I showed him my timeline, and got about a B response, since there were "still a lot of questions."

"Big article in the *Journal* this morning—the library expansion project has been approved and funded. I can't believe Byrne is surprised. So that means the big question is still what Byrne would gain by killing Yolanda. Other than simple revenge."

The phone saved me from reviewing the string of books, movies, and television shows that thrived on that "simple" notion.

"Good news," Elaine said. "I'm dating again."

"That's great, Elaine. But you got up pretty early to tell me."

"He just left."

I laughed. "Anyone I know?"

"It's Gil Hardin. You may remember him. He's a physicist in lasers."

I didn't know him, but I was happy for Elaine. "It's about time you tried a physicist. How many times did I tell you—?"

"I know, I know. I don't know why I didn't catch on. You're a physicist and I love you. We get along. We've been friends for longer than all my male relationships combined."

"My news is I think we've solved this case." I gave Matt a deliberate look, and a smile.

"Terrific. And the case of Matt Gennaro, also?"

"That, too, I think."

"He's there?"

"Yes."

Elaine sucked in her breath. "Call me."

BY THE END OF his second bagel and a look at Yolanda's Web sites, Matt was ready to put in a call to his partner George Berger. They agreed that Byrne should at least be interviewed—not an official interrogation, Matt noted—in connection with Yolanda's murder. As he pointed out, it would be a stretch to convince anyone to question him on a ten-year-old accident, and a fifty-five-year-old disappearance. We'd keep it as a police matter, not telling even the Galiganis.

Matt also admitted he had more reason to agree to a Byrne interview than my timeline.

"His alibi witnesses are questionable. Hector Gallerian, Dick Miller, a bunch of others. They're all telling a different story. One says pinochle, one says poker, one says no cards just drinks. Then, they're drinking beer, or they're drinking whiskey, or they're not drinking, and so on. I think the councilman's friends were all set to alibi him immediately after the murder, but after all this time they forgot their story—those guys are all pretty old.''

''These are Revere's statesmen of sorts. I can't believe they'd all agree to lie.''

Matt shrugged. ''Well, I hate to tell you, but it's pretty standard. Byrne probably told them he was in a compromising situation that night and he needs them to say he was with them. Something like that. Happens all the time.''

''Isn't that what Tony did?'' I mumbled.

''What?''

''Never mind.''

MATT LEFT AFTER breakfast, and I was free to read boron articles at leisure. No more case to think about. I could even apply for a library card. Or take up sewing as the men of Revere wished for their womenfolk.

On the third page of an article on new methods of storing spent fuel in dry casks instead of pools, I stopped to answer a phone call from Andrea.

''I'm going to have lunch with Peter today,'' she told me. ''I spent a couple of hours with him yesterday.''

''That's wonderful, Andrea. I'm glad that arrangement is working out. I'm sure he'll love your transparencies. And you can talk to him about your new idea—Gertrude Elion, Nobel Prize winner in medicine, was it?''

''Yes, in 1988, but—'' Her pause, and an *ahem* sound told me I'd missed the point of her call. ''Gloria, this thing with Peter, I think it's a date.''

My pause was longer. ''Oh, a date?'' was the best I could do.

One other time Peter had shown interest in a friend of mine—Elaine Cody, who was visiting me in Revere. It never went anywhere and Elaine and I both always assumed it was for my benefit. Elaine, of course, could handle Peter and four others simultaneously, but I wasn't sure Andrea could. I hoped I wasn't simply being egotistical, thinking Peter was showing off to me again.

"I thought he wanted to see my transparencies," she said. And at that point *my etchings* came to mind. "But he said, no, let's not do any business."

"It sounds like a wonderful idea. Where are you going?"

"It's a surprise. He's going to pick me up at the gate at noon." Andrea sighed heavily. "Gloria, I wish we'd already gone shopping for my new outfits."

"Well, Andrea, he asked you out based on your current wardrobe, so I don't think you have to worry. If you'd like a suggestion, why don't you wear that blue paisley top, with the lapis earrings? That's a nice combination."

"Thanks, Gloria. That's a great idea."

I hung up with Andrea and immediately called Peter, catching him in between classes.

"I'm just calling to see how it's going with Andrea," I told him. I didn't mention *test your sincerity.*

"Gloria, you won't believe this, well, you will believe this. She's really an amazing person. She's well read and very, very smart and incredibly organized."

I cleared my throat. "Really?"

Peter laughed. "I know, you told me all that. But I'm really delighted to get to know her, and I think it's going to be perfect. I probably should have called to thank you."

"No, no, that's fine, Peter."

And for the first time, Peter ended the conversation. "Got to go. Talk soon."

It took a few minutes of meditation to accept Peter's honorable intentions. First, I told myself, he didn't mention having a lunch date with her, which he would have if he was simply trying to make a point with me.

Good, I said to myself, and I'm not even jealous that Andrea could impress Peter so quickly. And a moment later, I believed it.

I poured a second cup of coffee. All was right in Revere. We'd exposed the perpetrator of three murders, John Galigani was on his way home, Rose and Frank would be happy, Elaine was dating a physicist, Andrea had a new friend, Peter would not be annoying me anymore. I added a picture of Derek Byrne, devastated at first to learn of his father's crimes, finally making peace with it and going off into the sunset with Frances Worthen.

I topped off the scenario with Matt and me holding hands in front of the Atlantic Ocean, not far from Kelly's Roast Beef stand.

Could life get any neater than this?

I was feeling so good and so generous, I decided to invite my cousin Mary Ann to the Galiganis' annual Fourth of July party. And I made the call in the middle of the morning, when I knew she'd be home.

THIRTY

I WAS READY for class on Friday afternoon with a briefcase full of notes and downloads from the Internet, including a listing of every nuclear power plant unit in the United States, and its current inventory of spent fuel rods. The long alphabetical tabulation, from *Arkansas 1* in Russellville, Arkansas, to *Wolf Creek* in Burlington, Kansas, itemized important parameters such as the core size, the number of assemblies stored in the pool, and the data on the plant's license.

Jamel was amused at the drawing that accompanied an explanation of PWR operation—behind the domed containment building was a lovely, full-color rainbow.

"Like these nuclear reactors are natural phenomena," Mi-Weh said. Her tiny outfit of black cotton pants and pink tank top hugged her body. I estimated she could fit her entire wardrobe into one fuel rod.

"Some spin doctor created this banner," Erin said, causing me to think of Tony Taruffi, the premier spinner of the Charger Street lab.

David and Mi-Weh had paired up and researched dry cask storage—a new method to store the fuel in metal containers instead of pools of water. They'd created a model out of soft clay, shaped to scale next to a small human figure.

I noticed the figure was in a skirt.

I LEFT THE SCHOOL feeling more carefree than I had in a long while, though from time to time I entertained an image of Councilman Brendan Byrne sweating it out in the basement of the police station, under a bare bulb. More likely sitting in the captain's office with a scotch and soda, I guessed. I was eager to hear how the interview was going and called Matt several times during the afternoon, but didn't reach him.

The only damper on my happy, normal day was that I'd kept Frank and Rose in the dark about John's whereabouts as well as the councilman's, but I knew it was the best choice. I wished I'd gotten a phone number from John so I could tell him he was no longer the prime suspect. I tried to picture him booking his flight, boarding a plane, being met at Logan. It might be less than twenty-four hours before their lives would be back together.

Then, I told myself, I'd focus on my own life.

DINNER AT RUSSO'S with Matt began as usual—a romantic briefing on the status of a criminal investigation.

"The councilman is standing firm on his alibi—some record number of judges and mayors came forward to defend his character. He's still being held for questioning, but I wouldn't be surprised if Revere's elite took turns playing pinochle with him."

"What about the other murders? When Scotto's body is dug up—"

"*If* Scotto's body is dug up, then yes, I think we might be able to push for an investigation that would include the councilman. Whether that would ripple to Irving Leonard is questionable, and then to Yolanda, it gets even shakier."

I nodded, a frowning and frustrated concession to reality. "There's nothing to tie him directly to the scene." I was aware my voice had gotten louder, just as our waitress arrived with two steaming plates of spinach tortellini. I gave her a sweet smile and a grandmotherly thank you. She left hurriedly.

"That's right," Matt said, his tone more even than mine. "And let's remember, even accusing the young Brendan Byrne of murdering Scotto won't necessarily lead to your idea of justice."

I raised my eyebrows. "What does that mean?"

Matt smiled. "You know, the civilian notion that the system always works."

"I thought I was a cop to you now."

He reached over and took my hand. "Sometimes a cop, sometimes a civilian, sometimes—"

I blushed. I was certain all the other Russo patrons had dropped their forks, aware what Matt and I were thinking at that moment. I withdrew my hand, wondering if I'd ever be comfortable with public displays of affection. I looked around Russo's, at the tables interspersed with plastic ferns and faux-marble statuary, satisfied that the other diners were caught up in their own worlds and not ours.

"You mean Byrne will get off?" I winced at the image of Byrne coming to the defendant's table at eighty years old— since he'd certainly be able to draw out the prosecution process for a few years—being tried as a juvenile.

"Maybe not scot-free. But the man has had five decades to prove himself an honorable and respected member of society. His life has been one of service to his country. He's a veteran, a family man, a public servant—"

I held up my hand, desperate to stop Matt's characterization of Byrne, as if he were the man's defense attorney. "Unless he killed twice again. Then he'd be a mass murderer."

"Technically, a serial killer. Mass murderer would be if he killed three people all at the same time."

I gave him a look that said, *picky, picky.* "Either way, it's a pretty sobering thought."

Matt nodded and dug into his pasta.

By the time we dipped chocolate frosted biscotti into our dessert cappuccinos my cheerful mood had dissipated significantly.

I WAS FURTHER DISAPPOINTED when Matt dropped me off at the mortuary around nine o'clock, with no plans to come upstairs. I'd tried to needle my way into his other principal case— the murder/suicide he was officially working on—but he'd assured me it was under control and had no science-related elements.

As I walked through the Galigani Mortuary lobby, I noticed Parlor A was empty. I pictured Mrs. Patira, uncomfortable in her facedown position in Holy Family cemetery.

Upstairs, I entered my apartment and picked up the pile of mail either Rose or her assistant, Martha, had slid under my door. Among the flyers and bills was a plain envelope without stamps or postmark. I sucked in my breath. Another note of questionable origin and threatening content? I carried the envelope to my rocker, holding the edges only, the way I used to transfer photographic plates from the developer into the fixing fluid so as not to get my fingerprints on the image.

I pulled out the single sheet of white paper, eight and a half by eleven. A note, typed on *Revere Journal* letterhead. I let out a breath. An innocuous ID.

Don't want to hang around your house right now.
Meet me in the library—John

I could believe John was leery of being seen around town. For all he knew his parents' home and business were being watched. Poor John, I thought—he doesn't know anything about the evidence we have on Councilman Byrne. Somehow I'd managed to convince myself that even though Matt doubted Byrne could be charged with Yolanda's murder, at least suspicion had shifted away from John Galigani.

I called the library, on the chance that John was in the building and not outside—if the press were issued passes, maybe they were also issued keys, I reasoned. I paced my living room listening to the recorded message. I thought John might have heard the ringing, and if I waited long enough he'd make his way to the phone and intercept my call. Hours of operation, directions to the building, and special programs—an impressive list, with children's hour, adult literacy classes, senior volunteers, family book exchange—but no pickup from John. Of course not, he's in hiding, I reminded myself.

Nothing to do but drive over and meet him.

I'd already parked my Cadillac inside for the night so I left the building through the garage. I jiggled my keys nervously, running questions through my head. How do I know the message is from John? It's on *Journal* letterhead, I answered. Why would John type a note to bring to my house before he knew he'd need one? He's efficient, thinking practically, like a fugitive. Should I call Matt and have him meet me? Don't bother him. This will be quick, once I tell John he can come back home.

My car purred into action, and I pulled out onto Tuttle Street, and drove to the library. I had a new question and answer at each intersection. What if Byrne is in the library, waiting in ambush? Byrne is in the city jail. Resting on specially provided pillows, maybe, but locked up nevertheless. Who else would want to lure me to an empty building for harm's sake? No one. The most likely scenario is the simple one—that John is inside, or outside in the shadows, waiting to come out and join me. With Byrne being detained, all was fine with the world.

The heat of the day had not dissipated much and I felt the muggy wash of air as I stepped out of my car in front of the library. The tall white flagpole, without its banner, caught the threads of moonlight and seemed to divide the building in half. I walked around the perimeter of the building, running my hand over the circular wooden picnic furniture as I passed. Nine-thirty and no sign of life. Not surprising, since the library had been closed for five hours—I'd learned more than I needed about the hours of operation during my recent phone call.

I stood at the corner of Beach Street and Library Street and glanced at the back lot. Where Sabatino Scotto's body was buried, I was certain. Had I walked on his bones the evening I strolled back here a week ago?

Nothing stirred on the library lot. I wondered how long I should wait. One more look on the other side of the building, I decided, and headed toward Beach Street.

Finally, a small light caught my eye near the back of the building on the north side. On and off, on and off, like Morse code. Or simply a flashlight. John's flashlight, I thought with relief, as I headed for the signal.

Closer to building, I saw the shadow of a person, leaning against an open door, arms waving me in.

I quickened my step and peered into the shadows at the figure. Taller than John. And heavier. How could that be?

I stopped short.

What had I been thinking, or not thinking? A flash of pale blue crossed my path as I remembered an important envelope—not the one with the message to meet John in the library, but an earlier one containing Yolanda's E-mails and the data on her Web use. The envelope from Tony Taruffi, with a pale blue note attached. The fashionably rough texture, the size, the slightly jagged edges. It had been a different hue, light blue instead of off-white, and I didn't recognize it as coming from the same batch as my original TAKE UP SEWING letter.

That advice was looking better and better. As a detective, I'd make a good quilter.

Tony Taruffi hurried to close the gap between us. His gun glinted in the light from the streetlamp. Or was it the moon? I tried to figure it out, as if it were an important calculation, a matter of life or death.

I'd been so stupid. Distracted and excited by the prospect of reading Yolanda's E-mails.

"I was stupid," Tony said, causing me to wonder if I'd confessed my dimwittedness out loud. He grabbed me roughly, cupped his hand over my mouth. "Using the same stationery—from that supply of my wife's." Mrs. Taruffi, the wedding coordinator, I remembered. "Stupid. Stupid. I knew it was just a matter of time before you'd figure it out."

He was right. I did figure it out. Just a little late.

THIRTY-ONE

TONY WAS MUCH heavier than I and had no trouble marching me, half carrying me, the few remaining steps to the building. I tried to squirm until I felt the butt of his gun in my back, one click away from ending my life. My heart pounded in my chest, my brain sending flashes of bright light across the optics of my eyes, as if a prism had been installed there.

I was still in the clothes I'd worn to dinner—lightweight pants and a raw silk short-sleeved top, all khaki, and now all soaking wet.

Up to now no other traffic had passed in the area, but at that moment an enormous white delivery truck pulled noisily up to the Beach Street entrance of the library. I took a deep breath and opened my mouth, prepared to scream, but Tony quickly tied a sweaty cloth around my face, covering my mouth. I gagged at the smell, at the same time relieved it wasn't soaked in chemicals.

He dragged me roughly inside the building through a trapdoor. The opening did not lead to the basement, as I'd thought, but only to a stairwell. I heard the heavy doors of the truck outside open and close. A delivery? More lions? Two other virtues? I knew my brain was rattled when I started to joke about a critical situation.

"Shit." Tony drew the word out so it became a hissing sound. "I'm going to have to take you upstairs. This may be the delivery entrance." He forced me up two flights of stairs to the attic mezzanine, opposite the level that held the administrative offices. I looked down on the area between the mezzanines—the circulation desks, now empty and fruitless as a source of help.

Tony pushed me down, and I landed between Patience and Fortitude, surrounded by other relics of the Historical Society. Photographs, fruit crates filled with scrolls, the old spinning wheels, part of the bootleg liquor still, a pile of old cloths that might once have adorned the dining-room tables of Revere's upper class. I looked at the artifacts, as if at the milieu of my final resting place.

"You have a short reprieve while I check on those men," he told me. Tony's eyes seemed to be bulging out of his head and perspiration had formed deep circles around the sleeves of his navy-blue polo shirt. He was out of breath, but not as much as I was.

I tried to plead with my eyes as Tony picked up a slat of wood from the old still and drew his arm back. I ducked, and the blow landed on the side of my head, hitting my right ear. The pain set off bells in my head—and also the beginnings of a plan. I collapsed onto my side and closed my eyes. If he thinks I'm dead, I thought, I have a chance.

When he prodded at my arms, attempting to tie them behind my back, I pressed my body into the wooden floor so that he was forced to bind my wrists in front. Acting like dead weight was not a stretch.

Below, the deliverymen banged on the front door of the building. *That's my car in front of your truck,* I wanted to scream—*don't you recognize it? I'm in here!*

The effort served only to make me nauseous.

In spite of my stellar performance, Tony added one more shackle—he tied my ankles together and twisted the remaining rope around the leg of a large walnut case halfway across the attic. Ironically, it was the cabinet with antique guns and ammunition, useless on this Friday night in the twentieth century.

Tony left me, with a warning. "Nothing funny, Gloria," he said to my utterly still body.

Or what? I wondered. Wasn't I going to be shot anyway? When I knew he'd reached the first floor, I hoisted myself up.

My limited range of motion—a radius of about eight feet, I guessed—allowed me to hop to the small window, high up on the brick wall. I could barely see over the sill. Two men, in white uniforms, black supports in place around their waists, one of them talking on a cell phone. Probably calling Derek Byrne or Dorothy Leonard.

I knew Tony wouldn't risk the sound of a gunshot while they were out there. I couldn't see my watch in the dark attic, but I estimated it was near ten o'clock, time for their shift to be over. As I realized my attempts to get their attention would never work, tears formed, clouding my vision, and adding to the sorry state of my face.

I wondered why Tony didn't just open the door and talk to them, make up an excuse about how he was in charge tonight, and they'd made an error—which I assumed they really had, since no one was on duty to receive a delivery. Then I realized Tony would not want anyone to see him, if it came to identifying him after...

The thought depressed me, and I fell back onto the floor. The window was too high up for me to open it and I couldn't see anything I could use to break it. I was doomed to die within the same few square yards as three other people. Not a quadruple homicide, however, but two doubles. One killer responsible for the deaths of Sabatino Scotto and Irving Leonard, the other for Yolanda Fiore and...

I shook the image away and allowed my rational side to take over. Tony Taruffi lined up perfectly in the places where Matt and I had problems fitting Councilman Byrne into our theory of Yolanda's murder. Eliminating her didn't help Byrne if the library project went through, but it did help Tony. It wasn't hard to figure a motive. I could easily imagine if I'd had an affair with my boss, and then he fired me, I might threaten to tell his wife. Not that I'd ever done that, nor would live long enough to do so.

And who knew what else Yolanda might have on an unscrupulous PR man. There might have been a controversy over boron safety practices after all. Possibly Tony just wanted to talk to her, make a bargain as he had with me. Another shudder as I remembered my meeting with a killer in the shadows of Tuttle Street.

Strangely, my faith in judges, mayors, and other elders of Suffolk County was renewed. Brendan Byrne really was playing pinochle with the boys while Yolanda was being sent to her death. He may have killed Sabatino Scotto and Irving Leonard, but it took another man, another motive, to murder Yolanda Fiore.

Not that I had time to work this out.

I took stock of the situation. I was in the attic, a dirty cloth in my mouth, a screaming headache, breathless from a crying jag, tied to a cabinet.

What was up here that I could use to survive? I wished, foolishly, that I had my cane—the cane that would split in two at the first contact with Tony's muscular frame. My eyes, adjusted to the moonlight streaming through the small window, landed on a stack of photographs. From one elaborate frame, a Victorian gentleman in a stiff white collar gave me a stern look, as if he were reprimanding me for getting into these straits. He had what I'd come to think of as a take up sewing look.

I stood up and peered into the glass-topped case I was tethered to. I'd admired the antique weapons when Derek Byrne had pointed them out on our tour. Now I wished they were functional. Long, sleek, black barrels, scratched wooden handles, boxes made of worn cardboard, with bullets, some shiny, some rusty. But useless. Through the glass, I examined the dull knives lined along the back edge of the case. Although the guns wouldn't fire, the knives would work, but it was a moot point since the top of the case was locked.

Patience and Fortitude had their eyes closed, as if to take the high road, and keep themselves above the flesh and blood incidents in the environment. Each lion had a paw on a ball about the size of a bowling ball. Patience had her right paw on the sphere; Fortitude her left. Or vice versa. I wasn't sure if they were boy and girl or the same gender. I wasn't even sure if lion's feet were called paws. The beasts were a pale green and had very curly manes and identical openmouthed expressions. I remembered Derek's stats—cast bronze, three hundred pounds each. Not something I could pick up and hurl at Tony when he came back upstairs.

I picked up the speaker from an old record player, holding it in my close-knit hands, and wondered, irrelevantly, what would be in the attics of the year 2020. Cell phones. Track balls. Keyboards. Pieces of satellite dishes. Why was I thinking twenty-five years into the future? Would I even be alive in the morning?

The thought sent an intensely cold shiver through me, competing with the extreme heat of the attic. I started to calculate my average temperature, as if to record it in a log book. Temperature, pressure, volume, density.

The roaring crank of the truck engine starting up startled me back to action. I tried once more to scream through the cloth, causing a massive fit of coughing that got me nowhere. Panicked, I hopped as far as I could with my tethered ankles, almost reaching the top of the stairs, when I ran into something that felt like a headless body.

My heart jumped in my chest, until I realized it was the dusty old dressmaker's form. Headless, naked, cut off at the thighs, but possibly enough of a body to save my life. My plan took shape. In the next moments my mind took over from my out-of-control pulse and I flew into action, limited though it was.

If I thought the dummy was a person, maybe Tony would, too. I pulled a large piece of cloth from a pile, ignoring the spiders and nameless insects that would otherwise repulse me, and draped it across the shoulders of the stiff, musty form. As I looked around for a head, I pictured Frank reattaching a little girl's head to her torso and calmed myself with thoughts of returning to my mortuary home.

I heard the delivery truck pull away.

In the corner was an old globe. I struggled to grab the sphere with the small angle afforded by my bound wrists. I dropped it several times before, finally, it stuck to the perspiration on my hands. I added another piece of fabric, over the globe. It fell loosely, like hair, I hoped, or an old-fashioned mantilla.

I heard Tony's footsteps, heading up the stairs. No time for artistic arrangement.

One more item and I'd be ready. I rehearsed my tactics as Tony's footsteps drew closer—hop into the shadows, wait until Tony approached the fake person, then whack him with... what? Something heavy? Something sharp?

My ankles were bruised from the rough rope that tied them together. I took a painful hop to survey the contents of the attic, pulling and pushing on possible weapons. I found the piece of wood Tony had slammed into my head. Next to it, attached to the old still, was another slab with a nail on the end of it. I heard Tony's labored breathing. Using all my strength, I wrestled with the still until I'd unhinged the stick with the nail and hopped back to the shadows near the top of the stairs.

I swallowed hard—a difficult process with the cloth still in my mouth, and shuddered at what I needed to do next. I'd struck more people in the last year in Revere than in my whole life. I crouched down, pulling the loose rope close around my feet and out of sight.

I'd positioned the dummy far enough away from the top of the stairs, in the shadows, and the first thing Tony would see. Since the lobby's night lights were fairly bright, his eyes would be less accommodated to the dark of the attic than mine were. His height was also to my advantage—like Derek Byrne, Tony had to hunch over to avoid hitting the beams on the low attic ceiling.

When he reached the top step he was so close I thought he would sense my position, but he took two steps toward the dummy. ''What the—''

Whack. Whack. I hit him with all my might. Once, twice, or maybe three times. Enough so that he stopped talking, dropped his gun, and fell to the floor.

THIRTY-TWO

"ROPE BURNS?" The young intern seemed to be as embarrassed as I was that I'd been taken to the ER at Whidden Hospital in Everett with nothing more than a sore throat, a few bruises on my wrists and ankles, and a raging headache.

Later, a female psychiatrist posing as a nurse asked me questions no doubt designed to determine the level of hysteria I'd reached in the library attic. *Do you have any plans for the Fourth of July?* probably meant *Are you suicidal?* And *How do you like this lovely plant?* was a ruse for *Do you think those green ferns are about to attack you?* I have no idea why she asked who the president of the United States was.

At least I'd won the battle of overnight or not overnight, and I was released from the hospital before midnight. Matt drove me home, and this time came upstairs with me.

"You don't have to stay," I said, without conviction.

He answered by serving me a glass of water and a pain pill and tucking me in. Then he took up residence on the upholstered chair next to my bed.

If I'd told Matt or the medics the whole truth about my last moments in the attic, they might have detained me.

For a while—I couldn't tell how long—I'd sat on the floor next to Tony's body, thinking I'd killed him. Beside me was the wooden slat, now splintered and bloody. Tony was facedown, blood from the back of his neck running onto the floor, seeping into the hem of my khaki pants.

I'd had the presence of mind to prod at his hand to shake his gun loose. I slid it next to me, my wrists still tied together, then gave it a shove that sent it hurtling down the stairs to the lobby. Finally, I stood and hopped around slowly, tears in my eyes, looking for an object sharp enough to cut through the rope that bound my ankles together and to the cabinet.

I found a pair of rusty garden shears under a pile of fabric, and sliced the rope apart, slowly, thread by thread.

Once my feet were free, I made my way painfully down the stairs, holding on to the banister, lest I fall from own weakness. I picked up the phone at the reference desk with my still-fettered hands and pushed 911.

Not until I knew Tony was alive, about an hour later, did I take a calm breath.

MATT'S PAGER went off in the middle of the night.

"I'm sorry," he said. "I hate to leave you."

"Hmmm?" I rolled over to face him, and the clock. Through sleep-filled eyes I saw 4:13. The little dot in the upper left corner told me it was a.m.

"Do you want me to see if I can raise Berger instead?"

"No, it's OK. I'd better get used to this."

"What?"

I gave him a groggy smile. "Well, if we're going to live together—"

Matt leaned closer. "Are you sure this is not the pills talking?"

I reached over and convinced him I was serious.

ROSE HAD GRACIOUSLY let me sleep most of the day on Saturday. By all appearances she'd needed the time to prepare the elaborate meal that accompanied the debriefing on the murder investigations for Sabatino Scotto, Irving Leonard, and Yolanda Fiore. And almost Gloria Lamerino, I thought.

A large tureen of cioppino dominated the long dining-room table, with bowls of salad and baskets of warm bread at each end. I was glad I'd slept through breakfast and lunch.

John Galigani, still a little tired from his Detroit-Boston trip, looked better than ever to us, nonetheless. He'd decided not to take Carolyn Verrico, or any other companion, on the upcoming charter trip to Bermuda, but instead to use the time to ''put some things behind me,'' as he'd called it. To straighten himself out, is what we would have said in the old days.

''Before we even get to the gory details, Gloria—I can't believe you were going through all this other stuff with Matt. You had to make this decision and I never knew. I feel so egotistic and self-absorbed, self-involved—'' Rose waved her hands, as if she needed to pull as many words out of the air as possible, to make up for her neglect of me.

''You had enough to deal with and, besides, it wasn't a tough decision.'' *Not once I'd made it.*

''Piece of cake,'' Matt said with a grin.

Glasses were raised—sparkling cider for Matt and me, a lovely rose-colored wine for the Galiganis.

''I heard about your headless torso,'' Frank said. ''I like to think I helped you figure that out.''

''You certainly did.'' I dipped my Italian bread in rosemary oil, no longer squeamish about the combination of dinner and mortuary talk. As Robert had told me after his first case, FUNERAL is an anagram for REAL FUN. I took it as the mortician's way of dealing with the heavy side of life on a daily basis.

''So fill us in,'' Rose said. ''Did someone actually convince Byrne to confess to the earlier murders?'' She scooped second helpings into everyone's bowl but her own.

Matt nodded. ''Covering up the Scotto murder worked for Byrne ten years ago. Killing Irving Leonard also killed the library project. He could put his own man in the director's job since he controlled the Council at the time. But Berger and Parker convinced him that if a body was dug up and IDed as Scotto, or if anything in the grave could be traced to him, he'd have no more bargaining power. So his lawyers—about six of them—advised him to tell the truth.''

''Apparently he'd been thinking about it anyway,'' I said, sharing what I'd learned from Matt earlier. ''They found several newspaper clippings in Byrne's desk—articles on how far we've come in being able to identify people from small amounts of DNA, from the tiniest flake of skin or fabric left behind.''

"And I suppose we all know how he got the entire Roman Catholic Church to back him," Frank said. Nods from everyone. "Money talks, even in the heavenly choirs." He rubbed his thumb and index finger together for emphasis.

"Then there's Tony Taruffi—" Rose put her hand on my arm. "If it's not too hard for you, Gloria?"

I shook my head. "I'm fine. Matt called the hospital before we came here. Tony's going to pull through. I'm not as strong as I thought." I smiled as if there were no ill effects from my violent encounter. "I guess Tony was responsible for the childish pranks on me, but we won't know for sure until he's well enough to answer questions. And it looks like he'll be good as new pretty soon."

"Except that he'll be in prison," Matt said.

"I keep thinking about Yolanda's grandmother," John said. "I want to keep in touch with her. I called her this morning to tell her all this and she was so happy. It was as if she's lived this long so she could vindicate her husband."

"Not that he wasn't a criminal," Matt said, spoiling things a bit.

"Oh, that," John said with a grin. "Nana Celia is sure her jewelry will be in the grave with Sabatino."

"Did you get the feeling she sent Yolanda to unmask Byrne in particular?" I asked.

John shook his head. "I don't think so. There were so many others who could have wanted Scotto out of the way—his partners in the business were afraid Scotto would turn them in under pressure, and a lot of people got sick or damaged in some way by the liquor, though none as severely as the Byrnes. Celia gave me several other names, which she'd apparently also given Yolanda. In fact, I might look into it—maybe do a feature on the Prohibition era in Revere."

His mother gave him a look that I suspect he'd seen before, perhaps as a teenager.

"Never mind," John said.

Rose CALLED ME OUT to the kitchen, to help prepare coffee and dessert, she said, but I knew she wanted some private girl talk.

She clapped her hands together and beamed. "This is going to be so wonderful. You and Matt. A wedding, maybe?"

"Hold on, Rose. Don't make me drop this *pizza dolce*."

"Well, just let me know if you want help with the guest list. I know MC will be here in a flash. She's been calling almost every day over this thing with John, and she would have come if I'd wanted her to. She's in love with an oilman."

"He's a petroleum chemist, Rose."

"I know. I'm just teasing. Don't lose your sense of humor just because you're engaged."

"I'm not exactly—"

"Have you told Elaine, Andrea, Peter, your cousin?"

Some of the above. I wasn't sure how to tell Mary Ann. My seventy-something cousin had expressed her displeasure many times about the wrong way things were done these days.

"It used to be we'd date, get pinned, announce an engagement, buy a hope chest, get married," she'd said.

One good thing—Mary Ann loved Matt. He often volunteered to make the round-trip to Worcester so she could attend "family" events in Revere. Maybe I'd let Matt, the professional interviewer, explain things to her. Right after he explained to his own sister, Jean, who was not my biggest fan.

Rose had gone off on another tangent. "Or if you need any wedding night consultation…"

"Rose!"

She laughed, in her easy way that had been missing for a while. "By the way, I ran into Annie Senato—the Civic Ladies had a meeting at her house. I told her you were back in town and she wants to get together."

"I don't remember her."

"Sure you do," Rose said.

I laughed. We'd had this conversation several times, with different names. Rose was always trying to jog my memory about our classmates, most of whom had lost their place in my brain cells long ago.

"I'm not getting any recollection of an Annie Senato." I tapped my head, as if to show her where the information would be if I had it.

"But you were in the same homeroom."

"I guess it was a big room."

Rose lowered her voice to a near-scolding tone. "Gloria, she showed me her yearbook. You wrote in it."

I swallowed hard, fairly sure what was coming next. "What did I write? 'I'll never forget you. Love, Gloria'?"

"Exactly."

"Oh, dear. Did I ever write in your yearbook, Rose?"

She leaned across the counter, dislodging a shower of powdered sugar from the *pizza dolce,* and slapped my arm, barely holding in her laughter.

BACK IN MY APARTMENT with Matt, I looked around with a new eye. What would I take with me to Fernwood Avenue, what would I leave behind? My two blue glide rockers were the only furniture that had traveled with me from California. I put them, with my computer system, on the list of *indispensable items.* I could do without nearly everything else.

In the corner, by the archway to the kitchen I saw a package I didn't recognize. A large package, about six inches thick, leaning against the wall.

"What's this?"

"Something for your new home."

I knew before I'd torn the paper all the way off. A set of prints of Revere Beach Boulevard, mounted, ready for hanging on my new walls. The largest poster showed the Cyclone rollercoaster, which had dominated the skyline of the Boulevard for many decades. A pale maroon car sat perched on the topmost hill, full of people with excited expressions, ready to plunge forward.

Like me. "It's a good thing I'm moving. These won't fit here. They need a bigger wall."

"I have a bigger wall."

I smiled at Matt. "What else do you have?"

"A driveway big enough for your Caddie. And a fireplace to keep you warm." He looked at the digital thermometer/clock on my desk. The outside temperature registered ninety-one degrees at ten o'clock at night.

"Wonderful. Let's go there now and throw some logs on."

"Maybe not. It hasn't been cleaned since last winter."

"No problem. I don't mind a little carbon."

"Whoa," he said, in an uncontrolled laugh. "I love you, Gloria."

"And I love you, Matt."

ED GORMAN
EVERYBODY'S SOMEBODY'S FOOL

A SAM McCAIN MYSTERY

When local bad boy David Egan is accused of murder, lawyer Sam McCain finds himself saddled with a new client...and another tale of small-town murder in Black River Falls, Iowa.

But McCain's client dies a fiery death in a car accident—an event that becomes murder when it's discovered the car's brake lines were cut. Working to clear Egan's name, McCain follows a trail of shattered dreams, cheating spouses, dark secrets to a body lying lifeless in a bath and to a tale of murder that embraces the vast human emotions that drive lovers to love...and killers to kill.

"...a fascinating time machine, recalling the arcana of a more innocent time.'
—*Publishers Weekly*

Available June 2004 at your favorite retail outlet.

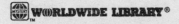 **WORLDWIDE LIBRARY** ®

WEG494

ACTS OF VENGEANCE

FRANK SMITH

Detective Chief Inspector Neil Paget lies unconscious in a hospital bed after an attacker slashed his throat. But the investigation is stalled until a recovering Paget sifts through his tortured flashbacks while receiving taunting calls from a killer who has struck again. To solve a crime that is more personal than he ever imagined, Paget must venture deep into the dark pain of his own past...and the twisted mind of a killer looking for revenge.

"... pleasurable Paget police procedural....
Smith makes this case personal as the audience
gets deep inside the mind of the hero."
—Harriet Klausner

Available July 2004 at your favorite retail outlet.

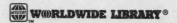

katie's gold

Tom Mitcheltree

When his office and apartment are ransacked and he's blindsided by an unknown assailant, Paul Fischer realizes that the saga of legendary pioneer Katie Baker is far from over! Returning to Oregon's Rogue River Valley to reopen a case he thought long closed, Paul must outsmart a brilliant and dangerous enemy long enough to find out what Katie Baker was so desperate to hide...and why.

> "Interesting characters, solid storytelling....
> works well as a stand-alone."
> —*Kirkus Reviews*

Available July 2004 at your favorite retail outlet.

WORLDWIDE LIBRARY®

WTM498

NANCY BELL

RESTORED TO DEATH

A JUDGE JACKSON CRAIN MYSTERY

Jackson Crain is devoted to being a judge in tiny Post Oak, Texas, where hard crime is rare. But that changes when Dora Hughes, Jackson's shrewish sister-in-law, is bludgeoned and strangled to death while sunbathing on her patio.

Dora's henpecked husband is accused of the crime and the case evolves into something decidedly sinister when a second body is found in a cornfield. Jackson connects both victims to a beautiful, exotic newcomer to Post Oak— a woman to whom he is dangerously attracted. The hunt for a clever killer exposes shattering secrets guaranteed to leave even the local gossips speechless.

"Quaint characters and locales,
frequent humor, and comfy prose..."
—*Library Journal*

Available June 2004 at your favorite retail outlet.

BETTY WEBB

DESERT WIVES

Arizona private investigator Lena Jones is hired by a frantic mother desperate to rescue her thirteen-year-old daughter from a polygamist sect. But when the compound's sixty-eight-year-old leader is found murdered, Lena's client is charged with his murder.

To find the real killer, Lena goes undercover and infiltrates the dark reality of Purity—where misogynistic men and frightened women share a deadly code of silence.

"...this book could do for polygamy what *Uncle Tom's Cabin* did for slavery."
—Publishers Weekly

Available July 2004
at your favorite retail outlet.